I raised the lid of the box and pushed it back against the wall.

And then I saw something which filled my soul with horror. There lay the Count, but his appearance was greatly changed. He looked years younger than before. The white hair and moustache were now a dark iron gray. The cheeks were fuller, and the skin, usually so pale, had a fresh pink-ness. The mouth was redder than ever, and drops of fresh blood trickled from the corners of the mouth and down over the chin and neck. Even the skin around the deep, burning eyes seemed swollen. It seemed as if the whole awful creature were simply stuffed with blood.

Dracula

BRAM STOKER

**Edited with an Afterword
by Beth Johnson**

 THE TOWNSEND LIBRARY

DRACULA

TP THE TOWNSEND LIBRARY

For more titles in the Townsend Library,
visit our website: **www.townsendpress.com**

All new material in this edition is
copyright © 2003 by Townsend Press.
Printed in the United States of America

0 9 8 7 6 5 4 3 2 1

Townsend Press, Inc.
1038 Industrial Drive
West Berlin, New Jersey 08091

ISBN 1-59194-003-6

Library of Congress Control Number:
2002114951

Chapter 1

May 3. I left Munich at 8:35 p.m. on May 1 and arrived in Vienna early the next morning. Next we stopped in Budapest, which looked like a wonderful place. I would have liked to get off the train and explore, but there was no time. But from my look out the window, I had the impression that I had left the Western world and entered the mysterious East.

By nightfall of the next day I had arrived at the city of Klausenburgh. I stopped for the night at the Hotel Royale, where I ordered a very good dish of chicken prepared with red pepper. (Note: Remember to get the recipe for Mina.) It is certainly lucky that I speak some

German. I don't know how I would get along here otherwise.

Before I left London, I visited the British Museum and looked at all the books and maps about Transylvania that I could find. I thought that knowing something about the region would help me make a good impression on Count Dracula, the nobleman with whom I will be dealing. From what I could make out, Transylvania is one of the wildest and least known portions of Europe. I couldn't find any map that gave the exact location of the Castle Dracula, but I did see that Bistritz, the town nearest the castle, is fairly well known. From my reading, it seems as though every superstition in the world is alive in this ancient region. If that is true, my stay may be very interesting. (Note: Ask the Count all about those old beliefs.)

I did not sleep well, although my bed was comfortable enough, for I had all sorts of odd dreams. There was a dog howling all night under my window, which may have had something to do with it; or it may have been all the red pepper in my dinner. After I awoke I had to hurry through breakfast, for my train was scheduled to leave a little before eight. At least it ought to have left then. Once I rushed to my seat, I had to sit there for more than an hour before we began to move. It seems to me that the further east you go, the less punctual are the trains. I wonder what they are like in China?

All day long we moved slowly through a country which was full of beauty of every kind. Sometimes we saw little towns or castles on the top of steep hills; sometimes we passed rivers and streams which had wide stony margins on each side of them, showing that great floods were frequent there.

It was on the dark side of twilight when we got to Bistritz, which is a very interesting old place. It has had a very stormy existence, and it shows the marks of it. Fifty years ago a series of great fires took place. At the very beginning of the seventeenth century, it underwent an attack by enemies that lasted three weeks. Between the fighting and the famine and disease that went along with it, 13,000 people lost their lives.

My letter from Count Dracula had instructed me to stay at the Golden Krone Hotel. The hotel was very old-fashioned, and this delighted me, for, of course, I want to see all the old traditions of this country.

At the hotel I was met by a cheery-looking elderly woman. She wore the peasant costume of the region—a white dress, topped with a long, brightly-colored apron. Apparently I was expected, for when I came up she bowed and said, "You are our English guest?"

"Yes," I said, "my name is Jonathan Harker."

She smiled, and spoke in her language to an elderly man who had followed her to the door. He left, but immediately returned with a letter, which he handed to me. It read:

"My friend—Welcome to my homeland. I am eagerly expecting you. Sleep well tonight. At three tomorrow the stagecoach will stop at your inn. I have reserved a seat on it for you. My own carriage will be waiting for you at the Borgo Pass, and it will bring you to me. I trust that your journey from London has been a happy one and that you will enjoy your stay in my beautiful land. —Your friend, Dracula."

May 4. Today I tried to have a chat with my host at the inn. But when I asked him a few questions about the Count and his castle, he became very quiet and claimed that he could not understand my German. I'm sure this wasn't true, because up until then he had understood it perfectly.

When I continued to try, he and his wife looked at each other in a frightened sort of way. He mumbled that the money for my room had been sent in a letter, and that was all he knew. When I asked him if he knew Count Dracula, both he and his wife crossed themselves and said that they knew nothing at all. It was nearly time for the stagecoach to arrive, and I had no time to ask anyone else. This was all very mysterious and not at all comforting.

But just before I was to leave, the host's wife came up to my room and said in a hysterical way: "Must you go? Oh, young man, must you go?" She was in such an excited state that she seemed to have forgotten the little German she knew, and mixed it all up with some other language. When I told her that I must go at once, and that I had important business, she asked, "Do you know what day it is?" I answered that it was the fourth of May. She shook her head as she said again, "Yes, I know that! I know that, but do you know what day it is?"

I said that I did not understand, and she went on: "It is the eve of St. George's Day. Don't you know that tonight, when the clock strikes midnight, all the evil things in the world will have their full power? Don't you know where you are going, and what you are going to?" She was so upset! I tried to comfort her, but I failed completely. Finally, she got down on her knees and begged me not to go, or at least to wait a day or two before starting.

It was all nonsense, of course, but it still made me nervous. However, there was nothing I could do. So I thanked her and said that my business could not wait, and that I must go.

She then rose and dried her eyes. Taking a crucifix on a chain from around her neck, she offered it to me.

I did not know what to do. The church I grew up in did not approve of symbols such as crucifixes, and yet it seemed rude to refuse the old lady's gift, especially when she was so upset.

I suppose she saw the doubt in my face, for she fastened the chain around my neck herself. "Wear it for your mother's sake," she said, and went out of the room.

I am writing this part of the diary while I wait for the coach—which is, of course, late— and the crucifix is still round my neck.

Whether it is the old lady's fear, or the many ghostly traditions of this place, I do not know, but I am not feeling nearly as relaxed as usual. But here comes the coach!

May 5. When I got on the coach, the driver was still outside talking to my landlady. They seemed to be speaking of me, for every now and then they looked at me. Then some other people who were sitting on the bench outside the door came and listened, and then stared at me too, most of them with pity in their eyes. I could hear words often repeated, strange words, for there were many nationalities in the crowd. I quietly got my European languages dictionary from my bag and looked them up.

I must say they did nothing to cheer me up, for among them were *Ordog*, which means "Satan," *Pokol*—"hell," *stregoica*—"witch," *vrolok* and *vlkoslak*—both meaning something that is either werewolf or vampire. (Note: Ask the Count about all this.)

When we started, the crowd around the inn door all made the sign of the cross and pointed two fingers towards me.

With some difficulty, I got a fellow passenger to tell me what they meant. He would not answer at first, but finally explained that the gesture was a charm against the evil eye.

This was not very pleasant for me, just starting out for an unknown place to meet an unknown man. But everyone seemed so kind-hearted that I was sure they meant well.

Then our driver cracked his big whip over his four small horses, and we set off on our journey.

I soon forgot my ghostly fears in the beauty of the scenery. Before us lay a green, sloping land full of forests and woods, with steep hills here and there, crowned with clumps of trees or with farmhouses. There were fruit blossoms everywhere—apple, plum, pear, cherry. And as we drove by, I could see the green grass under the trees dotted with the fallen petals. In and out among these green hills ran the road.

Beyond the hills rose the mighty slopes of the Carpathian Mountains. They towered on either side of us, with the afternoon sun bringing out all their glorious colors: deep blue and purple in the shadows of the peaks, green and brown where grass and rock mingled, and over all, the gleam of the snowy peaks.

As we continued on our endless way, and the sun sank lower and lower, the shadows of the evening began to creep around us. Sometimes the hills were so steep that the horses could only go slowly, no matter how the driver cracked his whip. I wanted to get out of the coach and walk, as we do at home, to make the load lighter, but the driver would not hear of it. "No, no," he said. "You must not walk here. The dogs are too fierce." And then he added, "And you may have enough of such trouble before you go to sleep." The only stop he would make was a moment's pause to light his lamps.

When it grew dark, the passengers seemed

to become very excited, and they kept speaking to him, as though telling him to go faster. He lashed the horses unmercifully with his long whip, and shouted at them to gallop harder. Then through the darkness I could see a sort of patch of gray light ahead of us. The excitement of the passengers grew greater. The coach rocked like a boat tossed on a stormy sea, so I was forced to hang on. Then the mountains seemed to come nearer to us on each side and to frown down upon us. We were entering the Borgo Pass.

Several of the passengers began to offer me gifts, refusing to take no for an answer. The gifts were an odd mixture, but each was given with great kindness, along with a blessing and that same strange gesture that I had seen in Bistritz. Then, as we flew along, the driver leaned forward, and on each side the passengers peered eagerly into the darkness. It was clear that something exciting was either happening or expected, but no one would explain it to me.

At last we saw the pass opening out on the eastern side. There were dark, rolling clouds overhead, and a heavy sense of thunder in the air. I looked for the carriage which was to take me to the Count. Each moment I expected to see the glare of lamps through the blackness, but all was dark. We could now see the sandy road lying white before us, but there was on it no sign of a vehicle. The passengers sat back with a sigh of relief, which contrasted with my own disappointment. I was wondering what I should do, when the driver, looking at his watch, said something to the others that I could hardly hear. I thought what he said was, "An hour early."

Then, turning to me, he spoke in German that was worse than my own: "There is no carriage here. There is no one to meet you after all. I will take you now to Bukovina, and bring you back tomorrow or the next day, better the next day."

But while he was speaking, the horses began to neigh and snort and plunge wildly. Then, among a chorus of screams from my fellow passengers, a carriage with four horses pulled up beside our coach. I could see from the light of our lamps that the horses were splendid, coal-black animals. They were driven by a tall man, with a long brown beard and a great black hat. I could see the gleam of his bright eyes, which seemed red in the lamplight, as he turned to us.

He said to the driver, "You are early tonight, my friend."

Our driver stammered in reply, "The

Englishman was in a hurry."

To which the stranger replied, "Is that why you wanted him to go on to Bukovina? You cannot deceive me, my friend. I know too much, and my horses are swift."

As he spoke he smiled. His lips were very red and his teeth, as white as ivory, looked sharp. "Give me the Englishman's luggage," he said, and the coach driver hurriedly did as he asked. As I climbed down from the side of the coach, the bearded man helped me with a hand that had a grip of steel. He must have been tremendously strong.

Without a word he shook his reins, the horses turned, and we swept into the darkness of the pass. As I looked back I saw the steam rise from the stagecoach horses. Their driver cracked his whip, and off they went on their way to Bukovina. As they disappeared into the darkness, I felt a strange chill, and a lonely feeling came over me. But a blanket was thrown over my shoulders, and another across my knees, and the driver said in excellent German, "The night is chilly, sir, and my master the Count told me to take good care of you. There is a bottle of brandy underneath the seat, if you should want some."

I did not want any, but it was a comfort to know it was there. I felt strange, even frightened, and I wished I was doing anything instead of making this night journey. The carriage went swiftly ahead; then we made a complete turn and went along another straight road. It seemed to me that we were simply going back and forth over the same ground again. I made myself notice a spot in the landscape and, when I saw it pass a second time, knew that I was correct. I wanted to ask the driver what this all meant, but I was really afraid to speak up. There was nothing I could do if he, for some reason, wanted to make our trip take longer than necessary.

Eventually, though, I was curious to know the time. I struck a match, and by its flame looked at my watch. It was a few minutes before midnight. This gave me a sort of shock. I suppose the general superstition about midnight was made worse by my recent experiences. I waited with a sick feeling of suspense.

Then a dog began to howl somewhere in a farmhouse far down the road—a long, agonized wailing, as if from fear. The sound was taken up by another dog, and then another and another. Through the gloom of night, the wild howling seemed to come from all over the country.

At the first howl the horses began to strain and rear. The driver spoke to them soothingly, and they quieted down, but shivered and sweated. Then, far off in the distance, there began a louder, sharper howling. It was the sound of wolves. The horses and I reacted in about the same way. I wanted to jump from the carriage and run, and the horses reared again and plunged madly. The driver had to use all his great strength to keep them from bolting. In a few minutes, however, my own ears got accustomed to the sound, and the horses became quiet enough that the driver was able to climb down and stand before them.

He petted and soothed them, and whispered something in their ears, as I have heard of horse-tamers doing. To my amazement, as they listened they became quite manageable again, though they still trembled. The driver again took his seat, and we started off at a fast pace. This time, after going to the far side of the pass, he turned down a narrow roadway which ran sharply to the right.

Soon we were hemmed in by trees, which in places arched over the roadway to form a tunnel. It grew colder and colder still, and fine, powdery snow began to fall. The wind still carried the howling of the dogs, though this grew fainter as we went on our way. The baying of the wolves sounded nearer and nearer, as though they were closing round on us from every side. I grew dreadfully afraid, and the horses shared my fear. The driver, however, did not seem the least bit disturbed.

Suddenly, away on our left I saw a faint flickering blue flame. The driver saw it at the same moment. He stopped the horses, and, jumping to the ground, disappeared into the darkness. I did not know what to do, especially since the howling of the wolves was growing closer. But while I wondered, the driver appeared again. Without a word he took his seat, and we resumed our journey. I think I must have fallen asleep and kept dreaming of the incident, for it seemed to be repeated endlessly, and now looking back, it is like a sort of awful nightmare.

A second time the driver left his seat and disappeared after the blue flame, and this time he was gone longer than before. The horses began to tremble worse than ever and to snort and scream with fright. I could not see why, for the howling of the wolves had stopped. But just then, the moon burst out from behind the black clouds. By its light I saw a ring of wolves around us, with white teeth, grinning red mouths, and shaggy hair. They were a hundred times more terrifying in silence than when they howled. I felt paralyzed with fear. It

is only when a man finds himself face to face with such horrors that he can understand how awful they are.

Then the wolves began to howl, as though the moonlight had had some strange effect on them. The horses jumped about and reared, and looked around helplessly with eyes that rolled wildly. But the living ring of terror imprisoned them on every side. I called to the coachman to come. I shouted and beat the side of the carriage, hoping by the noise to frighten the wolves away and give the driver a chance to return. I don't know where he came from, but suddenly he was there. I heard his voice shout in a commanding tone, and he raised his arms as though brushing something away. The wolves fell back and melted away into the darkness. The driver returned to his seat, and we set off once again.

This was all so strange that a dreadful fear came upon me, and I was afraid to speak or move. The ride seemed to go on forever, and we traveled now in complete darkness. Up and up the road climbed and then, suddenly, I realized we were turning into the courtyard of a vast ruined castle. From its tall black windows came no ray of light.

Chapter 2

May 5. I must have been asleep, for if I had been fully awake I certainly would have noticed we were approaching such a strange place. In the gloom the courtyard seemed very large, with several huge round arches leading out of it. Perhaps it seemed bigger than it really was. I have not yet seen it by daylight.

When the carriage stopped, the driver jumped down and then helped me to the ground. Again I couldn't help noticing his great strength. His hand felt like a steel vise that could have crushed mine if he had chosen. Then he took my suitcases and placed them on the ground. I stood close to a great door, old and studded with large iron nails, all set in a massive stone frame. Even in the dim light I could see that the stone was covered with carvings, but that they were worn by time and weather. As I stood, the driver jumped again into his seat and shook the reins. The horses started forward, and the carriage disappeared through one of the dark arches.

I didn't know what to do. There was no bell or knocker on the door. The walls looked so thick that I doubted that anyone inside would hear me call. I waited what seemed an endless time, and I felt doubts and fears crowding on me. What sort of place had I come to? What sort of grim adventure was this? Was this the normal experience of a lawyer's clerk, sent out to explain the purchase of a London home to a foreigner? "Lawyer's clerk"—Mina would not like that! I should say lawyer, for just before leaving London I learned that I had passed my examinations. I am now a full-blown lawyer myself. I began to rub my eyes and pinch myself to see if I were awake. It all seemed like a horrible nightmare to me, and I hoped that I would wake up and find myself at home. But I was indeed awake and in this strange place. All I could do now was to be patient.

Just as I had given up hope of getting

inside that night, I heard a heavy step approaching behind the great door. Then there was the sound of rattling chains and the clanking of bolts drawn back. A key was turned with a loud grating noise, and the door swung open.

There in the doorway stood a tall old man. He had a long white moustache, and he was dressed in black from head to foot. He held an antique silver lamp, which threw long quivering shadows as it flickered in the draft. The old man motioned me in, saying in excellent English, but with a strange accent, "Welcome to my house! Enter freely and of your own free will!"

He stood like a statue, as though his gesture of welcome had turned him into stone. The instant, however, that I had stepped over the threshold, he moved forward and grasped my hand with such strength that he hurt me. His hand felt cold as ice, more like the hand of a dead than a living man. Again he said. "Welcome to my house! Enter freely, and leave something of the happiness you bring!"

The strength of the handshake was so much like that of the carriage driver, whose face I had not seen, that for a moment I thought it must be the same man. So to make sure, I said questioningly, "Count Dracula?"

He bowed politely as he replied, "I am Dracula, and I welcome you, Mr. Harker, to my house. Come in; the night air is cold, and you need to eat and rest." As he spoke, he set down his lamp, and stepped out to take my luggage. I protested that I would carry it myself, but he insisted.

"No, sir, you are my guest. It is late, and my servants are not available. Let me help you." I followed him through the door, up a great winding staircase, then through a wide hallway on whose stone floor our steps rang. At the end of the hall, he threw open a heavy door. I was happy to see a well-lit room containing a table covered with food. In the fireplace a great fire burned warm and bright.

The Count opened another door, which led into a small eight-sided room lit by a single lamp, and without a window of any sort. Passing through this, he opened another door, and motioned me to enter. It was a welcome sight. For here was a large bedroom, well lighted and warmed with another log fire. The Count set down my luggage and said, "After your long trip, I'm sure you will want to wash up and relax for a few moments. When you are ready, come have some supper."

The light and warmth and the Count's welcome made all my fears melt away. I realized that I was half-starved, so I quickly tidied up and returned to the other room.

My supper was waiting. My host, who leaned against one side of the great fireplace, made a graceful wave of his hand towards the table and said, "Please, sit and eat. I have already dined, so I will not join you."

I handed him the sealed letter that my employer, Mr. Hawkins, had sent along. He opened it and read it gravely. Then, with a charming smile, he handed it to me to read. One passage pleased me very much. Mr. Hawkins had written, "I am so sorry that my health does not allow me to travel to see you myself. But I am confident Mr. Harker will do an excellent job. He is a young man full of energy and talent, and I have known him since he was a boy. You may trust him absolutely."

Dinner consisted of an excellent roast chicken, some cheese and salad, and a bottle of wine. As I ate, the Count asked me many questions about my journey, and I told him everything that had happened.

By this time I had finished my supper, and I accepted my host's invitation to draw a chair up to the fire and smoke a cigar. I now had a good chance to study him, and I found him a remarkable-looking man. He had an unforgettable face, with a high, thin nose and arched nostrils. His forehead was large and dome-shaped. His eyebrows were massive, almost meeting over the nose. The mouth, so far as I could see it under the heavy moustache, was hard and rather cruel-looking, with oddly sharp white teeth. The teeth showed a little over his lips, which were much redder than is usual in an elderly man. His skin was unusually pale.

I found myself looking at his hands as they

rested on his knees. They were broad, with thick fingers, and his long nails were cut to a point. Once as we talked, he leaned close to me and touched me on the arm. I could not help but shudder. A feeling of nausea had swept over me. The Count seemed to notice, and he drew back with a grim smile.

Eventually our conversation ceased. As we sat in silence, I saw the first dim streak of dawn through the window. Then, from the valley below, I heard the howling of many wolves. The Count's eyes gleamed, and he said, "Listen to them, the children of the night. What music they make!" I suppose he saw the expression on my face, for he added, "Ah, I forgot. You city people cannot understand how a hunter feels."

Then he rose and added, "But you must be tired. Your bedroom is all ready. Tomorrow, sleep as late as you like. I have to be away till the afternoon, so sleep well and dream well!" With a courteous bow, he left me.

May 7. I have rested well, and slept until late in the day. When I had dressed, I went into the room where I had eaten and found a cold breakfast laid out, with coffee kept hot over the fire. There was a note on the table, which read, "I have to be absent for a while. Do not wait for me. D."

I enjoyed a hearty meal. When finished, I looked for a bell, so that I could let the servants know, but I could not find one. It is odd what I do not find in the house, when it is obvious that the Count is very wealthy. The table service is of gold, and so beautifully made that it must be of immense value. The curtains and upholstery of the chairs are made of the costliest and most beautiful fabrics. Although they must be centuries old, they are in excellent condition. But still, I can't find a mirror anywhere. There is not even one in my bathroom—I had to get a small mirror from my suitcase before I could shave or brush my hair. I have not yet seen a servant, or heard a sound near the castle except the howling of wolves.

Some time after I had finished my meal, I looked about for something to read. I didn't want to wander about the castle without the Count's permission, but there was absolutely nothing in the room—not a book, newspaper, or even writing paper. One door in the room was locked. But another one opened, and behind it I found a sort of library.

To my delight, I found there a great number of books in English—whole shelves of them, and even English magazines and newspapers, although none of them was very recent. The books were on all subjects—history, geography, politics, political economy, botany, geology, law—but they all related to England and English life and English customs and manners. There was even a directory of London streets.

While I was looking at the books, the door opened and the Count entered. He greeted me cheerfully, and said he hoped that I had had a good night's rest. Then he went on.

"I am glad you found your way in here, for I am sure there is much that will interest you. These companions," and he laid his hand on some of the books, "have been good friends to me, ever since I had the idea of moving to London. Through them I have come to know and love your great England. I am anxious to reach London and experience it all for myself. I only wish I spoke English better."

"But, Count," I said, "your English is excellent!"

"I thank you, my friend, but I have barely begun. True, I know the grammar and the words, but yet I know not how to speak them."

"That's not so," I said, "You speak very well."

He shook his head. "If I were in London, everyone would recognize me as a foreigner.

That is not good enough for me. Here I am a nobleman. But in a strange land, a foreigner is a nobody. I want to speak so that no one in England who hears me will think, 'Ha ha! A foreigner!' I have been master too long, you see, and I will not let anyone else be master of me. And you will help me, Jonathan Harker. You are here not only to tell me about my new estate in London. You shall, I hope, stay with me a while, so that I may learn how to speak like an Englishman. And I ask you to tell me when I make error, even of the smallest, in my speaking."

Of course I said I would be glad to help, then asked if I could use the library whenever I chose. He answered, "Yes, certainly. You may go anywhere you wish in the castle, except where the doors are locked. I have my reasons for this." I said I understood, and then he went on. "We are in Transylvania, and Transylvania is not England. Our ways are not your ways, and you will find some things here strange. But from what you have told me of your trip, you have already begun to discover that."

We went on talking for a long time, for it was clear that he was in the mood for conversation. Eventually, I asked him about some of the strange things that had happened the night before, especially why the coachman went to the places where he had seen the blue flames. The Count explained that it was commonly believed that on the eve of St. George's Day, when all evil spirits are supposed to be loose on earth, a blue flame is seen over any place where treasure has been buried.

"But now," he said at last, "tell me of London and of the house which you have purchased for me." I went into my room to get the papers from my bag. While I was there, I heard a rattling of china and silver in the next room, and as I passed through, I noticed that the table had been cleared and the lamp lit. The lamps were also lit in the library, and I found the Count lying on the sofa, reading another of his guides to England.

When I came in, he cleared the books and papers from the table, and together we went over all the documents. He was interested in everything, and asked me a thousand questions about the place and its surroundings. As we talked, it became clear that he knew the neighborhood of his new home much better than I did. When I mentioned this, he said, "Well, but isn't it important that I know it? When I go there I shall be all alone, and my friend Jonathan Harker will not be by my side to correct and help me. He will be in Exeter, miles away!"

I described the estate, known as Carfax, to him in detail. Its twenty acres are surrounded by a high stone wall. Inside those walls are many trees, which make it quite gloomy in places. The house is very large and dates back to medieval times and contains an old chapel or church. There are only a few other houses nearby. One of them, a very large building, is now used as an insane asylum.

When I had finished, he said, "I am glad that it is old and big. I am of an old family, and to live in a new house would kill me. And I rejoice too that there is an ancient chapel. Even in death, we Transylvanian nobles do not want to lie among the common people. The house sounds exactly like what I seek."

He then left me again, but returned after an hour to say, "Aha! Still at your books? Good! But you must not work always. Come, I am told that your supper is ready." He took my arm, and we went into the next room, where I found an excellent supper on the table. Again, the Count did not join me, saying he had eaten dinner on the road that afternoon. But he sat with me, and chatted while I ate. After supper the Count stayed on, asking questions on every imaginable subject, hour after hour. It was getting very late indeed, but

I did not say anything, for I wanted to please my host. I was not sleepy, as I had slept so late the previous day, but sitting up all night still seemed unnatural. All at once we heard the crow of a rooster.

Count Dracula, jumping to his feet, said, "Why, there is the morning again! How rude of me to keep you up all night. Next time, you must make your conversation regarding my dear new country of England less interesting." With a bow, he quickly left me.

May 8. I thought perhaps as I wrote this journal that I was going into too much detail about unimportant things. But now I am glad I have written it, for there is something so strange about this place that I feel uneasy. I wish that I had never come. It may be that staying up all night is beginning to wear me out. If there were anyone I could talk to, it would help, but there is only the Count. And the Count . . . I begin to think I am the only living soul within this place. I do not want to let my imagination run wild. Let me just get the facts down, as clearly as I can.

I didn't sleep well, and I got up after just a few hours. I had hung my little mirror by the window and was beginning to shave. Suddenly I felt a hand on my shoulder, and I heard the

Count's voice say, "Good morning."

I jumped, for I hadn't seen him at all, even though the mirror showed the room behind me. As I jumped I nicked myself with the razor, although I didn't notice that right away. I answered the Count, and looked back in the mirror to see how I could have missed him. But there was no mistake. The Count was standing right there. I could see him over my shoulder. But there was no reflection of him in the mirror. There was no sign of any man but me.

This was startling enough. But at that instant I saw that the cut had bled a little, and the blood was trickling over my chin. I laid down the razor and turned to get a tissue. When the Count saw my face, his eyes blazed with a sort of devilish fury, and he suddenly made a grab at my throat. I pulled back and his hand touched the string of beads that which held the crucifix around my neck. In an instant the fury was gone from his face, so quickly that I could hardly believe it had been there.

"Be careful," he said, "be careful how you cut yourself. It is more dangerous than you think in this country." Then, grabbing the mirror, he went on. "And this is the useless piece of vanity that has done the mischief. Away with it!" And opening the window with one wrench of his hand, he threw out the mirror, which shattered into a thousand pieces on the stones of the courtyard far below. Then he left without a word. It is very annoying, for I don't know how I am going to shave.

When I went into the dining room, breakfast was prepared, but I could not find the Count anywhere. So I ate alone. It is strange that I have not yet seen him eat, or even drink. He is a very peculiar man!

After breakfast I did a little exploring in the castle. I went out on the stairs, and found a room looking towards the south. The view was magnificent, and where I stood was a wonderful place to see it. The castle is on the very edge of a terrifically high cliff. If I dropped a stone from the window, it would fall a thousand feet without touching anything. As far as I could see was a sea of green treetops. Here and there silver threads show where the rivers wind through the forest.

But I don't have the heart to describe the beauty. For after I had seen the view, I explored more of the castle. There are doors, doors everywhere, but all are locked tight. There is no exit available to me except for those awful windows. In other words, the castle is a prison, and I am a prisoner!

Chapter 3

Jonathan Harker's Journal
(continued)

When I found that I was imprisoned, a wild feeling came over me. I rushed up and down the stairs, trying every door and peering out of every window I could find. When I look back, I think I must have been crazy for a while, for I behaved just as a rat does in a trap.

But once I realized just how helpless I was, I sat down quietly and began to think. I am still thinking, and I have not reached any decision. There is only one thing that I know for sure: there is no use speaking to the Count. He knows very well that I am locked up, for he has done it himself.

So far as I can see, all I can do for now is keep quiet, and keep my eyes wide open. One of two things is happening: either I am being tricked by my own fears, or I am in desperate trouble. If the second is true, I will need to keep my wits about me to survive.

Just as I thought these words, I heard the great entry door below shut, and I knew that the Count had returned. He did not come into the library, so I went cautiously to my own room and saw him there, making the bed. This was odd, but it added to my belief that there are no servants in the house. When I later looked through a chink in the door and saw him setting the table, I knew I was correct. For if he does all these little jobs himself, surely it means there is no one else in the castle. It also means that it was the Count himself who was the driver of the coach that brought me here. This is a terrible thought. For what does it mean that he could control the wolves by holding up his hand? Why did the people at Bistritz and on the coach have such terrible fear for me? Why did they give me such strange gifts: a crucifix, garlic, a wild rose, a branch of mountain ash?

Bless that good woman who hung the crucifix round my neck! For it is a comfort and a strength to me whenever I touch it. It is odd that a thing which I have never put stock in should now, in a time of loneliness and trouble, be of help.

But for now, I must find out all I can about Count Dracula. It may help me to understand what is happening. Tonight I will try to make him talk about himself. I must be very careful, however, not to awaken his suspicion.

Midnight. I have had a long talk with the Count. I asked him a few questions on Transylvanian history, and he become very enthusiastic about the subject. In his speaking of things and people, and especially of battles, he spoke as if he had been present at them all. His pride in the Dracula name is immense. As he spoke of the bloody wars in which his family took a leading part, he grew excited. He walked about the room pulling his great white moustache and grasping anything he laid his hands on as though he would crush it to bits.

By the time he finished his tales, it was close to morning and we went to bed. (Note: This diary seems horribly like the beginning of the "Arabian Nights," for every story has to break off at dawn.)

May 12. Last evening, when the Count came from his room, he asked me questions about business and the law. The Count's questions were of a particular sort, so I will put them down here. Maybe they will be useful in some way.

First, he asked if a man in England could have two lawyers or more. I told him he could have a dozen if he wished, but that it would not be wise to have more than one lawyer working on a single matter, as only one could take action at a time. He seemed to understand. He went on to ask if that meant, for example, that he could have one lawyer taking care of his banking, and another of his shipping?

"Of course," I replied. "Men of business often do that, so that no one person knows all about their affairs."

"Good!" he said, and then went on to ask just how those various lawyers could be found and hired. I explained all these things to him as well as I could. He certainly would have made a wonderful lawyer himself, for there is nothing that he does not think of.

When we were finished talking, he said, "Have you written to our friend Mr. Peter Hawkins, or to anyone else?"

It was with some bitterness in my heart that I answered no, that I had not had a chance to send a letter to anyone.

"Then write now, my young friend," he

said, laying a heavy hand on my shoulder, "write to our friend and to any other, and say that you shall stay with me for another month."

"Do you wish me to stay so long?" I asked, for my heart grew cold at the thought.

"I desire it very much. In fact, I will take no refusal. When your master, employer, whatever you call him, arranged for someone to come here, it was understood that he would stay as long as I needed."

What could I do but accept? It was clear from the look in Count Dracula's eyes that I had no choice in the matter.

The Count continued. "And please, my good young friend, do not write of anything other than business in your letters. I'm sure it will please your friends to know that you are well, and that you look forward to getting home to them. Is it not so?" As he spoke he handed me three sheets of note paper and three envelopes. Looking at them, then at him, I noticed his quiet smile, with the sharp canine teeth lying over the red lower lip. I understood very well what he was saying. I should be careful what I wrote, for he would read it. So I decided to write as he asked now, but to find some way to write to Mr. Hawkins in secret. I would write to Mina as well, and I would write in shorthand, which the Count might be unable to read.

When I had written my two letters I sat quietly, reading a book, while the Count wrote several notes of his own. He then left the room to put away his writing materials. As quickly as I could, I leaned over to look at his letters. They were addressed to bankers and lawyers in England, in Budapest, and in the Bulgarian city of Varna. When I saw the door handle move, I sank back in my seat, quickly picking up my book before the Count entered the room. He took up the letters on the table, stamped them carefully, and said, "I hope you will forgive me if I work in private this evening. You will, I hope, find everything you need." At the door he turned, and after a moment's pause said, "Let me give you some advice, my dear young friend. If you leave these rooms, do not go to sleep in any other part of the castle. It is old, and there are bad dreams for those who sleep unwisely. Be warned! If you should find yourself falling asleep, then hurry to your own room or here, to the library. In either place you will be safe. But if you do not do this, then . . ." He finished his speech in a gruesome way, for he motioned with his hands as if he were washing them.

When he left me, I went to my room. After

a little while, not hearing any sound, I came out and went up the stone stair to where I could look out towards the south. This strange night existence is beginning to wear me out and make me horribly nervous. I jump at my own shadow, and my imagination runs wild. I stood looking out at the beautiful view, bathed in soft yellow moonlight till it was almost as light as day. The beauty seemed to cheer me, and to give me some peace and comfort.

As I leaned from the window, my eye was caught by something moving below me. The movement was a little to my left, about where I imagined the windows of the Count's own room would be. I drew back behind the great stone frame around the window I stood in, and looked carefully out.

What I saw was the Count's head coming out from the window. I did not see the face, but I knew the man by the neck and the movement of his back and arms. At first I was interested by the sight. You must understand, it takes very little to interest a man when he is a prisoner. But my feelings changed to terror at what I observed next. The whole man slowly emerged from the window and began to crawl down the castle wall. He was moving face down with his cloak spreading out around him like great wings.

At first I could not believe my eyes. I thought it was some trick of the moonlight, some weird effect of shadow. But I kept looking, and it was no trick. The Count's fingers and toes grasped the corners of the stones. He moved downwards quickly, just as a lizard moves along a wall.

What kind of man is this—or what kind of creature that appears to be a man? My dread of this horrible place is overpowering me. I am in awful fear, and there is no escape for me.

May 15.   Once more I have seen the Count go out in his lizard fashion. He moved downwards about a hundred feet, and a good deal to the left, then vanished into some hole or window.

I knew he had left the castle now, and I decided to explore more than I had dared to before. Taking a lamp with me, I tried the nearest doors. They were all locked, as I had expected. I went down the stone stairs to the hall where I had entered the night I arrived. That great exit door, too, was locked tight.

The keys to all the doors must be in the Count's room. I must wait and watch until he leaves his room open. Then I will get the keys and escape.

I went on to search the other stairs and

passages. One or two small rooms near the hall were unlocked, but there was nothing to see in them except old furniture, dusty with age. At last, however, I found one door at the top of the stairway which gave a little when I pushed at it. I realized that it was not really locked; it was just that the hinges had sagged a little, so that the heavy door rested on the floor. I knew I might not have this chance again. I pushed against the door as hard as I could and entered the room.

I was now in a wing of the castle, a story below the one I knew. I guessed that this had once been an area where ladies lived, for the furniture was more feminine and comfortable than any I had seen.

The windows had no curtains, and the yellow moonlight flooded in through the diamond panes of glass. As frightened as I was, the room had a comforting effect upon me. It was a relief to be away from the rooms where I had spent so much time with the Count. And so here I am, writing at a little oak table where in old times some fair lady may have sat to write a love-letter.

Later. The morning of May 16. God save my sanity, for that is all I can hope for. While I live here, there is only one thing to hope for— that

I may not go mad. Indeed, I may be mad already. Merciful God, let me be calm and record what has happened.

Last night, after I had written in my diary (and, fortunately, had replaced the book and pen in my pocket), I felt sleepy. I remembered the Count's warning about not sleeping in any other part of the castle, but I took pleasure in disobeying it. The soft moonlight soothed me, and the wide-open views from the windows gave me a sense of freedom. I decided not to return to my gloom-haunted room. Instead I would sleep here, where, in olden times, ladies had sat and sung and lived sweet lives. I pulled a great couch out of its place near the corner, so that I could lie looking at the lovely view. I suppose I must have fallen asleep. I hope so, but I fear that what happened next was not a dream, but all too real.

I was not alone. The room was the same, unchanged in any way since I came into it. In the brilliant moonlight, I could see my own footsteps in the dust along the floor. But opposite me were three young women, dressed like wealthy ladies. I thought that I must be dreaming when I saw them, for they threw no shadows on the floor.

They came close, looking at me and whispering together. Two of them were dark, and

had high thin noses, like the Count. Their large eyes, dark and piercing, seemed almost red in the yellow moonlight. The third was very blonde, with great masses of golden hair and eyes like pale blue sapphires. All three had brilliant white teeth that shone like pearls against the ruby of their full lips.

They made me feel an uneasy mix of emotions. They were lovely, and yet I felt a kind of deadly fear. In my heart was a wicked, burning desire that they would kiss me with those red lips. I should not write this down, in case some day Mina should read these words and be hurt by them, but it is the truth. They whispered together, and then all three laughed. Their laughter was silvery and musical, but it was also hard; too hard to have come through the softness of human lips. The fair girl shook her head flirtatiously, and the other two urged her on.

One said, "Go on! You first, and then us. It is your turn to begin."

The other added, "He is young and strong. There are kisses for us all."

I lay quiet, looking out from under my eyelashes, hardly able to breathe. I was inflamed by a sense of delightful anticipation. The fair girl advanced and bent down until I could feel her breath upon me. It smelled sweet as honey, but there was a bitter undertaste to it, like the scent of blood.

She sank to her knees, and bent over me. Her expression was both excited and triumphant. The slow, deliberate way she moved was both thrilling and repulsive. As she arched her neck, she licked her lips like an animal. I could see in the moonlight the moisture shining on her scarlet lips. Her head bent lower and lower. Her lips passed by my mouth. I could hear the wet sound of her tongue as it licked her teeth and lips, and I felt her hot breath on my neck. Then the skin of my throat began to tingle as one's skin does when another's hand is about to touch it. I could feel the soft touch of her lips on the sensitive skin of my throat, then the hardness of two sharp teeth, just touching and pausing there. I closed my eyes in sleepy ecstasy and waited, waited with beating heart.

But at that instant, another sensation swept through me as quick as lightning. The Count was there, and he was in a storm of fury. As my eyes opened, I saw his strong hand grasp the slender neck of the fair woman and hurl her away from me. Her blue eyes flashed with anger, her white teeth snapped together with rage, and her cheeks blazed red. But the Count! Never did I imagine such anger. His eyes were positively blazing. The red light in them shone brightly, as if the flames of hell fire burned behind them. He was deathly pale, and the lines of his face were hard as wires. With a fierce sweep of his arm, he motioned to the women, as though he were beating them back. It was the same commanding gesture I had seen him make to the wolves. In a voice which was almost a whisper, but seemed to cut through the air, he said, "How dare you touch him, any of you? How dare you look on him when I had forbidden it? Back, I tell you all! This man belongs to me! If you meddle with him, you'll have me to deal with."

The fair girl, with a laugh, turned to answer him. "You yourself never loved. You never love!" The other women joined in, and their humorless, hard laughter seemed like the laughter of fiends.

Then the Count turned, after looking at

my face carefully, and said in a soft whisper, "Yes, I too can love. You know that from the past. I promise that when I am done with him, you shall kiss him all you like. Now go! Go! I must awaken him, for there is work to be done."

"And is there nothing for us tonight?" said one of them, with a low laugh, as she pointed to the bag which he had thrown on the floor. It moved as though there were some live thing within it. He nodded his head. One of the women jumped forward and opened it. If I heard right, there was a gasp and a low wail, like that of a half-smothered child. The women gathered around it, while I felt dead with shock. But as I looked, they disappeared, taking with them the dreadful bag. There was no door near them, and they could not have passed me without my noticing. They simply seemed to fade into the moonlight and pass out through the window.

Then the horror overcame me, and I lost consciousness.

Chapter 4

I awoke in my own bed. If last night's horror was not a dream, then the Count must have carried me here. But I could not be sure. I did notice that my watch was not wound up, and I always wind it the last thing before going to bed. But this is no proof. In fact it might only mean that I was not in my right mind. I am glad about one thing. If the Count did indeed carry me in here, he must have been in a hurry, because my diary is still safe in my pocket. If he had found it, surely he would have either taken or destroyed it.

Although this room has been to me so full

of fear, it now seems like a place of safety. For nothing can be more dreadful than those awful women, who were—who are—waiting to suck my blood.

May 18. I have been down to look at that room again in daylight, for I must know the truth. When I got to the door at the top of the stairs, I found it closed and locked. It had been forced into place with such strength that the wood at its top was splintered. This was no dream.

May 19. My troubles grow worse. Last night the Count asked me, in the most polite way, to write three letters. The first was to say that my work here was nearly done, and that I would start for home within a few days. The second said that I was leaving the next morning from the time of the letter. And in the third I wrote that I had left the castle and arrived at Bistritz. I wanted to rebel, but I felt that it would be madness to quarrel with the Count while I am so absolutely in his power. And to refuse would be to make him suspicious. He would realize that I know too much, and that I must not live to tell anyone. My only chance is to play for more time. Something may occur which will give me a chance to escape. In explaining why he wanted me to write the letters, the Count said the chances of sending letters from this area were few and uncertain, and so that my writing now would make sure my friends did not worry unnecessarily later. I pretended to believe him, and asked what dates I should put on the letters.

He calculated a minute, and then said, "The first should be June 12, the second June 19, and the third June 29."

I know now how long he intends for me to live. God help me!

May 28. There is a chance of escape, or at any rate of my being able to send word home. A band of gypsies have come to the castle and are camped in the courtyard. I do not understand their language, but I shall write some letters home, and try to persuade the gypsies to send them for me. I have already spoken to them through my window. They took their hats off and bowed and made signs to me, although I could not understand anything that they meant . . .

I have written the letters. Mina's is in shorthand. I have explained to her my situation, very briefly. In my letter to Mr. Hawkins, I simply ask him to contact her. If the Count should see the letters, then, he would still not know how much I have learned about him.

I have given the gypsies the letters. I threw them through the bars of my window with a gold piece, and made what signs I could to have them mailed. The man who took them pressed them to his heart and bowed, and then put them in his cap. I can do no more. I went back to the study, and began to read.

The Count has come. He sat down beside me, and said in his smoothest voice as he opened two letters, "The gypsies have given me these. I don't know where they come from, but I shall, of course, take care of them. See here!" He must have looked at it—"One is from you, and to my friend Peter Hawkins. The other"—here he caught sight of the shorthand as he opened the envelope, and the dark look came into his face, and his eyes blazed wickedly—"The other is a vile thing, an outrage upon friendship and hospitality! It is not signed. Well! So it cannot matter to us." And he calmly held letter and envelope in the flame of the lamp till they were consumed.

Then he went on, "Of course I shall send on your letter to Hawkins. Your letters are sacred to me. Please pardon me, my friend, for opening it. Will you not address it again?" He held out the letter to me, and with a courteous bow handed me a clean envelope.

I could only do as he asked, and handed it to him in silence. When he went out of the room, I could hear the key turn softly. A minute later I went over and tried it, and the door was locked.

An hour or two later, the Count quietly returned to the room. His coming awakened me, for I had gone to sleep on the sofa. He was very courteous and cheery. Seeing that I had been sleeping, he said, "So, my friend, you are tired? Get to bed. I may not have the pleasure of talking with you tonight, since I have much work to do. I hope you will sleep well."

I went to my room and, strange to say, slept without dreaming. Despair has its own kind of calm.

May 31. This morning I thought I would take some papers and envelopes from my bag and keep them in my pocket, in case I have another chance to write a letter. But another shock! Every scrap of paper was gone, and with it all my notes, my records, my train schedules, in fact everything that might be useful to me if I were outside the castle. I sat and thought awhile. Then I had another thought, and I went to check my suitcase, and the closet in which I had placed my clothes.

The suit in which I had traveled was gone, and also my overcoat and traveling blanket. I could find no trace of them anywhere.

June 17. This morning, as I was sitting on the edge of my bed, I heard a cracking of whips and pounding and scraping of horses' hooves. With joy I hurried to the window, and saw two great wagons drive into the yard, each drawn by eight sturdy horses. Each wagon was driven by a peasant wearing a wide hat, dirty sheepskin, and high boots.

I ran to the window and called out to them. They looked up at me stupidly and pointed, but just then the head man of the gypsies came out. Seeing them pointing to my window, he said something, and they laughed.

After that, nothing I said or did would make them even look at me. They turned their backs. The wagons contained great square boxes with handles of thick rope. From the easy way the peasants handled them, and by the hollow noises they made as they banged on the ground, it was clear that they were empty. When the boxes were all unloaded and packed in a great heap in one corner of the yard, the gypsy gave the peasants some money. Shortly afterwards, I heard the cracking of their whips die away in the distance.

June 24. Last night the Count left me early, and locked himself into his own room. As soon as I dared, I ran up the winding stair and looked out of the window. I thought I would watch for the Count, for there is something going on. The gypsies are staying somewhere in the castle and are doing work of some kind. I know it, for now and then, I hear a faraway muffled sound, as of digging.

I had been at the window a little less than half an hour, when I saw something coming out of the Count's window. I drew back and watched carefully, and saw the whole man emerge. It was a new shock to me to find that he was wearing my traveling clothes, and slung over his shoulder was a traveling bag. I knew at once what he was up to. He will travel about, allowing others to see someone they think is me. That will create evidence that I have left the castle and gone into the towns, mailing my own letters. Furthermore, any wickedness which he may do will be blamed on me.

It makes me rage to think that this can go on while I am shut up here. Even a prisoner in jail has the protection of the law. I have none.

I thought I would watch for the Count's return, and for a long time I sat at the window. Then I began to notice that there were some little specks floating in the rays of the moonlight. They were like the tiniest grains of dust, and they whirled round and gathered in cloudy clusters. As I watched them, a sense of calm stole over me. I leaned back in a more comfortable position, so that I could enjoy the sight more fully.

Down below in the valley, the howling of dogs reached my ears. I sat up. The sound became louder, and the floating clouds of dust seemed to take new shapes as they danced in the moonlight. Even as sleep tugged at my eyelids, I felt myself struggling, fighting against something I didn't understand. I was becoming hypnotized!

Quicker and quicker danced the dust. The moonbeams seemed to quiver as they passed by me. More and more they gathered until they seemed to take dim, ghostly shapes. And then I jumped up, wide awake, and ran screaming from the place.

The phantom shapes which were gradually emerging from the moonbeams were those three ghostly women. I ran to my room, where there was no moonlight, and where the lamp was burning brightly.

When a couple of hours had passed, I heard something moving in the Count's room, and then a sharp wail which was quickly cut off. And then there was silence; deep, awful silence which chilled me. With a beating heart, I tried the door, but I was locked in my prison and could do nothing. I sat down and simply cried.

As I sat I heard an agonized cry in the courtyard below. I rushed to the window and looked out.

There was a woman with wild, disordered hair, holding her hands over her heart as though she were exhausted with running. She was leaning against the corner of the gate. When she saw my face at the window, she shouted in a voice full of hatred, "Monster, give me my child!"

She threw herself on her knees, and raising up her hands, cried the same words in tones which broke my heart. She tore at her hair, shrieking and sobbing. Finally, she ran forward, and though I could not see her, I could hear the beating of her hands against the door.

Somewhere high overhead, probably in the tower, I heard the high, metallic whisper of the Count. His call seemed to be answered from far and wide by the howling of wolves. Before many minutes had passed, a pack of them poured through the wide entrance and into the courtyard, like a pent-up river after a dam had broken.

There was no cry from the woman, and the howling of the wolves ended soon. Before long they streamed away, licking their lips.

I could not pity her, for I knew what had become of her child, and she was better off dead.

What shall I do? What can I do? How can I escape from this dreadful place of night, gloom, and fear?

June 25. Until he has lived through such a night, no man knows how sweet and dear the morning can be. When the sun climbed high in the sky this morning and shone down on the great gateway opposite my window, my fear somehow melted away. I must take action of some sort while this courage is with me. Last night I know the Count mailed one of my post-dated letters, the first of that series which is to blot out the very traces of my existence.

Let me not think of that. Action!

It has always been at night-time that these awful things have happened. I have never yet seen the Count in the daylight. Can it be that he sleeps when others wake, so that he may be awake while normal beings sleep? If I could only get into his room! But there is no possible way. The door is always locked.

And yet, there is a way, if I dare take it.

Why can't I do what he himself does? I have seen him crawl from his window. Couldn't I imitate him, and go in by his window? My chance of success is small, but my chances of surviving if I stay here are smaller still. At the worst I will die. God help me in my task! Goodbye, Mina, if I fail.

Same day, later. I have made the effort, and God helping me, I have safely returned to this room. While my courage was fresh I went straight to the window, took off my boots, and climbed outside. The stones are big and roughly cut, and the mortar has been washed away between them. I knew pretty well the direction and distance of the Count's window, and I headed for it as best I could. It seemed no time until I found myself standing on the windowsill. I was filled with fear, however, when I bent down and slid feet first in through the window. Then I looked around for the Count, but with surprise and gladness, I saw that the room was empty!

It was barely furnished with odd things which seemed to have never been used. The furniture was covered with dust. I looked for the key, but it was not in the lock, and I could not find it anywhere. The only thing I found was a great heap of gold in one corner. There were coins of all kinds—Roman, and British, and Austrian, and Hungarian, and Greek and Turkish—covered with a film of dust, as though they had lain there for a long time. None of the money was less than three hundred years old.

My main purpose was to find the key to the room or the key to the outer door, but I could not find either. At one corner of the room was a heavy door. It was open and led through a stone passage to a circular stairway, which went steeply down.

I descended carefully, for the stairs were dark. The only light was from a few holes in the heavy walls. At the bottom there was a dark, tunnel-like passage, through which came a sickly odor. It was the odor of freshly dug earth. As I went through the passage, the smell grew heavier. At last I pulled open a door that stood half-closed. I found myself in an old ruined chapel, which had evidently been used as a graveyard. The ground had recently been dug up, and the dirt had been placed in great wooden boxes. These were the boxes that I had recently seen brought to the castle.

Since there was nobody about, I searched every inch of the ground. I even went down into the burial vaults, although doing so made me fearful deep in my soul. In the first two vaults I saw nothing except fragments of old coffins and piles of dust. In the third, however, I made a discovery.

There, in one of the great boxes (there were fifty in all), on a pile of newly dug earth, lay the Count! He was either dead or asleep, but I could not say which. His eyes were open and stony, but they were not glazed over as dead eyes are. The cheeks had the warmth of life. The lips were as red as ever. But there was no sign of movement, no pulse, no breath, no beating of the heart.

I bent over him, trying to find any sign of life, but there was none. I thought he might have the keys on him, but when I went to search, I saw those eyes. In them was such a look of hate that I couldn't bear to be in their presence. I fled from the place. Leaving the Count's room by the window, I crawled up the castle wall. Back in my room, I threw myself upon the bed and tried to think.

June 29. Today is the date of my last letter. I am sure the Count has mailed it, for again I saw him leave the castle by the same window, and in my clothes. As he went down the wall, crawling like a lizard, I wished I had a gun so that I might destroy him. But I fear that no human weapon would have any effect on him.

I did not wait to see him return, for I was afraid of seeing those terrifying women. I came back to the library and read there till I fell asleep.

I was awakened by the Count. He looked at me as grimly as a man could look as he said, "Tomorrow, my friend, we must part. You return to your beautiful England, and I to some other work. I have already sent your letter home. Tomorrow I shall not be here, but everything shall be ready for your journey. In the morning some workmen will be arriving here. When they have gone, my carriage shall come for you, and shall take you to the Borgo Pass to meet the stagecoach, which will take you to Bistritz. But I hope that I shall see you again someday at Castle Dracula."

I asked him directly, "Why may I not go tonight?"

"Because, dear sir, my coachman and horses are away."

"But I would walk with pleasure. I want to get away at once."

He smiled, such a soft, smooth, diabolical smile that I knew there was some trick. He said, "And your baggage?"

"I do not care about it. I can send for it some other time."

The Count continued to smile with sweet

politeness. "Come with me, my dear young friend. You shall not wait another hour, although it makes me sad that you wish to leave. Come!" With great dignity, he led me down the stairs and along the hall. Suddenly he stopped. "Ah, listen!"

I heard the howling of many wolves. It was as if the sound sprang up at the rising of his hand, just as the music of an orchestra leaps under the baton of the conductor. After a pause of a moment, he walked to the door, drew back the bolts, unhooked the heavy chains, and began to open it.

The howling of the wolves outside grew louder and angrier. In my mind I could see their red jaws and snapping teeth. To struggle against the Count was useless. With wild beasts at his command, I could do nothing.

But still the door continued slowly to open, and only the Count's body stood in the gap. Suddenly I realized that this might be the moment of my death. I was to be given to the wolves. I cried out, "Shut the door! I shall wait till morning." And I covered my face with my hands to hide my tears of disappointment.

With one sweep of his powerful arm, the Count threw the door shut, and the great bolts clanged and echoed through the hall.

In silence we returned to the library, and

after a minute or two I went to my own room. When I last saw Count Dracula, he kissed his hand to me. There was a red light of triumph in his eyes, and a smile on his face that Judas in hell might be proud of.

When I was in my room and about to lie down, I heard whispering at my door. I went to it softly and listened, and I heard the voice of the Count.

"Back! Back to your own place! Your time has not yet come. Wait! Have patience! Tonight is mine. Tomorrow night is yours!"

There was a low, sweet ripple of laughter, and in a rage I threw open the door, and saw the three terrible women licking their lips. As I appeared, they all joined in a horrible laugh, and ran away.

I came back to my room and threw myself on my knees. Is my death so near? Tomorrow! Tomorrow! Lord, help me!

June 30. These may be the last words I ever write in this diary. I slept till just before the dawn, and when I woke threw myself on my knees to pray. I am determined that if Death comes, he will find me ready.

At last I heard the welcome crow of the rooster, and I felt that I was safe. I opened the door and ran down the hall. The night before

I had seen that the door was unlocked, and now escape was possible. With trembling hands, I unhooked the chains and threw back the massive bolts.

But the door would not move. I pulled and pulled at the massive thing and shook it until it rattled. It had been locked after I left the Count.

Wild with despair, I decided to scale the wall again and enter the Count's room. He might kill me, but at least I would die trying. I rushed to the east window, and scrambled down the wall and into the Count's room. It was empty, as I expected. I could not see a key anywhere, but the heap of gold remained. I went through the door in the corner and down the winding stair and along the dark passage to the old chapel. I knew now where to find the monster I was looking for.

The great box was in the same place, pushed against the wall. But this time the lid was on it. It was not yet fastened down, but nails lay in their places, ready to be hammered in.

I knew I must reach the body for the key. I raised the lid of the box and pushed it back against the wall. And then I saw something which filled my soul with horror. There lay the Count, but his appearance was greatly changed. He looked years younger than before. The white hair and moustache were now a dark iron gray. The cheeks were fuller, and the skin, usually so pale, had a fresh pinkness. The mouth was redder than ever, and drops of fresh blood trickled from the corners of the mouth and down over the chin and neck. Even the skin around the deep, burning eyes seemed swollen. It seemed as if the whole awful creature were simply stuffed with blood. He lay like a filthy leech, exhausted after its feast.

I shuddered. The idea of touching him was repulsive beyond belief, but I had no choice. I reminded myself that this very night, those three horrible women might feast like this on my own body. I searched everywhere, but I couldn't find the key. Then I stopped and looked at the Count. There was a mocking smile on the swollen face which almost drove me mad. This was the creature I was helping move to London. There, perhaps, for centuries, he could satisfy his lust for blood, while creating an ever-widening circle of demons like himself.

The very thought enraged me. A terrible desire came upon me to rid the world of such a monster. There was no weapon at hand, but I seized a shovel which the workmen had been using to fill the cases. Lifting it high, I struck at the hateful face with its sharp edge. But as I did so the head turned, and the eyes looked directly at me. The sight seemed to paralyze me. I nearly lost my grip on the shovel, and succeeded only in making a deep gash above the forehead. The shovel fell from my hand across the box. As I pulled it away, the blade caught the edge of the lid, which fell across the box again, hiding the horrid thing from my sight. The last glimpse I had was of the bloated, blood-stained face, grinning like the devil itself.

I tried to think of my next move, but my brain seemed on fire. In the distance I heard a gypsy song sung by merry voices coming closer, and through their song the rolling of heavy wheels and the cracking of whips. The workmen of whom the Count had spoken were coming. With a last look at the box which contained the vile body, I ran from the place and into the Count's room. I was determined to rush out at the moment the door was opened. I heard downstairs the grinding of the key in the great lock and the opening of the heavy front door.

Then there came the sound of many feet tramping and dying away in some hallway. I turned to run down again towards the vault, where I might find an escape, but at that moment there seemed to come a violent puff of wind, and the door to the winding stair blew shut. When I ran to push it open, I found that it was locked. I was again a prisoner, and the net of doom was closing around me more tightly.

As I write, I hear somewhere below me a sound of many feet and the crash of something being set down heavily. No doubt it is the boxes with their freight of earth. There is the sound of hammering. That must be the lid of the awful box containing the Count being nailed down. Now I can hear the heavy feet marching again along the hall.

The door is shut; the chains rattle. There is a grinding of the key in the lock. Another door opens and shuts. I hear the creaking of lock and bolt.

In the courtyard and down the rocky driveway I hear the roll of heavy wheels, the crack of whips, and the chorus of the work-men's voices as they pass into the distance.

I am alone in the castle with those horrible women. But no. Mina is a woman; I will not give them the same name. They are devils of hell itself!

I will not remain alone with them. I will try to climb the castle wall farther than before. I shall take some of the gold with me, in case

I need it later. I may find a way to leave this dreadful place.

And then I will head straight for home! Away to the quickest and nearest train! Away from this cursed spot, from this cursed land, where the devil and his children still walk!

At least God's mercy is better than that of those monsters. The cliff on which this castle sits is steep and high. At its foot a man may sleep, as a man. Goodbye, Mina . . .

Chapter 5

Letter from
Miss Mina Murray to Miss Lucy Westenra

May 9

My dearest Lucy,

Forgive me for taking so long to write. You know that I am teaching school, and I have been overwhelmed with work. I wish I were with you, by the sea, where we can really talk together. I have been working especially hard lately, practicing writing in shorthand. When Jonathan and I are married, he will be able to dictate his papers to me, and then I can write them out on the typewriter. He and I sometimes write letters in shorthand, and during his business trip he is keeping a shorthand journal. When you and I are vacationing together in Whitby, I will keep a diary in the same way. I don't suppose it will be very interesting to other people, but it is not intended for them. I may show it to Jonathan some day, but it is really more for practice than anything. I will try to do what journalists do, interviewing and writing descriptions and trying to remember conversations. I am told that with a little practice, one can remember almost everything that happens during a day.

However, we shall see. I will tell you of my little plans when we meet. I have just had a few hurried lines from Jonathan from Transylvania. He is well and will be returning in about a week. I can't wait to hear all his news. It must be nice to see strange countries. I wonder if we—I mean Jonathan and I—shall ever see them together. I must go now.

Goodbye,
from your loving Mina

P.S. Tell me all the news when you write. I hear rumors, especially of a tall, handsome, curly-haired man???

Letter from
Lucy Westenra to Mina Murray

May 15

My dearest Mina,

It's not fair to say I don't write! I've written you twice since we last saw each other. Besides, there really isn't any news. We just go to museums and for walks and rides in the park. As to the tall, curly-haired man, that must be Mr. Arthur Holmwood. He often comes to see us, and he and Mamma get along very well.

We recently met a man that would be perfect for you, if you were not already engaged to Jonathan. He really is a catch! His name is John Seward, and he is a handsome, pleasant doctor, very clever. He's only twenty-nine, but he is already the director of a huge lunatic asylum. He is an old friend of Mr. Holmwood's, and he often comes to visit now. He has an unusual habit of looking very intently at you, as if trying to read your mind. He tries this with me, but I don't think I let anyone know what I'm really thinking. I know this from looking at myself in the mirror. He says that I am a tough case for him, and in my humble opinion he is correct. As you know, I don't care about many things that young ladies are supposed to care about. I don't like to gossip, and clothes are a bore. Fortunately Arthur seems to like this about me . . .

There, I can't hold it in anymore, Mina. We have told all our secrets to each other since we were children. Oh, Mina, can't you guess? I'm in love with Arthur. I am blushing as I write these lines. Although I think he loves me, he has not told me so in words. But, oh, Mina, I love him. I love him!

I wish I were with you, Mina, sitting by the fire, and I would try to tell you what I feel. I should tear this letter up, but I don't want to, because I need to talk about this to someone! Let me hear from you at once, and tell me all that you think about it. Mina, pray for my happiness.

Lucy

P.S. Of course this is a secret. Goodnight again. L.

Letter from
Lucy Westenra to Mina Murray

May 24

My dearest Mina,

Many thanks again for your sweet letter. It was so nice to be able to tell you about Arthur and to have you understand it all.

You won't believe what has happened. As they say, it never rains but it pours. Here am I, only nineteen, and I've never had a marriage proposal—but today I had three. Can you imagine it? Three proposals in one day! Isn't it awful! I feel so sorry for two of the poor fellows. Oh, Mina, I am so happy that I don't know what to do with myself. And three! But, for goodness' sake, don't tell any of our other friends, or they will try to beat me out by getting at least six! Some girls are so vain—not like you and me, dear Mina, who will soon be serious married women!

Well, I must tell you about the three, but you must keep it a secret from every one except, of course, Jonathan. You will tell him, because if I were in your place, I would certainly tell Arthur. A woman ought to tell her husband everything. Don't you think so?

Well, my dear, Number One came just

before lunch. I told you about him, Dr. John Seward, the good-looking lunatic asylum man. He acted very cool, but I could tell he was nervous all the same. He almost managed to sit down on his hat, and then he kept playing with a pencil in a way that made me nearly scream. He told me how much he cared for me, even though he has not known me long, and how happy he would be if I would marry him. He began to say how unhappy he would be if I did not care for him, but when he saw me start to cry he stopped, saying he did not want to cause me pain. Then he asked if I thought I might learn to love him later. When I shook my head, he asked me if I already cared for someone else. He put it very nicely, Mina. He said, "I don't want to force your secrets out of you. It's just that, if your heart is free, I might still have hope." And then, Mina, I felt a sort of duty to tell him that there was someone. I only told him that much. He stood up, very serious, and he took both my hands in his. He said he hoped I would be happy, and that I would think of him as my best friend.

Oh, Mina dear, I can't help crying, and you must excuse this letter being all spotty. Being proposed to is all very nice, but it isn't at all a happy thing when you have to see a good man going away looking all broken-hearted. My dear, I must stop here now. I feel so miserable, though I am so happy.

Evening. Arthur has just gone, and I feel more cheerful than before, so I can go on telling you about the day.

Well, Number Two came after lunch. He is another friend of Arthur's, and such a nice fellow. He's an American from Texas, and he looks so young that it seems almost impossible that he has been to so many places and has had such adventures.

Mr. Quincy P. Morris found me alone. It seems that a man always finds a girl alone. No, that's not true, for Arthur tried twice to find me alone (with me helping him all I could, I am not ashamed to say). I must tell you beforehand that Mr. Morris doesn't always speak slang, for he is really well educated and has beautiful manners, but once he found out that it amused me to hear him talk American slang, he began doing it constantly.

Well, Mr. Morris sat down beside me and looked as happy as he could, but I could see all the same that he was very nervous. He took my hand in his, and said ever so sweetly . . .

"Miss Lucy, I know I ain't good enough to

tie your little shoes, but I guess if you wait till you find a man that is, you'll be waiting until the cows come home. Won't you just hitch up alongside of me and let us go down the long road together, driving in double harness?"

He looked so good-humored that it didn't seem half so hard to refuse him as it did poor Dr. Seward. So I said, as lightly as I could, that I did not know anything about hitching, and that I wasn't used to a harness at all. Then he said that he had spoken jokingly, and he hoped I would forgive him, because he really did mean to be serious. And then, before I could say a word, he began pouring out words of love, laying his heart and soul at my feet. I suppose he saw something in my face which alarmed him, for he suddenly stopped, and said . . .

"Lucy, you are an honest-hearted girl, I know. I wouldn't be here speaking to you like this if I didn't know you were. Tell me, like one good friend to another, is there another man that you care for? If there is, I'll never bother you like this again, but if you'll let me, I'll be your faithful friend."

Mina, I don't deserve such kindness. Here I was almost making fun of Mr. Morris, and he is such a big-hearted, wonderful man. I burst into tears, I'm afraid (you will think this a very sloppy letter in more ways than one), and I really felt very badly.

Why can't they let a girl marry three men, or as many as want her, and save all this trouble? But I mustn't think such things. I looked into Mr. Morris's eyes, and I told him straight . . .

"Yes, there is someone I love, though he has not yet told me that he loves me." I know I was right to tell him, for his face brightened up, and he put out both his hands and took mine. He said,

"That's my brave girl. It's better to be late for winning you than on time for any other girl in the world. Don't cry for me, my dear. I'm a tough one. If that other fellow doesn't speak up soon, well, he'll have to deal with me. You'll always have me for a friend, and they're harder to come by than sweethearts. Won't you give me one kiss? It'll be something sweet for me to remember. You can, you know, if you like, for that other good fellow hasn't spoken yet."

Wasn't that sweet of him, Mina, especially when he was feeling so sad? I leaned over and kissed him. He stood up with my hands in his and said, "Little girl, I hold your hand, and you've kissed me, and if these things don't make us friends nothing ever will. Thank you for your sweet honesty to me, and goodbye."

He squeezed my hand, and taking up his hat, went straight out of the room without looking back, and here I am crying like a baby.

Oh, why must a man like that be unhappy when there are lots of girls who would worship the ground he walked on? I know I would if I were free, only I don't want to be free. My dear, this has me so upset that I don't feel I can write about my happiness yet.

Your loving Lucy

P.S.   Oh, about number Three—do I really need to say anything? Besides, it was all so confused. It seems as though one moment Arthur was walking into the room, and the next he had his arms around me and was kissing me. I am very, very happy, and I don't know what I have done to deserve it.

Goodbye.

DR. SEWARD'S DIARY

May 25.   No appetite today. Can't eat, can't rest. Since Lucy turned me down yesterday I have such an empty feeling. Nothing seems important enough to do. The only cure for this sort of thing is work, I know, so I went to see the patients. I picked out one who interests me very much. His name is Renfield. He is so unusual that I am determined to understand him as well as I can. Today I seemed to make some progress. I asked him more questions than ever before, wanting to understand the facts of his madness. Perhaps it was cruel to do so, because I was actually encouraging him to spend time in his most insane state.

Letter from
Quincy R. Morris to Arthur Holmwood

May 25

My dear Art,

We've told stories by the campfire, and bandaged each other's wounds in the tropics, and drunk to each other's health on the shores of South America. There are more yarns to be told, and other wounds to be healed, and someone new to drink a toast to. Won't you join me at my campfire tomorrow night? Don't tell me that you are busy, for I happen to know that a certain lady is going to a certain dinner party, and that you are free. There will only be one other, our old pal Jack Seward. We both want to cry into our beer and to drink a toast to the luckiest man in all the whole wide world. We promise you a hearty welcome and true congratulations. But we swear to leave you at home if you drink too deep to a certain pair of eyes. Come!

> Yours, as ever and always,
> Quincy P. Morris

Telegram from
Arthur Holmwood to Quincy R. Morris

May 26

Count me in!

> Art

Chapter 6

MINA MURRAY'S JOURNAL

July 24, Whitby. Lucy met me at the station, looking prettier than ever, and we drove up to our rental house. This is a lovely place. A little river, the Esk, runs through a deep valley which is beautifully green. The houses of the old town are all red-roofed, and seem piled up on top of each other. Right over the town is an ancient abbey. It must have been very large, and even lying in ruins it looks very beautiful and romantic. There is a legend that a white ghost-lady is seen in one of the windows. Between the abbey and the town there is another church, surrounded by a big grave-yard all full of tombstones. I think this is the nicest spot in Whitby, for it has a view of the ocean. The graveyard descends so steeply over the harbor that part of the bank has fallen away, and some of the graves have been destroyed. There are walking paths with seats beside them, and people go and sit there all day long looking at the beautiful view and enjoying the breeze.

I come and sit here often myself. Indeed, I am writing here now and listening to the talk of three old men who are sitting near me.

They have a legend here that when a ship is lost, bells are heard out at sea. I must ask one of the old men about it. One is wandering this way just now . . .

He is a funny old man. He must be awfully old, for his face is gnarled and twisted like the bark of a tree. He tells me that he is nearly a hundred years old, and that he was a sailor in the Greenland fishing fleet when Waterloo was fought. He is a very skeptical person, for when I asked him about the bells at sea and the White Lady at the abbey, he said, "I wouldn't bother myself about them, miss. Them things be all wore out. Mind, I don't say that they never was true, but I do say that they wasn't in my time. They be all very well for day-trippers an' the like, but not for a nice young lady like you."

He was an interesting person to talk to, so I asked him about whale fishing in the old days. He was just settling himself to begin when the clock struck four. He struggled back to his feet and said, "I must be going homewards now, miss. My granddaughter doesn't like to be kept waitin' when the tea is ready."

He hobbled away, and I could see him hurrying, as well as he could, down the steps. The steps are wonderful. There are hundreds of them, leading from the town to the church. They wind up in a delicate curve on such a gentle slope that a horse could easily walk up and down them. I think they must originally have had something to do with the abbey. I shall go home, too. Lucy is out visiting friends with her mother.

August 1. I came up here to the graveyard an hour ago with Lucy, and we had a most interesting talk with my old friend and the two others who are always with him. He is evidently the biggest talker of them, and I think in his day he must have been a real dictator. He will never admit being wrong and argues with everyone.

Lucy was looking sweetly pretty in her white summer dress. She's developed beautiful pink cheeks since she has been here. I noticed that the old men did not lose any time in coming and sitting near her when we arrived. She is so sweet with old people; I think they all fell in love with her on the spot. Even my old man fell under her spell and did not contradict her, but argued with me twice as much. I got him on the subject of the legends, and he went off at once into a sort of sermon. I must try to remember it and write it down.

"It be all fool-talk, lock, stock, and barrel, that's what it be and nuthin' else. These ghosts and goblins are nuthin' but inventions to send the children a-cryin' and silly women worryin'. They be nuthin' but air. They're all invented by some preacher to scare some sinner into doing somethin' he don't want to do. It makes me mad to think o' them. Why, they're not content with printin' lies on paper an' preachin' them out of pulpits. They want to be cuttin' them on the tombstones!"

I could see from the way the old fellow looked around for the approval of his cronies that he was showing off, so I put in a word to keep him going.

"Oh, Mr. Swales, you can't be serious. Surely these tombstones are not all lies?"

"Sure enough! There may be a few not wrong, excepting where they make out the people to be too good. The place is full of lies.

Now look here. You come here a stranger, an' you see this cemetery."

I nodded, although I did not quite understand what he was getting at.

He went on, "And you'd think that under these stones lie the people whose names are on 'em, wouldn't you?" I nodded again. "Then that be just where the lie comes in. Why, there be dozens of these corpses that ain't never been here. And, my God, how could they be otherwise? Look at that one nearest us!"

I went over and read, "Here lies Edward Spencelagh, sailor, murdered by pirates off the coast of Andres, April, 1854, age 30."

When I came back Mr. Swales went on, "Who brought him home, I wonder, to put him here? He was murdered off the coast of Andres, for the love of God! His bones are scattered all over the Atlantic by now."

"Well," I said, "I see your point, but I suppose the tombstones are here to please the grieving relatives."

"To please the grieving relatives, you suppose!" He said this with intense scorn. "How will it please the relatives to know that lies is written on 'em, and that everybody in the place knows that they be lies?"

He pointed to the stone directly at our feet, which had been laid down as a slab.

"Read the lies on that one," he said.

The letters were upside down to me from where I sat, but Lucy was better positioned, so she leaned over and read. "It says, 'Sacred to the memory of George Canon, who died, in the hope of a glorious resurrection, on July 29, 1873, after a fall from the rocks at Kettleness. This tomb was erected by his sorrowing mother to her dearly beloved son. He was the only son of his mother, and she was a widow.' Really, Mr. Swales, why are you laughing? I don't see anything funny in that!"

"You don't see nothin' funny! Ha! But that's because you don't know that the sorrowin' mother was a hell-cat that hated Georgie because he was a drunk, and he hated her. He committed suicide so that she couldn't collect on the life insurance she'd taken out on him. He blew the top of his head off with an old gun that they had for scarin' crows with. That's the way he fell off the rocks. And, as to hopes of a glorious resurrection, I often heard him say myself that he hoped he'd go to hell, for his mother was such a church-goer that she'd be sure to go to heaven, and he didn't want to to spend eternity where she was. Now isn't that stone"—he hammered it with his stick as he spoke—"a pack of lies?"

I did not know what to say, but Lucy stood

up, saying, "Oh, why did you tell us such an awful story? It is my favorite seat, Mr. Swales, and now I find I am sitting over the grave of a poor suicide."

Mr. Swales softened at once. "That won't harm you, and it may please poor Georgie to have a pretty girl sittin' on his lap. Why, I've sat here off an' on for nearly twenty years, an' it hasn't done me no harm. Don't you worry about them that lies under you—or that doesn't lie there, either! Now, there's the clock, and I must be going. Good day, ladies!" And off he hobbled.

Lucy and I stayed for a while. She told me all over again about Arthur and their coming marriage. That made me feel a little heartsick, for I haven't heard from Jonathan for a whole month. I hope there is nothing the matter with him. I wonder where he is and if he is thinking of me.

Dr. Seward's Diary

June 5. The case of Renfield grows more interesting the more I get to understand the man. He has certain qualities that are very well-developed, namely: selfishness, secrecy, and purpose.

I wish I could understand, though, just what that purpose is. He seems to have some plan in mind, but what it is I do not know. One of his better qualities is a love of animals, although that love is such an odd sort that I sometimes think it is cruelty.

Just now his hobby is catching flies. He has so many that I have finally had to object. He did not break out into a fury, as I expected, but took my objection quite calmly. He thought for a moment, and then said, "May I have three days? I will get rid of them." Of course, I agreed. I must watch him.

June 18. He has now begun collecting spiders and has got several very big fellows in a box. He keeps feeding them his flies, which are shrinking in number, although he uses half his food to attract more flies from outside to his room.

July 1. His spiders are now becoming as great a nuisance as his flies, and today I told him that he must get rid of them.

He looked very sad at this, so I said that he could keep just a few. He cheerfully agreed, and I gave him another three days to carry out our agreement.

He did something very disgusting while I was with him. A nasty blowfly, swollen with

whatever garbage it had been eating, buzzed into the room. He caught it, held it triumphantly for a few moments between his finger and thumb, and then popped it in his mouth and ate it.

I scolded him, but he argued that the fly was very good and very wholesome, that it was "strong life," and gave life to him. This gave me an idea. I must watch how he gets rid of his spiders.

He seems to have some deep problem in his mind, for he keeps a little notebook in which he is always writing. Whole pages of it are filled with columns of figures, generally single numbers added up in batches, and then the totals added in batches again, as though he were an accountant.

July 8. There is a method in his madness, and the little idea in my mind is growing. It will be a whole idea soon, and then I believe I will have a better clue about our friend Renfield.

I kept away from him for a few days, so that I might notice if there were any changes. Things remain as they were except that he has parted with some of his pets and now has a new one. It is a sparrow, and he has already partially tamed it. His means of taming is simple, for he has fed it a number of his spiders. His remaining spiders are well fed, for he still brings in the flies by tempting them with his food.

July 19. We are making progress. My friend now has a whole colony of sparrows, and his flies and spiders are almost gone. When I came in, he ran to me and said he wanted to ask me a favor—a very, very great favor. His manner was so affectionate and excited that he reminded me of a pet dog.

I asked him what it was, and he said with rapture in his voice, "A kitten, a nice, little, sleek playful kitten, that I can play with, and teach, and feed, and feed, and feed!"

I was not surprised by this request, for I had noticed how his pets had been increasing in size. But I didn't like the idea that his pretty family of tame sparrows should be wiped out in the same manner as the flies and spiders. So I said I would see about it, and asked him if he wouldn't rather have a cat than a kitten.

His eagerness gave him away as he answered, "Oh, yes, a cat would be better! I only asked for a kitten because I thought you might say no to a cat. No one would refuse me a kitten, would they?" I realized my suspicion had been correct.

I shook my head, and said that it would not be possible now, but that I would see about it. His face fell, and I could see a warning of danger in it. There was a sudden fierce, sly look which meant killing. I believe the man is an undeveloped homicidal maniac. I shall test him about the cat. Then I shall know more.

10 p.m. I have visited him again and found him sitting in a corner sulking. When I came in, he threw himself on his knees and begged me to let him have a cat, saying that his salvation depended upon it.

I was firm, however, and told him that he could not have it. Without a word he returned to his corner and sat down, gnawing his fingers. I shall see him early in the morning.

July 20. Visited Renfield very early, before the attendant made his rounds. Found him up and humming a tune. He was spreading out his sugar, which he had saved, on the windowsill. He was clearly beginning his fly catching again.

I looked around for his birds, but I saw none. I asked him where they were. He replied, without turning round, that they had all flown away. There were a few feathers about the room and on his pillow was a drop of blood. I said nothing, but went and told the keeper to report to me if anything happened during the day.

11 a.m. The attendant has just come to say that Renfield has been very sick and has vomited a whole lot of feathers. "My belief is, doctor," he said, "that he has eaten his birds—that he just took and ate them raw!"

11 p.m. I gave Renfield a strong drug tonight, enough to make even him sleep, and then I took away his notebook to look at it. The thought that has been buzzing about my brain lately is complete.

My homicidal maniac is of a most unusual kind. I shall have to invent a new classification for him, and call him a "zoophagous" (life-eating) maniac. What he seemed to want is to absorb as many lives as he can. He gave many flies to one spider and many spiders to one bird, and then wanted a cat to eat the many birds. What would he have done with the cat?

It is almost tempting to allow him to continue, in order to see where it would lead. What might I discover from such an experiment! If I understand the secret of even one such mind, who knows what doors that understanding might open?

How well the man reasoned. Lunatics always do, within their own mad worlds. I wonder, in his mind, how many smaller lives equal one man's life.

Mina Murray's Journal

July 26. I am anxious, and it comforts me to write my thoughts here. I am unhappy about Lucy and about Jonathan. I had not heard from Jonathan for some time, and was very concerned. But yesterday dear Mr. Hawkins sent me a letter from him. It is only a line written at the Castle Dracula, and it says that he is just starting for home. That is not like Jonathan. I do not understand it and it makes me uneasy.

Then too, Lucy has lately begun her old habit of walking in her sleep lately. Her mother has spoken to me about it, and we have decided that I will lock the door of our room every night. Mrs. Westenra is afraid that she might walk out along the edge of the cliffs and fall to her death.

Lucy is to be married in the autumn, and she is already planning how her house is to be arranged. Her fiancé, Arthur Holmwood, is the only son of Lord Godalming, so one day he will be Lord Godalming himself. He is coming up here soon, as soon as he can leave London, for his father is not very well. I think dear Lucy is counting the moments till he comes. She wants to take him up on the churchyard cliff and show him the beauty of Whitby. I'm sure it is just the waiting for him that disturbs her. She will be all right when he arrives.

July 27. No news from Jonathan. I do wish that he would write, if it were only a single line.

Lucy sleepwalks more than ever, and each night I am awakened by her moving about the room. Fortunately, the weather is so hot that she cannot get chilled. But still, the anxiety along with being frequently awakened is wearing me out, and I am getting nervous and wakeful myself. Arthur's father has become quite seriously ill, so he cannot come as soon as he had planned. Lucy is sad that she has to wait.

August 3. Another week gone by, and no news from Jonathan, not even to Mr. Hawkins. Oh, I do hope he is not ill. He surely would have written. I look at that last letter of his, but somehow it does not satisfy me. It does not sound like him, and yet it is his writing. There is no mistake of that.

Lucy has not walked much in her sleep the last week, but there is an odd concentration about her which I do not understand. Even in her sleep she seems to be watching me. She tries the door and, finding it locked, wanders around the room searching for the key.

August 6. Another three days and no news. This suspense is getting dreadful. If I only knew where to write to or where to go, I would feel easier. But no one has heard a word of Jonathan since that last letter. I must pray to God for patience.

Lucy seems more nervous than ever, but is otherwise well. Last night was very threatening, and the fishermen say that we are in for a storm.

Today is a gray day, and as I write the sun is hidden in thick clouds. Everything is gray except the green grass, which seems like emeralds among gray earthy rock and gray clouds that hang over the gray sea. The sea is tumbling in over the sandy flats with a roar. The horizon is lost in a gray mist. Dark figures are on the beach here and there, sometimes half shrouded in the mist. The fishing boats are racing for home. Here comes old Mr. Swales. He is making straight for me, and I can see by the way he lifts his hat that he wants to talk.

Later. I am amazed and touched by the change in the old man. When he sat down beside me, he said in a very gentle way, "I want to say something to you, miss."

I could see he was uneasy, so I took his hand in mine and told him to go ahead.

He said, "I'm afraid, my deary, that I must have shocked you by the wicked things I've been sayin' about the dead. But I didn't mean them, and I want you to remember that when I'm gone. We old folks that have one foot in the grave, why, we don't much like to think of it, and we don't want to feel scared of it. That's why I've been makin' light of it, so to cheer up my own heart a bit. But, Lord love you, miss, I ain't afraid of dyin', not a bit, only

I don't want to die if I can help it. My time must be near at hand now, for a hundred years is too much for any man to expect. Some day soon the Angel of Death will sound his trumpet for me. But don't you grieve, my deary!"—for he saw that I was getting tearyeyed—"if he should come this very night, that'd be all right. After all, life is only a waitin' for something else, and death is all we can rightly expect. Maybe it's in that wind out over the sea. Look! Look!" he cried suddenly. "There's something out there that sounds, and looks, and tastes, and smells like death. It's in the air. I feel it comin'. Lord, make me answer cheerful, when my call comes!" He held up his arms, and his mouth moved as though he were praying. After a few minutes' silence, he got up, shook hands with me, blessed me, and hobbled off. It all touched me and upset me very much.

I was glad when the coastal guard came along with his telescope under his arm. He stopped to talk with me, as he always does, but all the time kept looking out at sea. A strange ship was visible.

"I can't figure her out," he said. "She's Russian, by the look of her. But she's knocking about in the strangest way. She doesn't know where she wants to go. She seems to see the storm coming, but can't decide whether to run up north into the open sea, or to put into harbor here. Look there again! She is steered mighty strange, for she changes about with every puff of wind. We'll hear more about her before this time tomorrow."

Chapter 7

Cutting from
The Daily Graph Newspaper,
pasted in Mina Murray's Journal
August 8

Whitby. We've just experienced one of the greatest storms here, with strange results.

The weather was fine until the afternoon, when it became apparent that a sudden storm was building up. More than one captain made up his mind that his boat would remain in the harbor till the storm had passed. The wind fell away entirely during the evening, and soon there was a dead calm, a sultry heat, and other signs of the approach of thunder.

The only ship visible was a foreign one

with all sails up, which seemed to be going westward. Many witnesses commented on the foolishness or ignorance of her officers, and many tried to signal her to lower her sails in the face of the storm's danger. But as night fell she was still there, her sails idly flapping as she gently rolled on the swell of the sea.

Shortly before ten o'clock the air grew completely still. The silence was so great that the bleating of a sheep inland or the barking of a dog in the town was distinctly heard. A little after midnight, the air began to carry a strange, faint, booming sound. Then, without warning, the tempest broke. With amazing speed, the waves rose in growing fury, until the recently glass-calm sea was like a roaring and devouring monster.

The wind roared like thunder, and blew with such force that it was difficult for even strong men to stay on their feet. Police cleared onlookers from the pier, certain that some would be swept to their deaths. To add to the danger, masses of sea fog came drifting inland. White, wet clouds swept by in a ghostly fashion. They were so dank and damp and cold that it was easy to imagine that the spirits of those lost at sea were touching the living with the clammy hands of death. At times the mist cleared, and the sea could be seen in the glare of the lightning, followed by such peals of thunder that the whole sky overhead seemed to tremble.

Fortunately, a searchlight had recently been purchased and installed on the summit of the East Cliff. Several times its service was most effective, as when a fishing boat rushed into the harbor, guided by the light. As each boat reached the safety of the port, there was a shout of joy from the mass of people there.

Before long the searchlight fell on the schooner which had been noticed earlier in the evening. There was a shudder among the watchers on the cliff as they realized she was in terrible danger.

Between her and the port lay the great flat reef on which so many ships have crashed, and with the wind blowing as it was, it seemed impossible that she would safely reach the harbor.

The schooner was rushing in the great wind with such speed that, in the words of one old sailor, "She must come to rest somewhere, if only in hell." Then came another rush of sea fog, greater than any before. The rays of the searchlight were kept fixed on the harbor mouth, and the crowd waited breathlessly.

The wind suddenly shifted, and the sea fog melted with in the blast. And then the strange schooner swept between the piers, reaching the safety of the harbor. The searchlight followed her, and a shudder ran through all who saw her. For tied to the steering gear was a dead man, whose drooping head swung horribly to and fro with each motion of the ship. Not another soul could be seen on the deck.

A sense of awe swept over the crowd as they realized that the ship, as if by a miracle, had reached the harbor steered by the hand of a dead man! All this took place in less time than it takes to write these words. The schooner didn't pause, but rushed across the harbor and pitched herself onto dry land. There was, of course, a huge shock of noise. But strangest of all, at the very instant the shore was touched, an immense dog appeared on the deck from below, ran forward, and jumped onto the sand. It disappeared in the darkness.

The coastal guard on duty was the first to climb aboard the ship, followed closely by a crowd of policemen. As a member of the press, I too was allowed on board. We saw the dead seaman while he was still lashed to his wheel. It was an unforgettable sight. The man was simply fastened by his hands, tied one over the other, to a spoke of the wheel. Between the inner hand and the wood was a crucifix. The poor fellow may have been seated at one time, but the motion of the ship had thrown him from his seat, and the cords with which he was

tied had cut the flesh to the bone. The local doctor on the scene said that the man must have been dead for at least two days. In his pocket was a bottle, carefully corked, which contained a little roll of paper. A search of the ship revealed no other sailors, dead or alive.

The coastal guard said the man must have tied up his own hands, fastening the knots with his teeth. The dead steersman has been respectfully removed from the place where he faithfully held his watch until death, and taken to the mortuary to await an autopsy.

I shall send, in time for the next issue, further details of the ship which found her way so miraculously into harbor.

August 9. What has happened next in the story of the ghost ship is almost more startling than its arrival. It turns out that the schooner is a Russian one, and it is called the *Demeter*. Her only cargo is a number of great wooden boxes filled with moldy earth.

Many people have asked about the dog that was aboard the ship, and a number of animal-lovers have been searching for it. To their general disappointment, however, it was not to be found. It may be that it was frightened and made its way into the hills, where it is still hiding in terror.

That possibility is a worrisome one, for the dog seems to be a fierce brute. Early this morning a large dog belonging to a coal merchant was found dead in its master's yard. It had been fighting, and clearly it had a savage opponent, for its throat was torn away and its belly was slit wide open.

Later. I have been permitted to look over the log book of the *Demeter*. Of more interest than that, however, is the paper found in the bottle, which was produced at the inquest today. I have never come across a stranger document.

I have been given permission to reproduce both of them for you here. I have omitted technical details that would be of little interest, and I am depending upon the translation kindly provided by a Russian clerk.

Log of the *Demeter*
Things are happening that are so strange that I shall keep accurate notes until we land.

July 6. We finished taking in cargo, silver sand and boxes of earth. At noon set sail. East wind, fresh. We have five sailors, plus two mates, cook, and myself (captain).

July 13. We passed Cape Matapan. Crew dissatisfied about something. Seemed scared, but would not speak out.

July 14. Am somewhat anxious about crew. Men all steady fellows, who have sailed with me before. First mate could not make out what was wrong. They only told him there was *something*, and crossed themselves. Mate lost temper with one of them that day and struck him. Expected fierce quarrel, but all was quiet.

July 16. Mate reported in the morning that one of the crew, Petrofsky, was missing. Could not account for it. Men more downcast than ever. All said they expected something of the kind, but would not say more than there was *something* on board. Mate getting very impatient with them. Fear some trouble ahead.

July 17. Yesterday, one of the men, Olgaren, came to my cabin and told me he thought there was a strange man on board. He said that when he stepped behind the deckhouse, he saw a tall, thin man come up from below. He followed cautiously, but when he got to where the man had been he found no one, and the hatchways were all closed. He was in a superstitious panic, and I am afraid the panic may spread. To calm the men, I shall search the entire ship carefully.

Later in the day I got together the whole crew, and told them that as they evidently thought there was someone on in the ship, we would search from stem to stern. First mate was angry; said it was foolish to give in to such idiotic ideas. I let him take the wheel, while the rest began a thorough search of the ship. As there were only the big wooden boxes, there were no odd corners where a man could hide. Men much relieved when search over, and went back to work cheerfully. First mate scowled, but said nothing.

July 22. Rough weather last three days, and everyone too busy to be frightened. Mate cheerful again and all on good terms. Praised men for work in bad weather. All well.

July 24. This trip does seem to be cursed. Last night another man disappeared. Like the first, he came off his watch and was not seen again. Men all in a panic, asking to work their watches in pairs, as they fear to be alone. Mate angry. Fear there will be some trouble, as either he or the men will do some violence.

July 28. Our days in hell, knocking about in a terrible storm. No sleep for anyone. Men all worn out.

July 29. Another tragedy. Had single watch tonight, as crew too tired to double. When morning watch came on deck there was no sign of second mate. Crew in utter panic. Mate and I agreed to carry our pistols and watch for trouble.

July 30. Final night. Rejoiced we are nearing England. Weather fine, all sails set. Retired worn out, slept soundly, awakened by mate telling me that both the man on watch and steersman missing. Only myself and mate and two sailors left to work ship.

August 1. Two days of fog, and not a sail sighted. Had hoped once in the English Channel to be able to signal for help. Not enough men to work sails, so we go where the wind takes us. Dare not lower sails, as could not raise them again. We seem to be drifting into some terrible doom.

August 2, midnight. Woke up from few minutes sleep hearing a cry. Could see nothing in fog. Rushed on deck, and ran against mate. Tells me he heard the cry as well and ran, but no sign of man on watch. One more gone. Lord, help us!

August 3. At midnight I went to relieve the man at the wheel, and when I got to it found no one there. I dared not leave it, so shouted for the mate. After a few seconds, he rushed up on deck. He looked wild-eyed, and I greatly fear his poor mind has cracked. He came close to me and whispered with his mouth to my ear as though fearing the very air might hear. "*It* is here. I know it now. I saw *It*, like a man, tall and thin, and ghastly pale. I crept behind *It* and stabbed *It*, but the knife went through *It* empty as the air." And as he spoke he took the knife and drove it savagely into space. Then he went on, "But *It* is here, and I'll find *It*. *It* is in the hold, perhaps in one of those boxes. I'll unscrew them one by one and see. You stay at the wheel." And with a warning look and his finger on his lip, he went below.

There was a choppy wind springing up, and I could not leave the wheel. I saw him come out on deck again with a tool chest and lantern, and go below. He is stark, raving mad, and it's no use my trying to stop him. He can't hurt those big boxes. They are filled with earth, and to pull them about is as harmless a thing as he can do. So here I stay and mind the helm, and write these notes. I can only trust in God and wait till the fog clears. Then, if I can't steer to any harbor with the existing wind, I shall cut down sails and signal for help . . .

It is nearly all over now. Just as I was beginning to hope that the mate would come out calmer, there came up the hatchway a sudden, startled scream, which made my blood run cold. Up on the deck he came as if shot from a gun, with his eyes rolling and his face convulsed with fear. "Save me! Save me!" he cried, and then looked round at the blanket of fog. His horror turned to calm, and in a steady voice he said," You had better come too, captain, before it is too late. He is there! I know the secret now. The sea will save me from Him!" Before I could say a word, he threw himself overboard. I suppose I know the secret too, now. The mate was the madman who had murdered the men one by one, and now he has followed them himself. God help me! How am

I to account for all these horrors when I get to port? When I get to port! Will that ever be?

August 4. Still fog, which the sunrise cannot pierce. I know there is sunrise because I am a sailor. I dared not go below, I dared not leave the helm, so here I stayed all night, and in the dimness of the night I saw it! God, forgive me, but the mate was right to jump overboard. It was better to die like a man. To die like a sailor in blue water. But I am captain, and I must not leave my ship. I shall baffle this fiend, for when my strength begins to fail I shall tie my hands to the wheel. Between them I shall tie that one thing which He—It—dares not touch. And then, come good wind or foul, I shall save my soul, and my honor as a captain. I am growing weaker, and the night is coming on. If we are wrecked, perhaps this bottle may be found, and those who find it may understand. If not . . . well, then all men shall know that I have tried. God and the Blessed Virgin and the Saints help a poor ignorant soul trying to do his duty . . .

(The reporter's story continues) Of course the mystery is unsolved. Whether the mate or the captain himself committed the murders, no one can say. The folks here believe that the captain is simply a hero, and he is to be given

a public funeral. An honor guard of boats will accompany him up the Esk River, and he will be brought up the abbey steps, for he is to be buried in the churchyard on the cliff.

No trace has ever been found of the great dog, which saddens people. They would like to see it adopted by the town. Tomorrow will be the funeral, and so will end this "mystery of the sea."

Mina Murray's Journal

August 8. Lucy was very restless all night, and I, too, could not sleep. The storm was fearful, and as it boomed loudly it made me shudder. Strangely enough, Lucy did not wake, but she got up twice and dressed herself. Fortunately, each time I woke in time and managed to undress her without waking her, and got her back to bed. This sleepwalking is a very strange thing, for as soon as I stop her, she gives in without any struggle.

August 10. The funeral of the poor sea captain today was most touching. Every boat in the harbor seemed to be there, and the coffin was carried by captains all the way from the pier up to the churchyard. Lucy came with me, and we went early to our old seat. We had a lovely view, and saw the procession nearly all the way.

Poor Lucy seemed quite much upset, very restless and uneasy. I think that sleepwalking is having a bad effect on her. In addition, our Mr. Swales was found dead this morning on our seat, his neck broken. He had evidently fallen back in the seat in some sort of fright, for there was a look of fear on his face that the men said made them shudder. Poor dear old man!

Lucy is so sweet and sensitive that she feels everything more than other people do. Just now she was quite upset by a little thing which I barely noticed, though I am fond of animals.

One of the men who came up to watch the procession was followed by his dog, which is always with him. They are both quiet, and I've never seen the man angry, nor heard the dog bark. But during the service the dog would not come to its master, who was on the seat with us. It kept a few yards away, barking and howling. Its master spoke to it gently, and then angrily. But it would neither come nor stop its barking. It was in a fury, with its eyes savage and all its hair bristling.

Finally the man, too, got angry, and kicked the dog and then took it by the scruff of the neck and dragged it onto the tombstone on which the seat rests. The moment it touched the stone, the poor thing began to tremble. It did not try to get away, but crouched down, quivering. It was so terrified that I tried to comfort it, but without success.

Lucy was full of pity, too. She did not try to touch the dog, but looked at it in an agonized sort of way. I am afraid for her. She is too sensitive for this world. She will be dreaming of this tonight, I am sure. Everything—the ship steered into port by a dead man, tied to the wheel with a crucifix; the funeral; the dog, first furious and then terrified; will all be material for nightmares.

I will take her for a long walk by the cliffs to Robin Hood's Bay and back. She ought to be too tired for sleepwalking then.

Chapter 8

MINA MURRAY'S JOURNAL

Same day, 11 p.m. Oh, but I am tired! If I hadn't promised to write in my diary every day, I wouldn't open it tonight. We had a lovely walk. Lucy, after a while, was in cheerful spirits, owing to some friendly cows who came towards us in a field, and frightened us out of our wits. We laughed and laughed, and it gave the day a fresh start. We had a good lunch at Robin Hood's Bay in a little old-fashioned inn. Then we walked home.

Lucy is asleep and breathing softly. She has more color in her cheeks than usual, and looks so sweet. I feel happy tonight, because dear

Lucy seems better. I really believe she has turned the corner, and that we are over her sleepwalking troubles. I would be entirely happy if I only knew what was going on with Jonathan.

August 11. No sleep now, so I may as well write. I am too upset to sleep. We have had such an adventure, such a terrible experience.

I fell asleep as soon as I had closed my diary. Suddenly I became wide awake, and sat up with a horrible sense of fear. The room was dark, so I could see nothing, but when I stumbled across to Lucy's bed I found it was empty. The door was shut but not locked, as I had left it. I didn't want to wake her mother, so I threw on some clothes to search for her. Her bathrobe and dress were still hanging in their places. "Thank God," I said to myself, "she cannot be far as she is only in her nightgown."

I searched all the rooms of the house, with an ever-growing fear chilling my heart. Finally, I came to the hall door and found it open.

I took a big, heavy shawl and ran out. The clock was striking one, and there was not a soul in sight. I ran along the road, but could see no sign of her. I looked across the harbor to the East Cliff, in the hope or fear, I don't know which, of seeing Lucy in our favorite seat.

There was a bright full moon with heavy black driving clouds. For a moment or two I could see nothing, as the shadow of a cloud hid St. Mary's Church and all around it. Then, as the cloud passed, I could see the ruins of the abbey coming into view, and the church and churchyard became gradually visible. There, on our favorite seat, was Lucy, half-sitting and half-lying. A cloud covered the moon too quickly for me to get a good look, but it seemed as though something dark was bending over the white figure.

I ran down the steep steps to the pier and along by the fish market to the bridge, which was the only way to reach the East Cliff. I was glad to meet no one, for I didn't want anyone to see poor Lucy in that state. The time and distance seemed endless, and my knees trembled as I climbed up the steps to the abbey. I must have gone fast, and yet it seemed to me as if my feet were made of lead.

When I got almost to the top, I could see the seat and the white figure. I had been right—there was something, long and black, bending over her. I called in fright, "Lucy! Lucy!" and the something raised its head, and from where I was I could see a white face and red, gleaming eyes.

Lucy did not answer, and I ran on to the

entrance of the churchyard. As I entered, the church was between me and Lucy, and for a minute or so I lost sight of her. When she came in view again the cloud had passed, and I could see Lucy, her head lying over the back of the seat. She was alone.

When I bent over her I could see that she was still asleep. Her lips were parted, and she was breathing in long, heavy gasps. As I came close, she raised her hand and pulled the collar of her nightgown close around her, as though she felt the cold. I wrapped her in the warm shawl, fastening it at her throat with a big safety pin. But I must have pricked her with it, for she put her hand to her throat and moaned. When I had her carefully wrapped up, I put my shoes on her feet and then began very gently to wake her.

At first she did not respond. Gradually she became more and more uneasy, moaning and sighing. Finally, I shook her hard until she opened her eyes and awoke. She trembled a little and clung to me. When I told her to come home with me, she rose with the obedience of a child. As we walked along, the gravel hurt my feet and Lucy noticed. She stopped and wanted to insist upon my taking back my shoes, but I would not.

Luckily we got home without meeting a

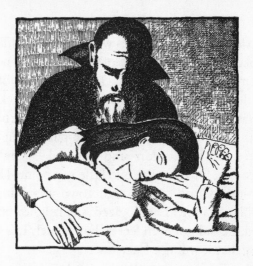

soul. My heart was beating so loudly that I thought I would faint. I was worried about Lucy, not only for her health, but for what people might say if they saw her out like this, half-dressed. When we got in, we washed our feet, said a prayer of thankfulness together, and I tucked her into bed. She begged me not to say a word to anyone, even her mother, about what had happened.

I hesitated at first to promise, but when I thought of how the story would worry her mother, I agreed. I hope what I did was right. I have locked the door, and the key is tied to my wrist, so perhaps I shall not be disturbed. Again Lucy is sleeping soundly.

Same day, noon. All goes well. Lucy slept till I woke her. The adventure of the night does not seem to have hurt her. In fact, she looks healthier this morning than she has for weeks. I was sorry to notice that I had indeed hurt her with the safety pin. I must have pinched up a piece of loose skin and pierced it right through, for there are two little red points like pin-pricks, and on her nightgown was a drop of blood. When I apologized, she laughed and said she did not even feel it. Fortunately it is so tiny that it will not leave a scar.

Same day, night. We enjoyed a happy day. The air was clear, sun bright, and there was a cool breeze. We had a picnic lunch in the woods with Mrs. Westenra. Lucy seems more relaxed than she has for some time, and fell asleep as soon as she lay down. I shall lock the door and tie the key to my wrist again, though I do not expect any trouble tonight.

August 12. My expectations were wrong, for twice during the night I was wakened by Lucy trying to get out. Even in her sleep, she seemed impatient to find the door shut. I woke at dawn and heard the birds chirping outside of the window. Lucy woke too, and was even better than on the previous morning.

All her old cheerfulness seemed to have come back, and she came and sat in bed with me and told me all about Arthur. I told her how anxious I was about Jonathan, and she tried to comfort me.

August 13. Another quiet day, and I went to bed with the key on my wrist as before. Again I awoke in the night, and found Lucy sitting up in bed, still asleep, pointing to the window. I got up quietly and looked out. It was brilliant moonlight. Between me and the moonlight flitted a large bat, coming and going in great whirling circles. Once or twice it came quite close, but I suppose it was frightened at seeing me, and it flitted away towards the abbey. When I came back from the window, Lucy had lain down again, and was sleeping peacefully. She did not move again all night.

August 14. On the East Cliff, reading and writing all day. Lucy seems to love the spot as much as I do, and it is hard to make her ever leave. This afternoon she made a strange remark. We were coming home for dinner and had stopped to look at the view. The setting sun was throwing its red light over the East Cliff and the old abbey, and seemed to bathe everything in a beautiful rosy glow. We were silent for a while, and suddenly Lucy murmured, "His red eyes again! They are just the same." I turned around a little, so I could see Lucy without seeming to stare at her. She looked dreamy and strange. I said nothing, but followed her eyes. She appeared to be looking over at our own seat, where a dark figure was seated alone. Then we went home to dinner. Lucy had a headache and went to bed early. Once she was asleep, I went out for a little stroll myself.

I walked along the cliffs, full of sweet sadness, for I was thinking of Jonathan. As I returned home it was bright moonlight. I glanced up at our window and saw Lucy leaning out. I waved and called to her. She did not notice me or make any movement. Straining my eyes, I saw that Lucy was lying with her head on the window sill and her eyes shut. Perched on the sill near her was what looked like a large bird. I ran upstairs, but as I came into the room she was moving back to her bed, still asleep, and breathing heavily. She was holding her hand to her throat, as though to protect it from the cold.

I did not wake her, but tucked her in warmly. I have made sure that the door is locked and the window securely fastened.

She looks so sweet as she sleeps, but she is

paler than usual, and there is a tired, haggard look under her eyes which I do not like. I think she is worrying about something. I wish I could find out what it is.

August 15. Got up later than usual. Lucy felt weak and tired, and slept on after we had been called to breakfast. We had a happy surprise at breakfast. Arthur's father is better and wants the wedding to happen soon. Lucy is full of quiet joy and her mother is glad and sorry at the same time. Later on in the day she told me why. She is sad to lose Lucy as her very own, but she is joyful that her beloved daughter will have someone to look after her. Poor, dear, sweet lady! She has told me a sad secret. Her doctor has warned her that she has no more than a few months to live. Any shock would be almost sure to kill her. She made me promise not to tell Lucy. We were wise after all, not to tell her about Lucy's dreadful night of sleep-walking.

August 17. No diary for two whole days. I haven't had the heart to write. Some sort of doom seems to be creeping over us. No news from Jonathan, and Lucy seems to be growing weaker, while her mother's life is slipping away. I do not understand what is happening.

Lucy eats well and sleeps well, and enjoys the fresh air, but all the time the roses in her cheeks are fading, and she gets weaker day by day. At night I hear her gasping for air.

I keep the key to our door always fastened to my wrist at night, but Lucy gets up and walks around the room and sits at the open window. Last night I found her leaning out when I woke up, and when I tried to wake her I could not. It was as though she had fainted. When she finally awoke, she was weak as water and cried silently. When I asked her why she had gone to the window, she shook her head and turned away.

Could her illness be from that unlucky prick of the safety pin? I looked at her throat just now as she lay asleep, and the tiny wounds have not healed. They are still open, and if anything, larger than before, and the edges of them are white. Unless they heal within a day or two, I shall insist that Lucy see a doctor.

Letter from Samuel F. Billington & Son,
Attorneys, Whitby
to the firm of Carter, Paterson & Co.

August 17

Dear Sirs,

I am enclosing a list of goods sent by Great

Northern Railway. Please deliver these to Carfax, a house near Purfleet, immediately. The house is empty, but I am enclosing a set of keys, all labeled.

Please place the fifty boxes in the partially ruined building marked as "A" on the diagram enclosed. The building is easily recognized, as it is the ancient chapel of the mansion. The boxes will leave by train at 9:30 tonight, and should arrive in your locality at 4:30 tomorrow afternoon. Leave the keys in the main hallway of the house, where the new owner will find them. I am depending upon you to carry out these instructions with the utmost speed.

> Yours truly,
> Samuel F. Billington

*Letter from Carter, Paterson & Co.
to Samuel F. Billington*

August 21

Dear Sir,

The goods have been received and delivered exactly as you instructed. The keys to the mansion were left in a parcel in the main hallway.

> Respectfully,
> Carter, Paterson & Co.

Mina Murray's Journal

August 18. Lucy is in cheerful spirits. This afternoon as we sat in the cemetery she reminded me, as if I needed any reminding, of the night that I found her asleep here. She tapped playfully with the heel of her boot on the stone slab and said, "My poor bare feet didn't make much noise then! Mr. Swales would have said it was because I didn't want to wake poor Georgie, resting so peacefully under the slab."

Since she seemed so talkative, I asked if she remembered anything about that night. She began hesitantly, as though she were trying to remember it all herself.

"I suppose I was dreaming, but it all seemed real," she said. "I wanted to be here in this spot, but I don't know why, for I was afraid to be here, too. I do remember walking through the streets and over the bridge. A fish jumped as I went by, and I leaned over to look at it. The whole town seemed full of dogs, all howling at once. Then there was something with me, something long and dark with red eyes, and I was surrounded with something very sweet and very bitter all at the same time. I felt I was sinking into deep green water, and there was a singing in my ears, as I have heard there is in drowning men. My soul seemed to go out from my body and float about the air. Then there was an agonizing feeling, as if I were in an earthquake, and I came back and found you shaking my body. I saw you do it before I felt you."

Then she began to laugh, in a way that didn't sound at all like her. I did not like it, so I changed the subject, and then Lucy was like her old self again.

August 19. Joy, joy, joy! Although not all joy. Finally, I have news of Jonathan. He has been ill, and that is why he did not write. Mr. Hawkins sent his letter to me, and I am leaving for Budapest in the morning to meet Jonathan and bring him home. I have cried over the good nurse's letter until I've nearly soaked it through.

Letter from the head nurse of the Hospital of St. Joseph and St. Mary, Budapest, Hungary, to Miss Wilhelmina Murray

August 12

Dear Madame,

I am writing on behalf of Mr. Jonathan

Harker, who is himself not strong enough to write, though progressing well. He has been in our hospital nearly six weeks, suffering from a dangerous fever. He asks me to send his love. He will still require a few weeks' rest here, but will then return home.

P.S. Mr. Harker is now asleep, so I open this to add a few words. He has told me all about you, and that you are to be his wife. All blessings to you both! He has had some fearful shock, and in his illness he has been raving about wolves and poison, blood and ghosts and demons. Please be careful to keep him calm. The effects of an illness like this will not disappear overnight. I am so sorry not to have contacted you before, but he was carrying no identification and we did not know who his friends were.

Please believe that he has been well cared for, and that we have all learned to love his sweet, gentle nature. He is truly getting much better, and I believe in a few weeks he will be entirely well. But be careful of him. I pray you will have many, many, happy years together.

DR. SEWARD'S DIARY

August 19. Strange and sudden change in Renfield last night. About eight o'clock he began to get excited and sniff about like a hunting dog. The attendant noticed the change, and encouraged him to talk. He is usually respectful to the attendant, but not tonight. He would not speak to the man at all, except to say, "I don't want to talk to you. You don't count now. The master is at hand."

The attendant thinks Renfield has developed some sort of religious mania. If so, we must be very careful, for a strong man with homicidal and religious tendencies together might be dangerous. It is a dreadful combination.

At nine o'clock I visited him myself. His treated me just as he had the attendant. It does look like religious mania, and I suspect he will soon announce that he is God.

For half an hour Renfield kept getting more and more excited. I pretended not to notice, but kept an eye on him. And then that shifty look came into his eyes, the look I always see when he has gotten an idea. He became quiet, and went and sat on the edge of his bed staring into space.

I tried to figure out what was happening. I asked him to talk of his pets, a subject which always interests him. At first he would not answer, but finally said, "To hell with them all! I don't care a pin about them."

"What?" I said. "You don't mean to tell me you don't care about spiders?" (Spiders are his hobby again, and the notebook is filling up with columns of small figures.)

To this he answered with a riddle. "The bridesmaids gladden the eyes of those who await the bride. But when the bride herself comes near, the maidens cease to shine."

He would not explain himself, but remained stubbornly seated on his bed all the time I remained with him.

I am tired tonight and depressed. I cannot help thinking of Lucy, and how different things might have been. I don't think I will sleep well tonight.

Later. Sure enough, I was lying awake in bed listening to the clock strike two when the night watchman came to say that Renfield had escaped. I threw on my clothes and ran down at once. Renfield is too dangerous a person to be roaming about. Those ideas of his might work out badly with strangers.

The attendant was waiting for me. He said he had seen Renfield not more than ten minutes before, seemingly asleep in his bed, when he had looked through the observation slot in the door. Minutes later he had heard the sound of the window being shattered. He ran back and saw feet disappear through the window. I followed through the window myself.

The attendant told me the patient had gone to the left, so I ran in that direction as quickly as I could. As I went through a grove of trees, I saw a white figure climbing the high wall which separates our grounds from those of Carfax, the deserted mansion.

I shouted back for the watchman to get three or four men immediately and follow me into the grounds of Carfax. I got a ladder and crossed the wall. Renfield was just disappearing behind the house. On the far side of the house, I found him pressed close against the old oak door of the chapel. He was talking, but I was afraid to go near enough to hear what he was saying, in case I might frighten him into running off.

After a few minutes, however, I realized he was paying no attention to anything around him, and my men had crossed the wall and were closing in on him. I walked nearer and heard him say, "I am here to do your bidding, Master. I am your slave, and you will reward me, for I shall be faithful. I have worshipped you long and from far away. Now that you are near, I wait your commands, and you will not forget me, will you, dear Master, as you give your gifts?"

When we closed in on him, he fought like a tiger. He is immensely strong, more like a wild beast than a man. I never saw a madman in such a rage before, and I hope I shall not again. It is fortunate that we have found out how strong and how dangerous he is. He is safe now, at any rate. Houdini himself couldn't get free from the straitjacket Renfield's locked in, and he's chained to the wall in the padded room as well.

His cries are awful to hear. Just now he spoke understandable words for the first time. "I shall be patient, Master. It is coming, coming, coming!"

Chapter 9

Letter from
Mina Harker to Lucy Westenra

Budapest
August 24

My dearest Lucy,

I know you want to hear everything that has happened since I left Whitby. I found Jonathan so thin and pale and weak looking. He is a wreck, and he does not remember anything that has happened to him for a long time. At least he says he does not remember, and I don't ask him questions. He has had some terrible shock, and I'm afraid it might do him harm to try to remember. The nurse who wrote says that he wanted her to tell me about it, but she refuses. She says that the things a sick person says are secrets between him and God.

I am sitting by Jonathan's bedside now, where I can see his face while he sleeps. He is waking!

Later. When he woke, he asked me for his coat as he wanted to get something from the pocket. The nurse brought him all his things, and I saw a notebook with them. I was going to ask him if I could see it, but he sent me over to the window, saying he wanted to be alone for a moment.

Then he called me back, and said to me very seriously, "Wilhelmina?" That surprised me, for the only time he has ever used my full name is when he asked me to marry him. Then he said, "I don't believe there should be any secrets between a husband and wife. I have had a great shock, and I don't know what I am imagining and what I truly do remember. The truth is in this notebook, but I don't want to read it. I want to begin life here, now, with our marriage. I'm going to give the book to you, Wilhelmina. Read it if you want to, but don't tell me what is in it unless the day comes when you have no other choice." He fell back on his pillows exhausted. I put the book under his pillow and kissed him. We have gotten permission to be married, here, this very afternoon, in the hospital.

. . . Lucy, we are married. I am very, very happy. When the chaplain left and I was alone with my husband—that is the first time I have written those words, "my husband"!—I took the book from under his pillow. I wrapped it in white paper and sealed it with sealing wax, and pressed my wedding ring into the warm wax. Then I kissed it and showed it to Jonathan, and told him that I would keep it like that and that I would never open it unless it was for his sake.

Goodbye, my dear. I must stop, for Jonathan is waking up. I will write again soon!

Your ever loving,
Mina Harker

Letter from
Lucy Westenra to Mina Harker

Whitby
August 30

My dearest Mina,

Oceans of love and millions of hugs, and I can't wait until you're in your own home with your husband. I wish you were here with us. The healthy sea air would soon heal Jonathan, as it has me. I'm eating like a horse, and I don't sleepwalk at all anymore. Arthur is here, and we are having so much fun going for walks and drives, and rides, and rowing, and tennis, and fishing together, and I love him more than ever. We are leaving Whitby for my mother's house soon, and we will be married on September 28. There he is, calling to me, so no more just now from your loving,

Lucy

Dr. Seward's Diary

August 20. The case of Renfield grows even more interesting. For a week after his escape,he was violent all the time. Then one night, just as the moon rose, he grew quiet, murmuring to himself: "Now I can wait. Now I can wait." The attendant told me, so I ran down to have a look at him. He was still in the straitjacket, but he was quiet enough that I ordered him released. Tonight he will not speak. Even the offer of a kitten or a full-grown cat does not interest him. He will only say, "I don't care about cats. I have more to think of now, and I can wait. I can wait."

After a while I left him. The attendant tells me that he was quiet until just before dawn, and that then he began to get uneasy, and finally had a sort of fit that exhausted him.

. . . For three nights the same thing has happened. He is violent all day, then quiet from moonrise to sunrise. I wonder why. I've had an idea that might help me find out. Tonight we shall "accidentally" give him a chance to escape, with men ready to follow him to see where he goes and what he does.

August 23. Mad or not, Renfield is not stupid. When our bird found the cage open, he would not fly. At least we know his schedule now, and we do not have to keep him in the straitjacket around the clock. The poor man's body will appreciate the rest, even if his mind cannot.

Later. Another night adventure. Renfield slyly waited until the attendant was entering the room to inspect. Then he dashed out past him and ran down the hallway. The attendants chased him, and again we found him pressed against the chapel door of the old mansion. When he saw me he became furious, and if the attendants had not grabbed him in time, he certainly would have tried to kill me. As we were holding him, a strange thing happened. He was fighting harder than ever, but suddenly grew calm. I saw him staring into the sky, but when I looked in that direction I saw nothing but a big bat, flapping its silent way to the west. Renfield grew calmer, saying, "You don't have to tie me up. I shall go quietly." We came back to the house without trouble. Something about his calm frightens me.

LUCY WESTENRA'S DIARY

August 24. I wish Mina were with me again, for I feel so unhappy. Last night I think I sleepwalked again, just as I did at Whitby. Perhaps it is the change of air, or getting home again. Everything seems dark and horrid, and I can't remember what I do in my dreams. When Arthur came for lunch, he looked worried when he saw me, and I didn't have the energy to try to be cheerful. I wonder if Mother would let me sleep in her room tonight.

August 25. Another bad night. Mother did not think it was a good idea for me to sleep in her room. She doesn't seem very well herself, and I think she's afraid of worrying me. I tried to stay awake, but when the clock struck midnight it woke me. There was a sort of scratching or flapping at the window, but I ignored it, and I suppose I fell asleep again. More bad dreams. I wish I could remember them. This morning I am horribly weak. I am white as a sheet and my throat hurts. There must be something wrong with my lungs, for I don't seem able to get enough air. I must try to cheer up when Arthur comes.

Letter from
Arthur Holmwood to Dr. Seward

August 31

My dear Jack,

I want you to do me a favor. Something is wrong with Lucy; she looks awful, and is getting worse every day. I can't worry her mother about it, because the poor old lady has heart disease and could go off at any moment. I told Lucy I would ask you to come see her. I know being with her is painful for you, my dear old friend, but I wouldn't ask you this if it wasn't important. Please come to lunch at Mrs. Westenra's house tomorrow at two o'clock. That way her mother will think it is just a social visit. After lunch Lucy will see you alone.

With many thanks,
Arthur

Telegram from
Arthur Holmwood to Dr. Seward

September 1
Must go to my father, who is worse. Write or telegraph me tonight.

Letter from
Dr. Seward to Arthur Holmwood

September 2

My dear old fellow,

Let me say right away that I do not find any sign of serious physical disease in Miss Westenra. At the same time, I am not at all happy with her health. She is very different from when I saw her last. I will tell you exactly what happened so you can draw your own conclusions. I will then say what I think we should do.

Miss Westenra seemed cheerful during lunch, but I suspected she was trying hard to be so in order to mislead her mother. Then Mrs. Westenra went to lie down, and Lucy was left with me. We went to her room, and as soon as the door was closed, she sank down into a chair with a great sigh and covered her eyes with her hand.

She said to me very sweetly, "I can't tell you how I hate talking about myself!" I reminded her that she could tell me anything privately, but also that you were greatly worried about her. She immediately said, "Tell Arthur everything! I am more worried about him than me."

Clearly, she looks bloodless and anemic, and yet my test showed that her blood is in quite normal, healthy condition. But something is certainly wrong, and I suspect the problem is a mental one. Her symptoms include an inability to breathe normally at times and abnormally heavy sleep with dreams that frighten her but that she cannot remember. She says that as a child she used to walk in her sleep, and that when she was in Whitby the habit came back. Once she walked out in the night all the way to East Cliff, where Miss Murray found her.

In response, I have done the best thing I know of. I have written to my old friend and teacher, Professor Van Helsing of Amsterdam. Van Helsing knows as much about unusual diseases as any one in the world, and I have asked him to examine Miss Westenra. I was once able to save Van Helsing's life, and he has often said he wished he could do a favor for me in return.

I must prepare you for Van Helsing. Some of the things he does may seem unusual, but we must trust what he says is for the best because he knows what he is talking about better than anyone else. He is one of the most brilliant scientists living today as well as the kindest and best man ever born. I have complete confidence in him. I have asked him to come at once. I will see Miss Westenra tomorrow and will keep you fully informed.

Yours always,

Jack

*Letter from
Dr. Seward to Arthur Holmwood*

September 3

My dear Art,

Van Helsing has come and gone. He came with me to see Lucy while her mother was out so that we were alone with her.

The professor made a very careful examination, and he will report to you. I can tell that he is very concerned, but he says he must think before he speaks. You must not be angry with him or with me for making you wait, Art, because his silence means that all his thoughts are working for her good. He will speak plainly when the time comes, believe me.

Well, about the visit. Lucy was more cheerful than on the day I first saw her and certainly looked better. She had lost some of the ghastly look that so upset you, and her breathing was normal. She was very sweet to the Professor (as she always is) and tried to make him feel at home, although I could see the poor girl was struggling.

I believe Van Helsing saw it, too, for he began to chat about everything except ourselves and diseases. He was so cheerful and amusing that Lucy became genuinely cheerful herself. Then he brought the conversation gently around to the purpose of his visit. He said, in his funny Dutch-English, "My dear young miss, I have the so great pleasure to see you are so much beloved. They told me you were down in the spirits and that you were ghastly pale. To them I say 'Pooh-pooh!'" And he snapped his fingers at me and went on. "But you and I shall show them how wrong they are. How can he"—and he pointed at me— "know anything about young ladies? He has his madmen to play with. But he has no wife nor daughter, and the young do not tell their secrets to the young! They tell them to the old, like me, who have known more about life and its sorrows. So, my dear, we will send him away to smoke a cigarette in the garden, while you and I have a little talk all to ourselves."

I took the hint and strolled around outside. Finally the professor came to the window and called me in. He looked serious but said, "I agree with you that there has been much blood lost. But I can find no cause. And yet there is cause. There is always cause for everything. I must go back home and think. You must send me a telegram every day, and if you think I should return, I shall. The disease, whatever it is, interests me, and this sweet, young dear, she interests me, too. She charms me, and I would come for her sake, if not for yours."

And he would not say a word more, even when we were alone. And now, Art, you know everything that I know. I shall watch over her. I hope your poor father is better. It must be terrible for you to be torn between two people who are both so dear to you. I respect your feeling of duty to your father. Please don't worry too much about Lucy. If I think you must come to her, I will let you know.

Dr. Seward's Diary

September 4. Our zoophagous patient continues

to be interesting. His outburst yesterday came at an unusual time. Just before noon he began to grow restless. The attendant knew the symptoms, and called for help at once. Fortunately the men came quickly, for at the stroke of noon he became so violent that it took all their strength to hold him. In only about five minutes, however, he began to get more quiet, and has been sitting staring into space ever since. My hands were full when I got in, for some of the other patients had been badly frightened by his screams. I can understand why, for the sounds disturbed even me, and I was quite far away at the time. It is now after the asylum's dinner hour, and Renfield remains sitting in a corner with a dull, woebegone look on his face.

Later. Another change. At five o'clock I looked in on him and found him seeming as happy and contented as he used to be. He was catching flies and eating them, and was counting them by making marks on the edge of the door. When he saw me, he came over and apologized for his bad behavior. He asked in a very humble way to be allowed back to his own room and to have his notebook again. I granted both requests, so he is in his room with the window open. He has some sugar spread out on the window sill, and is catching quite a supply of flies. He is not now eating them, but is putting them into a box, and searching the corners of his room for a spider. I tried to get him to talk about the past few days, but he would not respond. For a moment or two he looked very sad. Then he said in a sort of faraway voice, as though saying it rather to himself than to me: "All over! All over! He has deserted me. No hope for me now unless I do it myself!" Then he asked me, "Doctor, won't you be very good to me and let me have a little more sugar? I think it would be very good for me."

"And the flies?" I said.

"Yes! The flies like it, too, and I like the flies; therefore I like it." I got him a double supply of sugar, and left him as happy as any man in the world. I wish I could figure him out.

Midnight. Another change in Renfield. I had been to see Miss Westenra (who seemed much better), and had just returned, when I heard him yelling. I reached his room just as the sun was going down, and from his window I saw the red glow disappear below the horizon. As it sank, he became less and less excited, and then as it vanished, he crumpled onto the floor. Within just a few minutes, though, he stood up quite calmly and looked around. I signaled to the attendants not to hold him, for I wanted to see what he would do. He went straight over to the window and brushed out the crumbs of sugar. Then he took his fly box and emptied it outside, and threw away the box. Then he shut the window, and crossing over, sat down on his bed. All this surprised me, so I asked him, "Aren't you going to keep flies any more?"

"No," said he. "I am sick of all that rubbish!" He certainly is an interesting case. His greatest excitements come on at high noon and at sunset. Can it be that the sun has some evil influence on him? We shall see.

Telegram from
Seward, London to Van Helsing, Amsterdam

September 4
Patient even better today.

Telegram from
Seward, London to Van Helsing, Amsterdam

September 5
Patient greatly improved. Good appetite, sleeps normally, good spirits, color coming back.

*Telegram from
Seward, London to Van Helsing, Amsterdam*

September 6
Terrible change for the worse. Come at once.
Do not lose an hour.

Chapter 10

Letter from
Dr. Seward to Arthur Holmwood

September 6

My dear Art,

My news today is not so good. Lucy is a bit worse. There is, however, one good thing which has come from it. Mrs. Westenra was anxious about Lucy, and asked me my advice, as a doctor. So I was able to tell her that my old teacher, the great specialist Van Helsing, was coming to visit me and that he and I would look after Lucy. So now we can come and go without alarming her too much.

Yours,
John Seward

Dr. Seward's Diary

September 7. When Van Helsing and I arrived at the house, Mrs. Westenra met us and showed us up to Lucy's room. If I was shocked when I saw her yesterday, I was horrified when I saw her today.

She was ghastly, chalky pale. The red color had left even her lips and gums, and the bones of her face stood out sharply. Her breathing was painful to see or hear. Van Helsing's face grew hard as marble, and he frowned so that his eyebrows almost touched over his nose. Lucy lay motionless and did not seem to have strength to speak. Then Van Helsing motioned to me, and we went out of the room. "My God!" he said. "This is dreadful. There is no time to be lost. She will die for want of blood. There must be a transfusion at once. Is it you or me?"

"I am younger and stronger, Professor. It must be me."

"Then get ready at once. I will bring up my bag. I am prepared."

I went downstairs with him, and as we were going there was a knock at the hall door. When we reached the hall, Arthur was there. He rushed up to me, whispering, "Jack, I was so worried. I read between the lines of your letter. Dad was better, so here I am. Is this Dr. Van Helsing? I am so thankful to you, sir, for coming."

Van Helsing held out his hand. "Sir, you have come in time. Our dear miss is bad, very, very bad. But you can help her, and you will need your courage."

"What can I do?" asked Arthur hoarsely. "Tell me, and I shall do it. I would give the last drop of blood in my body for her."

The Professor nearly chuckled at that, saying, "My dear young man, I do not ask that much, not the last drop!" Arthur looked bewildered, and the Professor explained in a kindly way. "Our Miss Lucy needs blood, or she will die. My friend John and I are about to perform a transfusion. John was to give his blood, as he is younger and stronger than I, but now you are here. . ."

Arthur interrupted. "I would gladly die for her. Let us begin."

"Good boy!" said Van Helsing. "Soon, you will be happy that you have done this for her. Come now. You shall kiss her once before it is done, but then you must go. Say nothing to her mother. You know how she is."

We all went up to Lucy's room. Van Helsing asked Arthur to remain outside. Lucy turned her head and looked at us, but she was too weak to speak.

Van Helsing mixed a sleeping drug, and coming over to the bed said cheerily, "Now, little miss, here is your medicine. Drink it up, like a good child. See, I lift your head so you can swallow easily." Once she had fallen into a deep sleep, the Professor called Arthur into the room and began the transfusion. As the transfusion went on, something like life seemed to come back to poor Lucy's cheeks. Although Arthur grew pale, his face shone with joy. After a bit I began to worry, for the loss of blood was obviously weakening Arthur, even though he was a strong man. It gave me an idea of what a terrible strain Lucy's system had been under.

When it was over and I was bandaging Arthur's wound, Van Helsing adjusted the pillow under Lucy's head. Lucy always wore a narrow black velvet band around her throat, fastened with a diamond pin Arthur had given her. As the professor shifted her head, the velvet ribbon slipped a little. I heard Van Helsing suck in his breath with a hiss. He said nothing, but turned to me, saying, "Now take our brave young lover downstairs. Give him a glass of wine and let him lie down a little. He must then go home and rest, sleep much, and eat much."

When Arthur had gone, I went back to the

room. Lucy was sleeping gently, but her breathing was stronger. Van Helsing sat by the bedside looking at her intently. The velvet band was again in place. I asked the Professor in a whisper, "What did you see?"

"I have not examined it yet," he answered, and then loosened the band. Just over the jugular vein there were two punctures, not large, but nasty looking. The edges were white and seemed worn. Of course it occurred to me that this wound, or whatever it was, might explain the loss of blood. But it was ridiculous to think she could have bled so much from such tiny wounds. In order to leave Lucy as pale and nearly dead as she had been before the transfusion, the whole bed would have had to be drenched in blood.

"Well?" said Van Helsing.

"Well," I said, "I don't understand it."

The Professor stood up. "I must go back to Amsterdam tonight," he said. "There are books and things there which I want. You must stay here all night, and you must not let her out of your sight. I shall be back as soon as possible. And then we may begin."

"May begin?" I said. "What on earth do you mean?"

"We shall see!" he answered, as he hurried out. He came back a moment later and put his head inside the door. "Remember, she is your responsibility. If you leave her, and she is harmed, you will not forgive yourself later!"

September 8. I sat up all night with Lucy. When she woke in the morning, she looked like a different person. Her spirits were good, and she was full of happy energy. When I told Mrs. Westenra that Dr. Van Helsing had ordered that I should stay with Lucy, she almost pooh-poohed the idea, because her daughter looked so well. I was firm, however. After her maid had gotten her ready for bed that evening, I came in and sat down by her bed.

She did not ask any questions, but gave me a grateful look. After a long time she seemed to be dozing off, but then sat up, as though to shake off her sleepiness. It was clear that she was trying to force herself to stay awake, so I tackled the subject at once.

"You do not want to sleep?"

"No. I am afraid."

"Afraid to go to sleep! Why? It is rest we all need."

"But for me, sleep opens the door to horrible things."

"What kind of horrible things?"

"I don't know. Oh, I don't know. And that

is what is so terrible. All these bad things happen when I sleep, until I dread the very thought."

"But, my dear girl, you may sleep tonight. I am here watching you, and I can promise that nothing will happen."

"Ah, I can trust you!" she said.

"I promise that if you seem to be having any bad dreams, I will wake you at once."

"You will? Oh, will you really? That would be wonderful. Then I can sleep!" Almost immediately she gave a deep sigh of relief, and sank back, asleep.

All night long I watched her. She never moved, but slept on and on in a deep, peaceful, health-giving sleep. There was a smile on her face, and it was clear that no bad dreams were disturbing her.

In the early morning her maid came in. I left her to watch Lucy and went back home. I sent telegrams to Van Helsing and to Arthur, telling them of the excellent result of the transfusion. My own work at the asylum took me all day, so it was dark when I was able to inquire about Renfield. The report was good. He had been quiet for the past day and night. A telegram came from Van Helsing in Amsterdam while I was at dinner, asking me to spend the night at the Westenras', and saying that he would meet me there early in the morning.

September 9. I was pretty worn out when I got to the Westenras' house. For two nights I had hardly had a wink of sleep, and my brain felt numb with exhaustion. Lucy was up and in cheerful spirits. She gave me one look and said, "No sitting up for you tonight. You are worn out, and I am quite well again. In fact, if there is any sitting up, I will sit up with you."

I could not argue with that but went and had my supper. Lucy came with me, and I had an excellent meal and two glasses of more than excellent wine. Then Lucy took me upstairs and showed me a room next to her own, where a cozy fire was burning.

"Now," she said, "you must stay here. I shall leave this door open and my door too. You can lie on the sofa. If I need anything I will call out, and you can come to me at once."

I had no choice; I could not have stayed awake if I had tried. Making her promise again to call me if she needed anything, I lay on the sofa and forgot about everything.

LUCY WESTENRA'S DIARY

September 9. I feel so happy tonight. I have been so miserably weak, and now to be able to think clearly and move about is like feeling sunshine after a long spell of bad weather. Somehow Arthur feels very, very close to me. I seem to sense his presence warm about me. What a wonderful sleep I had last night, with good Dr. Seward watching me. And tonight I will not be afraid to sleep, with him just in the next room. Thank everybody for being so good to me. Thank God! Goodnight, Arthur.

DR. SEWARD'S DIARY

September 10. I woke up to feel the Professor's hand on my head. "And how is our patient?" he asked.

"Very well when I left her, or rather when she left me," I answered.

"Come, let us see," he said. And together we went into the room. The blind was down, and I went over to it while Van Helsing stepped over to the bed.

As I raised the blind, and the morning sunlight flooded the room, I heard the Professor's hissing intake of breath. Deadly fear shot through my heart. "God in Heaven!" he exclaimed, his face a mask of horror. I felt my knees begin to tremble.

There on the bed, lying as if she had fainted, was poor Lucy. She was more horribly white and weak-looking than ever before. Even her lips were white, and her gums seemed to have shrunk back from the teeth, as we sometimes see in a dead body after a lengthy illness.

Van Helsing raised his foot to stamp in anger, but he regained control of himself and put it down again softly.

"Quick!" he said. "Bring the brandy."

I ran to the dining room, and returned with the bottle. He wetted the poor white lips with it, and together we rubbed the alcohol into her palms and wrists. He felt her heart, and after a few moments of agonizing suspense said, "It is not too late. It beats, but only weakly. All our work is undone. We must begin again. There is no young Arthur here now. I have to call on you yourself this time, friend John." As he spoke, he was reaching into his bag, and pulling out the instruments of transfusion. I had taken off my coat and rolled up my shirt sleeve. And so, without a moment's delay, we began the operation.

After a time—it did not seem a short time either, for the draining away of one's blood, even if it is willingly given, is a terrible feeling—Van Helsing held up a warning finger. "Do not move," he said. "But I fear that she may wake, and that would be dangerous. I shall give her an injection of morphine."

The transfusion was having a good effect on Lucy. I felt proud to see a faint tinge of color steal back into the pale cheeks and lips. It is a strange and wonderful feeling for a man to watch his own lifeblood fill the veins of the woman he loves.

When we stopped the procedure, he attended to Lucy, and I applied pressure to my own incision. I lay down, for I felt faint and a little sick. When he was finished with Lucy, he bandaged my wound, and sent me downstairs to get a glass of wine for myself. As I was leaving the room, he came after me, and half whispered.

"Tell Arthur nothing of this. It would at frighten him and make him jealous as well. So not a word!"

When I came back, he looked at me carefully, and then said, "You do not look too bad. Go into the room, and lie on the sofa, and rest a while; then have a big breakfast and come back here."

I followed his orders. I had done my part, and now my duty was to keep up my strength. I fell asleep on the sofa, wondering over and over again how Lucy could have relapsed so quickly. How could she have lost so much blood with no sign to show for it? I think I must have continued my wonder in my dreams, for even in my sleep my thoughts came back to the little punctures in her throat, tiny though they were.

Lucy slept most of the day. When she woke she was fairly strong, though not nearly as well as the day before. Once Van Helsing had seen her, he went out for a walk, leaving me with strict orders not to leave her for a moment. I could hear his voice in the hall, asking the way to the nearest telegraph office.

Lucy chatted with me freely, and seemed quite unaware that anything had happened. I tried to keep her amused. When her mother came up to see her, she said to me gratefully, "We owe you so much, Dr. Seward, for all you have done, but you really must now take care of yourself. You are looking pale yourself. You need a wife to look after you, that you do!" As she spoke, Lucy blushed, and a jolt of pain went through my heart. Van Helsing returned in a few hours, and said to me "Now you go home, and eat a good dinner. Make yourself strong. I stay here tonight, and I shall sit up with little miss myself. Don't talk to anyone about this case. I have my reasons."

September 11. This afternoon I found Van Helsing in excellent spirits, and Lucy much better. Shortly after I arrived, a big parcel arrived for the Professor. He opened it and took out a great bundle of white flowers.

"These are for you, Miss Lucy," he said.

"For me? Oh, Dr. Van Helsing!"

"Yes, my dear, but not just to look at. These are medicines." Here Lucy made a wry face. "No, I won't make you eat or drink them, so you don't have to wrinkle your pretty nose. This is a different kind of medicine. This flower, I put him in your window, I make pretty wreath, and hang him round your neck, so you sleep well."

While he was speaking, Lucy had been looking at the flowers and smelling them. Now she threw them down, saying with laughing disgust, "Oh, Professor, you are joking! These are garlic flowers!"

To my surprise, Van Helsing stood up and said sternly, "I am not joking! Do as I say, for the sake of others if not for your own sake." Then, seeing poor Lucy's frightened face, he went on more gently, "Oh, little miss, my dear, do not fear me. I do this only for your good. There is much good in those flowers. See, I place them myself in your room. I make myself the wreath that you are to wear. Come, friend John, help me deck the room with my garlic, which is all the way from my friend

Vanderpool's greenhouse. I had to telegraph yesterday, or they would not have been here."

The Professor's actions were certainly odd, and not mentioned in any medical classes I had ever attended. First he locked all the windows securely. Next, taking a handful of the flowers, he rubbed them all over the window frames, as though he wanted every whiff of air that got in to be scented with garlic. He did the same on the doorframe, and even around the fireplace. It all seemed bizarre to me. Finally I said, "Well, Professor, I know you always have a reason for what you do, but this certainly puzzles me. One would think you were working a spell to keep out an evil spirit."

"Perhaps I am!" he answered quietly, as he began to make a wreath of garlic flowers.

We then waited while Lucy got ready for bed. Once she was tucked in, he fixed the wreath of garlic around her neck. The last words he said to her were, "Take care you do not disturb it. And even if the room feels warm, do not open the window or the door."

"I promise," said Lucy. "And thank you both for all your kindness to me!"

As we left the house, Van Helsing said, "Tonight I can sleep in peace, and sleep I need. Tomorrow morning early you pick me up, and we come together to see our pretty miss. She will be much more strong for my 'spell' which I have worked. Ha!"

He seemed so confident. I remembered my own confidence of two nights before, and how wrong I had been. I did not have the courage to tell Van Helsing my fears, but I felt them like unshed tears.

Chapter 11

Lucy Westenra's Diary

September 12. Why was kind Dr. Van Helsing so fierce about these flowers? And yet he must be right, for I feel comforted by them. I am not afraid to be alone tonight. I never liked garlic before, but somehow this is delightful! There is peace in its smell. I feel sleepy already.

Dr. Seward's Diary

September 13. I picked up Van Helsing from his hotel, and we arrived at the Westenras' at eight o'clock. It was a lovely, bright autumn morning. When we entered, we met Mrs. Westenra, who is always an early riser. She greeted us warmly and said, "Lucy is better. The dear child is still asleep. I looked into her room and saw her, but I didn't want to wake her." The Professor smiled joyously. He rubbed his hands together, and said, "Aha! My treatment is working."

Mrs. Westenra replied, with a smile, "You must not take all the credit, doctor! I have helped Lucy as well."

"How do you mean, ma'am?" asked the Professor.

"Well, I was worried about her during the night, so I went into her room. She was sleeping soundly, but the room was awfully stuffy. There were a lot of strong-smelling flowers everywhere, and she actually had a bunch of them round her neck. I thought that the heavy odor would be bad for her, so I took them all away and opened the window to let in a little fresh air. You will be pleased with her condition, I'm sure."

She walked away toward her breakfast. As she spoke, the Professor's face had turned gray as ashes. He controlled himself in front of her, and he actually smiled as he held open the door for her to leave the room. But the instant she had disappeared he pulled me into the dining room and closed the door.

Then, for the first time in my life, I saw Van Helsing break down. He raised his hands over his head in silent despair, and then beat them together in a helpless way. Finally he sank down on a chair. Putting his hands before his face, he began to sob out loud. "God! God! God!" he said. "What have we done, what has this poor girl done? This poor mother, meaning nothing but good, may have destroyed her daughter body and soul, and we must not tell her! We must not even warn her, or she will die; then both will die. Oh, how the powers of the devil act against us!"

Then he jumped to his feet. "Come," he said, "come, we must see. Devils or no devils, or all the devils at once, we must fight him." Together we went up to Lucy's room.

Once again I drew up the blind, while Van Helsing went towards the bed. This time neither of us was surprised to see the poor face with its awful, waxen whiteness. Without a word he went and locked the door, and then began to set out the instruments for yet another transfusion. I had begun to take off my coat, but he stopped me. "No!" he said. "Today I shall provide. You are weakened already." As he spoke, he took off his coat and rolled up his shirtsleeve.

Again the transfusion. Again the narcotic. Again some return of color to her ashy cheeks, and the regular breathing of healthy sleep.

After Van Helsing had rested a while, he told Mrs. Westenra that she must not remove anything from Lucy's room without asking him. He explained that the flowers were a form of medicine, and that breathing their scent would help cure Lucy. Then he said that he would watch her for the next two nights and would call me when he needed me.

After another hour Lucy awoke from her sleep, fresh and bright and seemingly not badly weakened.

LUCY WESTENRA'S DIARY

September 17. Four days and nights of peace. I am getting so strong again! Since Dr. Van Helsing has been with me, it is as if I have awakened from a long nightmare and found the beautiful sunshine and fresh air around me. The noises that used to frighten me out of my wits, the distant voices that commanded me to do things I didn't understand, have all gone away. I go to bed now without any fear. I have grown quite fond of the garlic, and a boxful arrives for me every day from Holland.

Tonight Dr. Van Helsing is going away, as he has to be in Amsterdam for a day. But I am well enough to be left alone. I will sleep as well as I did last night, even though the trees or bats or something flapped almost angrily against the window panes.

The Pall Mall Gazette
Zoo Wolf Escapes, Returns
September 18

A gray wolf, by the name of Bersicker, escaped earlier this week from the Zoological Gardens. Zookeeper Thomas Bilder, who looks after the wolves, described the wolf as gentle and nearly tame, and said he was greatly surprised by the animal's actions.

Bilder mentioned that all his wolves had seemed greatly disturbed early in the day of Bersicker's escape. Hearing the racket they were making, he came to investigate, and found a stranger standing before their cages. He described the man as a tall, thin gentleman whose presence seemed to greatly excite the animals. What particularly surprised Bilder was that when the zookeeper approached Bersicker and petted him to quiet him, the strange man did likewise, and Bersicker (who Bilder says would not usually let a stranger near him) lay down quietly and allowed the man to touch him.

Later that night, Bilder reports that all the zoo's wolves began howling madly. When the zookeeper went to see the cause, he found Bersicker gone.

Most surprisingly of all, the wolf later returned voluntarily to Bilder's cottage, located on the grounds of the zoo. He had suffered a number of small cuts on his head, and there were bits of glass embedded in his skin. His cuts were cleaned and he was safely returned to his cage.

Dr. Seward's Diary

September 17. I was working in my study after dinner when the door burst open and in rushed Renfield. He ran straight at me, a dinner knife in his hand. I had no chance to defend myself before he had struck at me, cutting my left wrist badly.

Before he could strike again, I managed to hit him with my right hand, sending him sprawling on the floor. My wrist bled freely, and a little pool was forming on the carpet. Renfield did not attempt to get up. As the attendants rushed in, he was behaving in a sickening manner. He was lying on his belly on the floor licking up the blood just as a dog would. To my surprise, he went with the attendants quite easily, simply repeating over and over again, "The blood is the life! The blood is the life!"

I can't afford to lose any more blood. The transfusions and the strain of Lucy's illness are making me feel half-mad myself. I need rest, rest, rest. Fortunately, Van Helsing has not called me, so I can sleep tonight.

Telegram from
Van Helsing, Amsterdam to John Seward. M.D.
(Due to mistake at telegraph office, delivered twenty-two hours late.)

September 17
Go to Lucy tonight. If not watching all the time, frequently visit and see that flowers are as placed. Very important, do not fail. Shall be with you as soon as possible after arrival.

DR. SEWARD'S DIARY

September 18. The arrival of Van Helsing's telegram filled me with dismay. I had lost a whole night, and I know by awful experience what can happen in a night. Surely there is some horrible doom hanging over us.

Note left by Lucy Westenra

September 17-18, night. I am writing this so that no one may get into trouble because of me. I feel so weak I am afraid I am dying, but I must leave this record of what has happened.

I went to bed as usual, making sure that the flowers were placed as Dr. Van Helsing told me, and I soon fell asleep. I was wakened by the flapping at the window, which had begun after my night of sleepwalking to the cliff at Whitby. I was not exactly afraid, but I did wish that Dr. Seward was in the next room, as Dr. Van Helsing said he would be. I tried to sleep, but I could not. Then I began to feel afraid that I would fall asleep, and wished that someone was with me. I opened my door and called out, "Is anybody there?" but there was no answer. I was afraid to wake mother, so I closed my door again.

Then outside in the bushes I heard a sort of howl like a dog's, but deeper and fiercer. I looked out the window, but all I could see was a big bat, which I suppose had been flapping its wings against my window. After a bit, the

door opened, and mother came in. She said to me, "I was worried about you, dear, and came in to see that you were all right." She lay down beside me, still wearing her bathrobe, because she said she would only stay a few minutes. But then the flapping began at the window again. She was frightened, and cried out, "What is that?"

I calmed her, telling her it was only a bat, but I could hear her poor dear heart beating so hard. And then there was the howl again, a crash at the window, and a shower of broken glass as the head of a great, gray wolf broke through the window pane.

Mother screamed, grabbing wildly at anything that would help her. She tore away the wreath of flowers that I wore around my throat. For a second or two she sat up, pointing at the wolf, and there was a strange, horrible gurgling in her throat. Then she fell over, as if struck with lightning. Her falling head hit my forehead and made me dizzy.

Everything was spinning, but I tried to keep my eyes on the window. The wolf pulled its head back, and something like a cloud of little, shining specks seemed to come floating into the room. I tried to move, but it was as if I were under a spell. I felt helpless under the weight of poor Mother's body, which was already growing cold. I can't remember anything that happened for a while.

Finally I seemed to wake up again. Dogs all over the neighborhood were howling, and I felt dazed with pain and terror. The sounds must have awakened the maids, too, for I could hear them outside my door. I called to them, and when they came in and saw what had happened, they began to scream and cry. They lifted Mother's body to the side of the bed and covered it with a sheet. They were nearly hysterical, so I told them to go to the dining room and each have a glass of wine. I stayed with Mother's body, but as time went on and the maids did not return, I went to the dining room to look for them.

My heart sank when I saw what had happened. All four maids lay helpless on the floor, breathing heavily. The bottle of wine was on the table, half full, but there was a queer, burning smell coming from it. When I examined the bottle, I realized it smelled of the sleeping-medicine that Mother's doctor gives her—I should say, used to give her. Looking around, I found the little medicine bottle, empty.

What can I do? What can I do? I am back in the room with Mother. I cannot leave her, and I am alone, except for the drugged servants. I do not dare go out, for I can still hear the howling of the wolf through the broken window.

The air seems full of specks, floating and circling in the breeze that blows through the broken window. What am I to do? I shall hide this paper in my pocket, where they shall find it if I die. My dear mother is gone! It is time that I go too. Goodbye, dear Arthur, if I should not survive this night. God keep you, dear, and God help me!

Chapter 12

DR. SEWARD'S DIARY
(continued)

September 18. I drove immediately to the Westenras' house. I knocked as softly as I could, hoping not to disturb Lucy or her mother. When no one answered, I knocked and rang more loudly. I cursed the laziness of the servants for still sleeping at this hour, for it was almost ten o'clock.

As I continued knocking, however, a terrible fear came over me. Was I too late? I went around the house, searching for an open door or window, but everything was locked. As I did so I heard the pit-pat of horse's feet, and

Van Helsing appeared, out of breath. "How is she?" he gasped. "Are we in time? Didn't you get my telegram?"

I explained everything as quickly as I could. His face turned pale as he said, "Then I fear we are too late. But come, we must find a way in."

We went around to the back of the house, where there was a kitchen window. The Professor took a small surgical saw from his case, and I managed to cut through the iron bars which guarded it. We pushed back the lock with the handle of a long, thin knife, and crawled inside.

There was no one in the kitchen or in the servants' rooms, but in the dining room we found four servant women lying on the floor. We could hear their loud snores, and smell the odor of the narcotic, so we realized they were drugged. "We will help them later," Van Helsing said. Then we climbed the stairs to Lucy's room. We listened for an instant or two at the door, but there was no sound. With white faces and trembling hands, we opened the door gently and entered the room.

And oh, the awful sight that met our eyes. Broken glass littered the floor, and the breeze came freely through a shattered window. On the bed lay two women, Lucy and her mother.

Mrs. Westenra was covered with a white sheet, the edge of which had blown back to show the look of terror on her cold, dead face. By her side lay Lucy. Her wreath of flowers was missing from her neck, and the two little wounds on her neck were horribly white and ragged. Without a word the Professor bent over the bed, listening for Lucy's heartbeat. Leaping to his feet, he cried out to me, "It is not yet too late! Quick! Quick! Bring the brandy!"

I ran downstairs and returned with it, being careful to smell and taste it, in case it too, was drugged. The maids were beginning to mutter and moan in their sleep. As he had done once before, Van Helsing rubbed the brandy onto Lucy's lips and gums and on her wrists and the palms of her hands. He said to me, "I can do this alone. Go wake the maids. Tell them to make a fire and prepare a hot bath. This poor soul is nearly as cold as her mother. She needs to be warmed before we can do anything."

The maids were dazed at first, then they began to cry hysterically as they remembered what they had seen. I scolded them, telling them that it was too late to save Mrs. Westenra, but they still had time to help Lucy. So they went sobbing on their way to heat water for a bath. Once Lucy was in it, one of the maids hurried in, whispering that there was a gentleman at the door with a message from Mr. Holmwood. I told her we could not see anyone now, and promptly forgot all about it.

The heat was beginning to have some effect on Lucy. Her heart beat a little more strongly, and her breathing steadied a bit. Van Helsing's face almost beamed as we lifted her from the bath and rolled her in a warm towel to dry her.

We took Lucy into another room, put her in bed, and forced a few drops of brandy down her throat. I noticed that Van Helsing had tied a soft silk handkerchief around her throat. She was still unconscious, and she looked worse than we had ever seen her.

Van Helsing called in one of the women, and told her to not take her eyes off her until we returned, and then led me out of the room. "We must think what to do," he said as we went downstairs. "Where can we get help? We must have another transfusion of blood, and soon, or that poor girl will die. You and I are exhausted. I don't trust these panicky maids. Who can help us now?"

"What's the matter with me?" The voice came from the sofa across the room. The sound brought joy to my heart, for it was Quincy Morris.

"Quincy! What brought you here?" I cried, taking his hand.

"This did," he said, handing me a telegram. It was from Arthur, and it read: "Have not heard from Seward for three days and am terribly anxious. Cannot leave. Father still very ill. Send me news how Lucy is. Do not delay.—Holmwood."

"I think I came just in the nick of time. Just tell me what to do," said Quincy.

Van Helsing came forward and took his hand, looking him straight in the eyes. "The devil may work against us, but God sends us good men when we need them," he said. Once again we went through the transfusion. I don't have the heart to describe it. Lucy was weaker than ever before, and although plenty of blood went into her veins, her body barely responded. Finally though, her heart and lungs were working a little more strongly, and I sent Quincy downstairs to eat and rest.

When I returned to the bedroom, I found Van Helsing reading a sheet of paper. He handed it to me saying only, "It dropped from Lucy's pocket when we carried her to the bath."

When I had read it, I asked the Professor, "In God's name, what does it all mean? Is she mad? Or what sort of horrible danger is it?"

Van Helsing took the paper, saying, "Don't worry about it now. You will understand it all in good time."

Next, I hurried out to notify the undertaker of Mrs. Westenra's death. The poor lady's heart disease was enough explanation; I did not feel it was necessary to reveal what had caused her final shock. When I returned I met Quincy, who was putting together a telegram for Arthur telling him that Mrs. Westenra was dead.

"Jack, may I have a word with you?" Quincy asked. We sat down to talk. "I don't want to push myself in where I don't belong, but this is no ordinary case. You know I loved that girl and wanted to marry her, and though that's over and done, I can't help worrying about her. Just what is it that is wrong with her? That fine old Dutchman of yours said that she must have another transfusion of blood and that both you and he were exhausted. Didn't he?"

"He did," I said, and he went on.

"Then I take it that you and Van Helsing have both done already what I did today?"

"That's right."

"And I guess Art has, too. When I saw him four days ago, he looked awful. I have not seen anyone get run-down so quickly since I was in

South America. A mare of mine was outside all night, and one of those big bats that they call vampires got her. In the morning there wasn't enough blood in her to let her stand up. I had to put a bullet through her as she lay there. How long has this been going on?"

"About ten days."

"Ten days! You're telling me that in ten days, that poor pretty creature has had the blood of four men put into her veins?" Then coming close to me, he spoke in a fierce half-whisper. "What took it out?"

I shook my head. "That," I said, "is the mystery. Van Helsing is frantic about it, and I can't even begin to guess."

When she woke late in the afternoon, Lucy's first movement was to feel in her pocket and pull out the paper which Van Helsing replaced there. Her eyes turned to Van Helsing and then to me, too. Then she looked round the room, and seeing where she was, shuddered. She moaned and held her poor, thin hands to her pale face.

We both understood what she meant, that she had remembered her mother's death. We tried to comfort her, but she seemed very sad and wept silently and weakly for a long time. We told her that either or both of us would stay with her all the time, and that seemed to comfort her. Towards dusk she fell asleep, and then a very odd thing happened. As she slept she took the paper from her pocket and tore it in two. Van Helsing stepped over and took the pieces from her. But she went on making tearing movements, as if she still had the paper. Finally she lifted her hands and opened them as though scattering the fragments.

September 19. All last night she slept uneasily and seemed weaker every time she awoke. The Professor and I took turns watching, never leaving her for a moment. All night Quincy patrolled around the house.

When the day came, it was clear that the poor girl was losing the battle. She was hardly able to turn her head, and the little food which she ate didn't seem to do her any good. Van Helsing and I both noticed the difference in her, depending on whether she was asleep or awake. While she slept she looked somehow stronger. Her pale gums must have been pulling away from her teeth, for the teeth looked longer and sharper than usual. When she was awake she looked more like her sweet self, although a dying self. In the afternoon she asked for Arthur, and we telegraphed for him. When he arrived it was nearly six o'clock. His presence seemed to cheer her up, and she spoke to him a little.

It is now nearly one o'clock, and he and Van Helsing are with her. I will begin my shift in a quarter hour. I am afraid that the end will come tomorrow. The poor child cannot recover. God help us all.

Letter from Mina Harker to Lucy Westenra
(Unopened by her)

September 17

My dearest Lucy,

It seems an age since I have written, and I have plenty of news. Jonathan and I returned safely to England. When we arrived at Exeter, Mr. Hawkins met us, even though he has been so ill. He took us to his lovely house where we had dinner together. After we ate, Mr. Hawkins said, "My dears, I want to drink a toast to you. I have known you both since you were children, and I love you like my own. Now, will you live here with me? I have left you this house and everything else in my will and I want to see you enjoy it now." Wasn't that wonderful of him, Lucy? Our evening was a very, very happy one.

So here we are, installed in this beautiful old house. I am busy arranging things and housekeeping, and Jonathan and Mr. Hawkins are busy all day at their law firm.

How is your mother getting on? I wish I could come see you, but I don't feel that I can yet, with so much to do and Jonathan still weakened by his illness. He is beginning to put on a little weight, thank God, but he still sometimes jumps in his sleep and wakes up shaking. These things happen less frequently, though, and I hope they will soon stop forever. And now that I have told you my news, let me ask yours. When will you be married, and where, and who is to perform the ceremony, and what will you wear, and is it to be a large or small wedding? Tell me all about it, for there is nothing which interests you which does not interest me. Goodbye, my dearest Lucy, and blessings on you.

Yours,
Mina

*Report from
Patrick Hennessey, M.D. to John Seward, M.D*

September 20

My dear Sir:

As you asked, I am sending on the daily reports from the asylum. Regarding Renfield, there is more to say. He has had another peculiar outbreak, but fortunately no one was badly hurt.

This afternoon two men driving a mover's cart headed to the empty mansion near these grounds. The men stopped at our gate to ask directions.

I happened to see the men myself, as I was in my study having a cigarette after dinner. As one of them passed by the window of Renfield's room, the patient began to shout at him, calling him all the foul names he could think of. The man, who seemed like a nice enough fellow, only told Renfield to quiet down. Then Renfield raved on, accusing the man of robbing him and wanting to murder him, and said that he, Renfield, would stop the man even if it meant he would hang for it. The man paid him no mind, but continued on his way to the gates of the old house while Renfield continued to curse and scream at him.

I went down to see if I could discover why Renfield was so angry. To my surprise, I found him very quiet and well behaved. I tried to get him to talk about what had happened, but he pretended not to know what I was talking about. This was clearly just a trick of his; half an hour later he had broken through the window in his room and was running down the road. The attendants and I followed after him, and soon we met the same moving cart, only this time it was loaded with some big wooden boxes. Before I could reach them, Renfield leaped out, pulled one of the men off the cart, and began to knock his head against the ground. It was clear he meant to kill him. The other fellow jumped down and struck Renfield over the head with the butt end of his heavy whip. It was a horrible blow, but he did not seem to feel it. He grabbed the second man also, and struggled with the three of us, pulling us around as if we were kittens. You know I am no lightweight, and the others were both burly men. At first he fought silently, but as we got the better of him, he began to shout, "I'll fix them! They won't rob me! I'll fight for my Lord and Master!" and all sorts of similar crazy stuff. It was hard work to get him back to the house and put him in the padded room. One of the attendants, Hardy, had his finger broken.

The two movers threatened all kinds of lawsuits at first, but when I gave them each some money and paid for a round of beer, they said they didn't hold a grudge. I think they were mostly embarrassed at being beaten by a single lunatic. I did take down their names and addresses in case they might be needed later.

They are as follows: Jack Smollet, of King George's Road, and Thomas Snelling, of Bethnal Green. They both work for Harris & Sons, Moving and Shipment Company, Soho.

I will report if anything more of interest happens here.

Yours faithfully,
Patrick Hennessey

Letter from Mina Harker to Lucy Westenra
(Unopened by her)

September 18

My dearest Lucy,

Such a sad thing has happened. Mr. Hawkins has died very suddenly. I never knew my own father or mother, so it really feels to me that I have lost a parent. Jonathan is very upset. It is not just that he misses his lifelong friend who was so good to us. It is also that Jonathan says he is nervous about the greater responsibility he will now have at the law office. He is full of doubts about himself, and these feelings are all the result of his illness. It is so awful that a sweet, strong man like him should have so little confidence. It worries me greatly, and it is hard to keep up a brave and cheerful front for his sake. I dread coming up to London, as we must day after tomorrow, for poor Mr. Hawkins wanted to be buried beside his father. I shall try to come see you, if only for a few minutes.

Your loving,
Mina

Dr. Seward's Diary

September 20. I am miserable, low spirited, and sick of the world and of life itself. Just now I would not care if I heard the angel of death drawing near me. And it seems he has been hovering over us lately. Arthur's father has died, and Lucy's mother, and now . . .

I took my turn watching over Lucy. We wanted Arthur to rest, but he refused at first. I convinced him by telling him that we would need his help during the day.

Van Helsing was very kind to him. "Come, my child," he said. "You are sick and weak, and have had much sorrow. You must not be alone, for to be alone is to be full of fears. Come to the drawing room where there is a big fire and there are two sofas. You shall lie on one and I on the other. We will keep each other company even though we do not speak and even if we sleep."

Arthur went off with him, casting back a heartsick look on Lucy's face, which looked whiter than her pillow. She was breathing with a harsh, gasping sound, and her face was at its worst. Her open mouth showed its pale gums, and her teeth seemed even longer and sharper than they had been in the morning.

As I sat down beside her, she moved uneasily. There was a dull flapping at the window. Looking out into the full moonlight, I could see that the noise was made by a huge bat, which was probably attracted by the light. When I came back to my seat, I found that Lucy had torn away the garlic flowers from her throat. I replaced them and sat watching her.

After a bit she awoke, and I tried to interest her in eating. She took almost nothing. She no longer seemed to have the will to live that we had seen earlier in her illness. Oddly, when she awoke, she automatically held the garlic flowers close to her. But when she slept and made that harsh, gasping sound, she pushed them away.

At six o'clock, Van Helsing came to relieve me. Arthur had then fallen into a doze, and the Professor had left him in the other room. When he saw Lucy's face, I could hear the hiss of his breath, and he said to me in a sharp whisper, "Open up the blind. I want light!"

Then he bent down and examined her carefully. He removed the flowers and lifted the silk handkerchief from her throat. As he did so, he seemed greatly startled. "My God!" he said. I bent over and looked, too, and a chill came over me. The wounds on the throat had absolutely disappeared.

For five long minutes Van Helsing stood looking at her, his face at its most serious. Then he turned to me and said calmly, "She is dying. It will not be long now. Wake that poor boy and let him come and be with her at the end."

I went to the dining room and woke up Arthur. I told him that Lucy was still asleep but warned him as gently as I could that the end was near. He covered his face with his hands and slid down to his knees by the sofa. There he stayed, praying, while his shoulders shook with grief. I took him by the hand and pulled him up. "Come, Art," I said, "be brave. It will make things easier for her."

We came into Lucy's room. Van Helsing had, with his usual kindness, made everything look as pleasant as possible. He had even brushed Lucy's hair so that it lay on the pillow in dark ripples. When we came into the room, she opened her eyes and, seeing him, whispered softly, "Arthur! Oh, my love, I am so glad you have come!"

Arthur took her hand and knelt beside her. Her face was soft with love and sadness. Then, gradually, her eyes closed and she sank to sleep. For a little bit her breath came and went gently like a tired child's. And then came the strange change which I had noticed in the night. Her breathing grew harsh, her mouth opened, and the pale gums, drawn back, made the teeth look long and sharp as an animal's. She opened her eyes, which now seemed dull and hard. In a soft, husky voice, such as I had never heard from her, she said, "Arthur! Oh, my love, I am so glad you have come! Kiss me!"

Arthur bent down eagerly. But at that instant Van Helsing swooped upon him. Grabbing him by the neck with both hands, he dragged him back and actually hurled him across the room. "Not on your life!" he said, "Not for your soul and hers!" And he stood between them like an angry lion.

Arthur was so shocked that he did not know what to do or say. I kept watching Lucy, as did Van Helsing. We saw a look of ugly rage flit like a shadow over her face. The sharp teeth snapped together. Then her eyes closed and she breathed heavily.

After a few moments she opened her eyes, which were once again soft and loving. Putting out her pale, thin hand, she took Van Helsing's great brown one, and gently kissed it. "My true friend," she said, in a faint voice. "My true friend, and Arthur's! Oh, protect him and give me peace!"

"I swear it!" he said solemnly, kneeling beside her. Then he turned to Arthur and said to him, "Come, my child, take her hand, and kiss her—on the forehead."

Their eyes met instead of their lips, and so they parted. Lucy's eyes closed, and Van Helsing, who had been watching closely, took Arthur's arm. Lucy's breathing became harsh again, and all at once it stopped. "It is over," said Van Helsing. "She is dead."

I led Arthur to the drawing room, where he sat down and covered his face with his hands, sobbing in a way that nearly broke my heart. Back in the bedroom, I found Van Helsing looking at poor Lucy, and his face was sterner than ever.

I stood beside him and said, "Poor girl, there is peace for her at last. It is over."

He turned to me, and said solemnly, "Not true, sadly! Not so. It is only the beginning!"

When I asked him what he meant, he only shook his head and answered, "We can do nothing yet. Wait and see."

Chapter 13

DR. SEWARD'S DIARY
(continued)

The funeral was arranged for the next day so that Lucy and her mother might be buried together. I took care of all the horrible details. Before turning in, Van Helsing and I went together to look at poor Lucy. The undertaker had certainly done his work well. There was a wilderness of beautiful white flowers. When the Professor and I looked at Lucy's face, we were both startled by its beauty. All Lucy's loveliness, and more, had come back to her in death. I absolutely could not believe that I was looking at a corpse.

The Professor looked stern. He said to me, "Stay until I return," and left the room. He came back with a handful of wild garlic from the box waiting in the hall and placed the flowers among the others on the bed. Then he took a little gold crucifix from around his neck and placed it over Lucy's mouth.

He came to my room that night. "Tomorrow, before dark, I want you to bring me a set of surgical knives."

"Must we do an autopsy?" I asked, surprised.

"Yes and no. I want to operate, but not as you think. I want to cut off her head and take out her heart. Ah, John, you are a surgeon, and yet you are so shocked! But I must not forget, my dear friend, that you loved her. And I do not forget, for I am the one who will operate and you will not help. I would like to do it tonight, but for Arthur's sake I must not. He will be free after his father's funeral tomorrow and he will want to see her. Then, when she is in her coffin ready for burial, you and I shall come when everyone else sleeps. We shall unscrew the coffin lid, do our operation, and then replace the lid, so that no one knows but you and me."

"But ... but ... why? The girl is dead. Why mutilate her poor body? This is monstrous!"

He put his hand on my shoulder and said with great tenderness, "John, I pity your poor bleeding heart. If I could, I would take on myself the sadness that you feel. But there are things that you do not know. When you do know them, you shall bless me for knowing them first. Did you ever know me to do anything without good reason? Isn't that why you sent for me when this trouble began? Weren't you horrified when I would not let Arthur kiss his dying love? Yes! And yet you saw how she thanked me with her beautiful dying eyes. And didn't you hear me promise to continue to help her? You did. My friend, there are strange and terrible days ahead of us. I will need your faith and your help. Will I have them?"

I took his hand and promised. As I watched him walk to his room, I saw one of the maids go silently along the hallway and into the room when Lucy lay. She had her back to me, so she did not see me watching her. I was touched by the girl's devotion—to go sit alone with her poor dead mistress so that she would not be lonely.

I must have slept well, for it was broad daylight when Van Helsing woke me up by coming into my room. He came over to my bedside and said, "Don't bother about the knives. We shall not do it."

"Why not?" I asked.

"Because," he said sternly, "it is too late, or, too early. See!" Here he held up the little golden crucifix. "This was stolen in the night."

"Stolen?" I asked in wonder. "Then how do you have it?"

"Because I got it back from the worthless maid who stole it from the dead. Now we must wait." He went away, leaving me with a new puzzle to think of.

When Arthur arrived he looked terribly sad and broken. I knew he had loved his father very much, and to lose him and Lucy in the same week was a bitter blow. I led him to the room where Lucy lay and left him at the door, feeling that he would want to be alone with her. But he took my arm and led me in, saying huskily, "You loved her too, old fellow. She told me all about it, and your friendship was precious to her. I don't know how to thank you for all you have done. I can't think yet . . ."

Here he suddenly broke down and threw his arms around my shoulders, crying, "Oh, Jack, what will I do? There is nothing in the wide world for me to live for."

I comforted him as well as I could, as men do, without many words. I stood still, my arm around him, until his sobs died away, and then I said softly to him, "Come and look at her."

Together we moved over to her. God! How beautiful she was. Every hour seemed to be making her lovelier. It frightened and amazed me. And as for Arthur, he began to tremble. At last, after a long pause, he said in a faint whisper, "Jack, is she really dead?"

I promised him sadly that she was. After kneeling by the bed for a while and looking at her lovingly, he turned to go. I reminded him that this was goodbye, since the coffin lid would be fastened down next. He went back and took her dead hand and kissed it, and bent to kiss her forehead. He came away, fondly looking back over his shoulder at her.

We ate dinner together, and I could see that poor Art was trying to make the best of things. Van Helsing had been silent all through dinner, but when we had lit our cigars, he began to speak to Arthur.

"Now, Lord Godalming . . ." (for, since the death of his father, Arthur had that title), but Arthur interrupted him.

"No, no, don't call me that, for God's sake! Not yet, anyway. Forgive me, sir. I don't mean to be rude. It is only because my loss is so recent."

The Professor answered kindly, "I wasn't sure whether I should or not, but I cannot call you 'Mr.' when I have grown to know and love you as Arthur."

Arthur held out his hand and took the old man's warmly. "Call me whatever you want," he said, "as long as you will call me your friend. And let me say that I cannot thank you enough for your goodness." He paused a moment, and went on, "I know that Lucy understood your goodness even better than I do. If I ever seemed to doubt you, you must forgive me. Please believe that I trust you in every way. You are Jack's friend and you were hers."

The Professor cleared his throat a couple of times, as though about to speak, and finally said, "May I ask you something now?"

"Certainly."

"Did you know that Mrs. Westenra left you all her property?"

"No, poor dear; this is the first I have heard of it," Arthur replied.

"Since it is all yours, you have a right to do whatever you want with it. I am asking you to give me permission to read all Miss Lucy's papers and letters. Believe me, I am not merely curious. I have a reason, of which she would approve. I have them all here. I took them before we knew that all was yours, so that no stranger might read her words and look into her soul. If you will allow me, I shall keep them. Even you may not see them yet, but I shall keep them safe, and in good time I shall give them back to you. It is a hard thing that I ask, but will you do it, for Lucy's sake?"

Arthur answered heartily, like his old self, "Dr. Van Helsing, do what you like. Lucy would want you to. I shall not bother you with questions until the time comes."

The old Professor stood up, saying solemnly, "Thank you. There will be pain for us all, but it will not be all pain. We all will have to pass through the bitter water before we reach the sweet. But we must be brave and unselfish, and do our duty, and all will be well!"

I slept on a sofa in Arthur's room that night. Van Helsing did not go to bed at all. He walked endlessly, as if he were a night watch-man. He was never out of sight of the room where Lucy lay in her coffin, covered with the wild garlic flowers which sent a heavy, over-powering smell through the odor of lily and rose and into the night.

MINA HARKER'S JOURNAL

September 22. In the train to Exeter. Jonathan is asleep.

Mr. Hawkins's service was very simple. It was only Jonathan and me, the servants, one or two old friends of his from Exeter, and a few friends from the legal world.

Jonathan thought it would interest me to sightsee in London a little. We walked down Piccadilly for a bit, and I was looking at a very beautiful girl in a big hat sitting in a carriage outside a dress shop, when I felt Jonathan clutch my arm so tight that he hurt me. He said under his breath, "My God!" I turned to him quickly and asked him what was the matter.

He was very pale, and his eyes seemed to be bulging out of his head. I saw that he was staring at a tall, thin man, with a great beak of a nose, black moustache, and pointed beard. He, too, was looking at the pretty girl, so hard that he did not notice either of us. I did not like his face. It was hard and cruel, with unnaturally red lips that made his pointed white teeth even more noticeable. Jonathan kept staring at him, until I was afraid he would notice. I asked Jonathan again why he was disturbed, and he answered, "Don't you see who it is?"

"No, dear," I said. "I don't know him, who is it?"

"It is the man himself!" he said. The poor man was obviously terrified. I believe that if he hadn't been leaning on me, he would have collapsed. He kept staring. A man came out of the shop with a parcel and gave it to the lady, who then drove off. The dark man kept his eyes on her and moved off in the same direction. Jonathan kept staring after him. He said, as if to himself, "I believe it is the Count, but he has grown young. My God, how could it be? Oh, my God! My God! If only I knew!" He was so upset that I didn't want to make him worse by asking him questions, so I remained silent. We walked a little further, and then went in and sat for a while in a park. It was a hot day for autumn, and there was a seat in a shady place. After a few minutes staring at nothing, Jonathan's eyes closed, and he went to sleep with his head on my shoulder. In about twenty minutes he woke up, and said to me quite cheerfully, "Why, Mina, have I been asleep? How rude of me. Come, let's get a cup of tea somewhere."

He had forgotten all about the stranger. I worry about these lapses of memory. I worry about everything. I must learn what happened on his journey. The time has come, I am afraid, when I must open the notebook and know what is written there. Oh, Jonathan, I know you will forgive me. It is for your own sake.

Later. A sad homecoming in every way. The house is empty of the dear man who was so good to us. Jonathan is still pale and dizzy. And now a telegram from a Dr. Van Helsing, whoever he may be. "I am sorry to inform you that Mrs. Westenra died five days ago and that Lucy died the day before yesterday. They were both buried today."

Oh, what a weight of sorrow in a few words! Poor Mrs. Westenra! Poor Lucy! And poor, poor Arthur, to have lost such sweetness out of his life! God help us bear our troubles.

DR. SEWARD'S DIARY

September 22. It is all over. Arthur has gone back to his home and has taken Quincy Morris with him. What a fine fellow Quincy is! I believe that he suffered as much about Lucy's death as any of us, but he never broke down. Van Helsing is lying down, resting before his journey. He goes to Amsterdam tonight but says he will return tomorrow night. Poor old fellow! The strain of the past week has broken even his iron strength.

So, for now, we are scattered in all directions. Lucy lies in the tomb of her family, a noble tomb in a lonely churchyard, away from busy London.

And with this I finish this diary, and God only knows if I shall ever begin another. If I do or if I even open this again, it will be to write about different people and different themes.

The Westminster Gazette
A Hampstead Mystery: 'A Booful Lady'
September 25

The residents of Hampstead are nervous about the safety of their children. During the past two or three days, several toddlers have briefly disappeared from their homes. In all these cases the children were too young to explain what had happened, but all have mentioned being with someone that, in their childish way, they refer to as a "booful lady."

It has always been late in the evening when they have disappeared. On two occasions the children have not been found until early the next morning. When the first child who disappeared was found, he explained that he had gone for a walk with a beautiful lady. Perhaps the other children picked up the phrase and are using it as they play hide-and-seek.

There is, however, a serious side to the question. The children who have been missing have been found with a very minor wound to the throat. The wounds seem such as might be made by a rat or a small dog. Local police are keeping a sharp lookout for stray children.

The Westminster Gazette
The Booful Lady: Another Child
September 25. Special Edition

Another child, missing since last night, was discovered late this morning in a deserted area of Shooter's Hill. The little boy has the same tiny wound in the throat as has been noticed in other cases, but his injury was more serious than that of the others. He seemed extremely weak. Once he had rested, he too told of being lured away by a "booful lady."

Chapter 14

MINA HARKER'S JOURNAL

September 23. Jonathan is better after a bad night. I am glad that he is so busy at the office, for that keeps his mind occupied. He will be home quite late tonight. My household work is done, so I shall take his travel journal and lock myself up in my room and read it.

September 24. I didn't have the heart to write last night, Jonathan's notebook upset me so. Poor man! Whether it is real or imagined, how he must have suffered! I wonder if there is any truth in it at all. Was he ill from the beginning, and is that why he wrote all those terrible things? Or did something happen to begin this train of thought? It cannot be true . . . and yet that man we saw yesterday! Jonathan seemed so certain about him! I suppose the funeral upset him and started him thinking about those awful days.

One thing is certain: he believes it all himself. On our wedding day, I remember how he said, "Read it if you want to, but don't tell me what is in it unless the day comes that you have no other choice." I don't know what to make of any of it, but when I read of that fearful Count and his plans to come to London . . . the day may come when I have no choice. If that hour comes, I must be prepared. I shall get my typewriter out today and begin translating the shorthand. Then the story can be ready for others to read, if necessary. That way, I can provide it to others and not worry or upset Jonathan at all.

Letter from Van Helsing to Mina Harker

September 24

Dear Madame,

Please forgive this letter from a stranger. In fact, I am not quite a stranger, as it was I who sent you the sad news of Miss Lucy Westenra's death. By permission of her fiancé, Lord Godalming (you know him as Arthur Holmwood), I have read her letters and papers, for I am deeply concerned about certain matters. In them I find some letters from you which show how great friends you were and how you love her. Madame Mina, in the name of that love, I beg you to help me. May I come to see you? You can trust me. I am a friend of Dr. John Seward as well as of Lord Godalming. If you will agree to see me, I shall come to Exeter at once. Again, please forgive this intrusion, Madame. I have read your letters to poor Lucy, and know how good you are and how your husband has suffered. So I ask you, if it is possible, do not speak to him of my coming in case it may harm him.

Abraham Van Helsing

Telegram from Mrs. Harker to Van Helsing

September 25

Come today by quarter past ten train if you can catch it. Can see you any time after that.

Wilhelmina Harker

Mina Harker's Journal

September 25. I am excited about this visit of Dr. Van Helsing, for somehow I think it might help explain Jonathan's experience. And, if he took care of Lucy in her last illness, he can tell me all about her. But of course that is why he is coming, to talk about Lucy and her sleepwalking, not about Jonathan. How silly I am. That dreadful journal gets hold of my imagination and colors all my thoughts. That awful night on the cliff must have somehow made Lucy ill, and Dr. Van Helsing wants to know what I remember of it. I hope I did the right thing in not telling Mrs. Westenra about it and that Dr. Van Helsing will not blame me. I will not even mention Jonathan's journal unless the doctor asks about it. I am glad I've typewritten out my own journal, so that the doctor can read for himself my account of Lucy's sleepwalking.

Later. He has come and gone. Oh, what a strange meeting; it has made my head spin. Can it be all possible, or even a part of it? If I hadn't read Jonathan's journal first, I couldn't begin to believe it. Poor Jonathan! How he must have suffered! I hope this will not bring all his terror back. But it may be a comfort to him to know that his eyes and ears and brain did not deceive him and that it is all true.

But I will try to put down just what happened. I liked the doctor as soon as I saw him. He is a strongly built man, with reddish hair and big, dark blue eyes. He gives the impression of kindness and great intelligence.

"You must be Mrs. Harker," he said to me. I nodded, and he added, "But you were Miss Mina Murray before, and it is Miss Murray, the friend of that poor, dear child Lucy Westenra, that I come to see."

I asked him how I could help him, and he began at once. "I have read your letters to Miss Lucy. Forgive me, but I had to begin my investigation somewhere, and there was no one to ask. I know that you were with her at Whitby. She sometimes kept a diary. Do not look surprised, Madame Mina. She began it after you left, in imitation of you. In it, she suggests that certain things began after the night she sleepwalked to the cliff in Whitby. So I come to you and ask you out of your so great kindness to tell me all of it that you can remember."

"I can tell you all about it," I said. "I wrote it all down at the time, and I can show it to you if you like."

"Oh, Madame Mina, I will be grateful. You will do me much favor."

I could not resist puzzling him a bit, so I handed him the shorthand diary. He opened it, and for an instant his face fell. Then he chuckled. "Oh, you so clever woman!" he said. "Will you not help me and read it for me? I know not the shorthand."

A little ashamed of myself, I took the type-written copy and handed it to him.

"You are so good," he said. "May I read it now? I may want to ask you some things when I am done."

"By all means," I said. "Read it while I prepare lunch, and then we can talk while we eat."

He settled himself in a chair and became deeply absorbed in the papers. When I came back from the kitchen, I found him walking up and down the room, his face blazing with excitement. He rushed up to me and took me by both hands.

"Oh, Madame Mina," he said, "how can I repay you? This paper is as sunshine. It opens the gate to me. I am dazed. I am dazzled with so much light. I am grateful to you, you so clever woman. Madame"—he said this very solemnly—"if ever Abraham Van Helsing can do anything for you or yours, you must let me know. It will be pleasure and delight if I may serve you as a friend. There are darknesses in life, and there are lights. You are one of the lights. You will have a happy life and a good life, and your husband will be blessed in you."

I was almost embarrassed. "But, Doctor, you praise me too much. You don't even know me."

"I know enough, from your letters and diary, and now from meeting you. Now, tell me of your husband. Is he quite well? Is the fever gone, and is he strong and healthy?"

I answered, "He was much better, but he has been greatly upset by Mr. Hawkins's death. You must know of that from my letters to Lucy." He nodded and I continued, "I suppose it upset him, for when we were in town on Thursday, he had a sort of shock."

"Another shock, so soon! That is not good. What kind of shock was it?"

"He thought he saw someone who reminded him of terrible things, the things that led to his illness." And here, somehow, the whole thing seemed to overwhelm me. I began to cry, quite helplessly, and begged Dr. Van Helsing to help Jonathan if he could. The doctor said to me with great sweetness, "I will be so happy if I can be of some use to you. For your husband's suffering—yes, this is a suffering that I know something about. I promise that I will gladly do all for him that I can, to make him strong and well, and your life together a happy one. Now you must eat. Husband Jonathan would not like to see you so pale and unhappy. Therefore, for his sake, you must eat and smile.

"You have told me about Lucy, and so now we shall not talk about her any more, in case it would make you sad. I shall stay in Exeter tonight, for I want to think over what you have told me. Later, I will ask you more questions, if I may. Then too, you will tell me of Jonathan's trouble, but not yet. You must eat now; afterwards you shall tell me all."

After lunch, when we went back to the living room, he said to me, "And now tell me all about him." When I began, I was afraid he would think me a weak fool, and Jonathan a madman. But he was so sweet and kind and I felt such trust in him that I said, "If you will let me, I shall give you a paper to read. It is the copy of the journal he kept in Transylvania. I don't want to tell you anything about it. You will read for yourself and judge. And then when I see you, please, you tell me what you think."

"I promise," he said as I gave him the papers. "If I may, I shall come in the morning to see you and your husband."

So he took the papers with him and went away, and I sit here thinking, thinking . . . I don't know what.

Note from Van Helsing to Mrs. Harker
(delivered by messenger)

September 25, 6 p.m.

Dear Madame Mina,

I have read your husband's so wonderful diary. You may sleep without doubt. Strange and terrible as it is, it is true! I will pledge my life on it. He is a brave fellow, and let me tell you that a man who would do what he did—going down that wall and to that room, not once but twice—is a man who will not be permanently injured by shock. I shall have many questions to ask him.

Yours the most faithful,
Abraham Van Helsing

Letter from Mrs. Harker to Van Helsing

September 25, 6:30 p.m.

My dear Dr. Van Helsing,

A thousand thanks for your kind letter. You have taken a great weight off my mind. And yet, if it is all true, what terrible things there are in the world, and what an awful thing if that monster is really in London! I will so look forward to seeing you tomorrow.

Your faithful and grateful friend,
Mina Harker

Jonathan Harker's Journal

September 26. I thought I would never write in this diary again, but the time has come. When I got home last night, Mina told me of Van Helsing's visit. She showed me the doctor's letter, saying that all I wrote down was true. I feel like a new man. It was my doubts about my own sanity that were tearing me apart. But now that I know, I am not afraid, even of the Count. He has succeeded in getting to London, and it was he that I saw. He has become younger, but how? Van Helsing is the man to explain it and hunt him down, if he is anything like what Mina says. We sat up late talking it all over. Now Mina is dressing, and I will go to the hotel to meet Dr. Van Helsing and bring him here.

I think he was surprised to see me. When I came into his room and introduced myself, he took me by the shoulder, turned my face to the light, looked at me sharply, and said, "But Madame Mina told me you were ill, that you

had had a shock." I smiled and said, "I was ill, I have had a shock, but you have cured me already."

"And how?"

"By your letter to Mina last night. I did not know what to believe, even what I myself, saw or heard. Now you have given me back my faith in myself, and I am quite well again."

He seemed pleased and began praising Mina to the skies. I could only agree with every word he said. He ended by saying, "And you, sir . . . I have read all the letters to poor Miss Lucy, and some of them speak of you, so I feel I know you already. You will give me your hand, will you not? And let us be friends for all our lives."

We shook hands, and he was so earnest and so kind that I felt quite choked up.

"And now," he said, "may I ask you for some more help? I have a great job to do, and the more information I have at hand, the better. Can you give me details of the business that took you to Transylvania?"

"I can," I said. "I shall give you the bundle of papers, and you can read them on the train."

After breakfast I took him to the station. When we were parting, he said, "If I need you and Madame Mina in London, will you come?"

"We shall both come whenever you ask," I promised.

I had picked up copies of the local and London newspapers, and while we were waiting for the train to start, he was glancing through them. His eyes suddenly seemed to catch something in one of them, the *Westminster Gazette*, and he grew quite white. He read intently, groaning to himself, "My God! So soon! So soon!" I think he forgot I was standing there. Just then the whistle blew and the train moved off. This brought him back to himself, and he waved his hand, calling out, "Love to Madame Mina. I shall write as soon as I can."

Dr. Seward's Diary

September 26. Truly there is no such thing as finality. It hasn't been a week since I said I was closing my diary forever, and yet here I am starting fresh again, or rather, going on with the same story. Until this afternoon I was concentrating on forgetting all that has happened. Renfield seemed as sane as he ever was. I had a letter from Arthur, written on Sunday, and he seemed to be doing well enough. Quincy Morris is with him, and that is a great help, for he would cheer anyone up. As for myself, I was settling down to my work with my old enthusiasm. The wound which poor Lucy left on me was beginning to heal.

It is now, however, torn wide open again, and God knows how this will all end. Van Helsing went to Exeter yesterday and stayed the night. Today he came back and almost bounded into the room, thrusting last night's *Westminster Gazette* into my hand.

"What do you think of that?" he asked, as he stood back and folded his arms.

I did not know what he meant, but he took it from me and pointed out a paragraph about children being lured away at Hampstead. It did not mean much to me until it mentioned small puncture wounds on their throats. I looked up.

"Well?" he said.

"It is like poor Lucy's."

"And what do you make of it?" he demanded.

"Whatever injured her has injured them."

"That is true indirectly, but not directly."

"How do you mean, Professor?" I asked. I wanted to take this conversation lightly, for four days of rest and freedom from burning anxiety had helped to restore my spirits. But when I saw his face, my smile died away. Never, even in the worst of our despair about poor Lucy, had he looked more stern.

"Tell me!" I insisted. "I have no opinion. I don't know what to think. I don't have enough information to think anything."

"Do you mean to tell me, John, that you still have no suspicion as to what poor Lucy died of?"

"Of organ failure, following a great loss of blood," I answered automatically.

"And how was the blood lost?" he asked. I shook my head.

He sat down beside me, and went on, "You are a clever man, friend John. You reason well, and you have great intelligence, but you are too narrow-minded. You do not let yourself believe the evidence of your own eyes and ears. Don't you think that there are things which you cannot understand, but which do exist? Do you believe, say, in hypnotism?

"Certainly," I said, "that has been well proven . . ."

"And yet do we understand it? We do not. Do you believe there are people who can read your thoughts?"

"Of course not," I sputtered.

"Why? Why? Tell me, for I am a student of the mind, how you accept hypnotism and reject mind reading? Let me tell you, my friend, that there are things done today in electrical science by men who, not so long ago, would have been burned as wizards. There are always mysteries in life. Why was it that Methuselah lived nine hundred years and that one man in France lived to one hundred and sixty-nine, and yet that poor Lucy, with four men's blood in her poor veins, could not live even one day? Can you tell me why in South America there are bats that come out at night and open the veins of cattle and horses and suck their veins dry? Or how in some islands there are bats which hang in the trees all day and on hot nights, when the sailors sleep on the deck, the bats flit down on them and in the morning the men are found dead, white as even Miss Lucy was?"

"Good God, Professor!" I said. "Do you mean that Lucy was bitten by such a bat? That such a thing is here in London in the nineteenth century?"

He waved his hand for silence and went on. "Can you tell me why the tortoise lives for generations of men, why the elephant goes on and on? Can you tell me why in all lands, in all ages, people have believed in men and women who cannot die? There have been toads, living toads, shut up in rocks for thousands of years. There are Indian holy men who can themselves die and be buried, and their graves sealed and corn planted on them, and the corn is harvested and planted again, and harvested, and planted, and harvested a third time, and then men come and open the grave and there lies the holy man, not dead, who rises up and walks among them as before?"

Here I interrupted him. I was getting bewildered. "But what does it all add up to? What are you trying to teach me?"

"I want you to believe," he answered me.

"To believe what?"

"To believe in things that you are not prepared to believe. It is the first step. Now, think again. You believe that those small holes in the children's throats were made by the same creature that made the holes in Miss Lucy?"

"I suppose so," I agreed.

He stood up and said solemnly, "Then you are wrong. It is worse, far, far worse."

"In God's name, Van Helsing, what do you mean?" I cried.

He threw himself into a chair, covering his face with his hands as he spoke.

"They were made by Miss Lucy!"

Chapter 15

DR. SEWARD'S DIARY
(continued)

Anger boiled through me. It was as if he had struck the living Lucy on the face. I hit the table with my fist and shouted, "Dr. Van Helsing, are you mad?"

He raised his head and looked at me, and somehow the tenderness of his face calmed me at once. "I wish I were," he said. "Madness would be easier to bear than truth like this. Oh, my friend, why have I taken so long to tell you? Do I hate you? Do I wish to give you pain?"

"No," I murmured. "Forgive me."

He went on, "My friend, it was because I wanted to break it to you gently, for I know you loved that sweet lady. But even now I do not expect you to believe. Tonight, though, I will prove it to you. Do you dare to come with me?"

This staggered me. I did not want to see such a thing proven.

"Come, I tell you what I want to do," he continued. "First, we go and see that child in the hospital. Dr. Vincent, who is attending him, is a friend of mine. He will let two scientists see his case. We shall tell him nothing but only that we wish to learn. And then . . ."

"And then?"

He took a key from his pocket and held it up. "And then we spend the night, you and I, in the churchyard where Lucy lies. This is the key to her tomb."

My heart sank, but I agreed to go with him.

The child was awake when we arrived. He had slept and eaten and was doing well. Dr. Vincent took the bandage from his throat and showed us the punctures. No mistake, they were almost identical to Lucy's wounds. They were smaller, and the edges looked fresher, but that was all. Dr. Vincent said the child had been quite cheerful. When he woke up, he had immediately asked if he could go play with the "booful lady" again.

Our visit to the hospital took longer than we had expected, and the sun had set before we came out. When Van Helsing saw how dark it was, he said, "There is no hurry. It is later than I thought. Come, let us find something to eat, and then we will be on our way."

We ate at a restaurant with a cheerful, noisy crowd of bicyclists. It was about ten o'clock when we left, and very dark. As we walked along we met fewer and fewer people, until at last we reached the wall of the church-yard, which we climbed over. It took us a while to find the Westenra tomb in the dark. The Professor took the key, opened the creaky door, and, standing back, politely motioned me to enter first. I had to choke back a hyster-ical laugh at his good manners on such an awful occasion.

We lit a candle. In the daytime, even filled with flowers, the tomb had looked awful enough. Now, with the flowers hanging limp and dead, their whites turning to rust color and their greens to browns, and spiders and beetles scurrying everywhere, it was a miser-able place.

Van Helsing went straight to work.

Holding his candle so that he could read the coffin nameplates, he quickly located Lucy's. He pulled a screwdriver from his bag.

"What are you going to do?" I asked.

"Open the coffin. I will convince you yet."

He quickly began taking out the screws and finally lifted off the lid, showing the inner case of lead. The sight was almost too much for me. It seemed as insulting to the dead as stripping her as she slept would have been to the living. I actually took hold of his hand to stop him.

He only said, "You shall see," and, again fumbling in his bag, took out a tiny saw. Striking the screwdriver through the lead, he made a small hole, just big enough to let in the point of the saw. I stepped back, expecting a rush of foul-smelling gas from the week-old corpse. But the Professor never stopped for a moment. He sawed down a couple of feet along one side of the lead coffin, and then across and down the other side. Taking the loose edge, he bent it back towards the foot of the coffin. He held the candle high and motioned me to look.

The coffin was empty. I stood staring, shocked into silence. Van Helsing showed no surprise whatsoever. "Are you satisfied now, John?" he asked.

My stubborn nature made me answer as I did. "I am satisfied that Lucy's body is not in that coffin, but that only proves one thing."

"And what is that?"

"That it is not there."

"That is good logic," he said, "so far as it goes. But how do you explain its not being there?"

"Perhaps a body snatcher," I suggested. "Some undertaker's employee may have stolen it." I knew I was talking nonsense, but it was the only explanation I could come up with.

The Professor sighed. "Ah, well!" he said, "we must have more proof. Come with me."

He put on the coffin lid again, gathered up all his things, and placed them in the bag. We opened the door and went out. Behind us he closed the door and locked it. Then he told me to watch at one side of the graveyard while he watched the other.

I sat behind a tree, and he headed out of sight in the other direction. Just after I had taken my place, I heard a distant clock strike midnight. In time I heard the chime for one o'clock, then two. I was cold and nervous, and angry with the Professor for bringing me here, and angry with myself for coming. Altogether I was having a miserable time.

Suddenly, I thought I saw something like a

white streak, moving between two dark trees at the side of the churchyard farthest from the tomb. At the same time, a dark shape moved from the Professor's side of the cemetery and hurried towards the whiteness. I moved as well, but I had to weave my way around tombstones and I stumbled over graves. A little ways off, beyond a line of scattered trees, a dim white figure flitted towards the Westenra tomb. The tomb itself was hidden by trees, and I could not see where the figure had gone. Stumbling in that direction, I found the Professor. He was holding a tiny, sleeping child in his arms. When he saw me he held it out to me, and said, "Are you satisfied now?"

"No!" I said, still angry.

"Do you not see this child?"

"Yes, it is a child, but who brought it here? And is it hurt?"

"We shall see," said the Professor. We headed out of the churchyard, he carrying the child. Once we had got a little distance away, we struck a match, and looked at the child's throat. There was not even a scratch.

"You see, I was right," I said triumphantly.

"We were just in time," said the Professor thankfully.

Now we had to decide what to do with the child. If we took it to a police station, we would have to explain what we were doing in the cemetery all night. Finally we decided to take it to the park and leave it where a policeman would find it. That worked well. At the edge of the park we waited until we heard the patrolling officer coming. We placed the child on the pathway, then hid and watched until the officer saw it. As soon as we heard his exclamation of astonishment, we went away silently towards home.

I cannot sleep, so I am writing this. But I must try to get a few hours' sleep, as Van Helsing is to pick me up at noon. He insists that I go with him again.

September 27. It was two o'clock before we could make our move. A funeral held at noon finally ended, and the last mourners had wandered away. Looking from behind a clump of trees, we saw the caretaker lock the cemetery gate behind him. I felt heavy with dread. What was the use of this? It had been outrageous enough to open a coffin, to see if a woman dead nearly a week were really dead. Now it seemed absolute madness to open the tomb again, when we knew that the coffin was empty.

But I said nothing. Van Helsing would go his own way, no matter who objected. He took the key, opened the vault, and again politely motioned me to go in first. Van Helsing walked over to Lucy's coffin and I followed. He bent down and again forced back the leaden top, and a shock of surprise and dismay shot through me.

There lay Lucy, just as we had seen her the night before her funeral. She was, if possible, more radiantly beautiful than ever. The lips were redder than before, and the cheeks were a delicate wild-rose pink.

"Are you convinced now?" said the Professor—it seemed for the fiftieth time. As he spoke, he put out his hand and pulled back the dead lips to show the white teeth. "See," he went on, "they are even sharper than before. With this and this"—and he touched one of the canine teeth, then another—"the little children can be bitten. Do you believe now, friend John?"

Once more, I was filled with rage and disbelief. I could not accept the idea he suggested. "She may have been placed here since last night," I insisted.

"Indeed?" Van Helsing replied politely. "That is so, and by whom?"

"I do not know. Someone has done it."

"And yet," he responded, "she has been dead one week. Most people in that time would not look like this."

I had no answer for this. Van Helsing did not seem to notice my silence. He was looking intently at the face of the dead woman, raising the eyelids and looking at the eyes, and once more examining the teeth. Then he turned to me and said sadly, "Usually when the Undead—for that is what she is, friend John—sleep, their faces show what they are. But this Miss Lucy, she was so sweet that nothing bad can be in her face. There is nothing evil showing there. So that makes it hard that I must kill her in her sleep."

This turned my blood cold. It began to dawn upon me that I was accepting Van Helsing's theories. But if she were really dead, why should killing her be such a terrifying idea?

He looked up at me. Apparently he saw the change in my face, for he said almost joyously, "Ah, you believe now?"

I answered, "Don't push me too hard just yet. I am trying to believe. How will you do this bloody work?"

"I shall cut off her head and fill her mouth with garlic, and I shall drive a stake through her body."

It made me cold to think of destroying the body of the woman I had loved. And yet the feeling was not so strong as I had expected. I was, in fact, beginning to shudder at the presence of this thing, this Undead, as Van Helsing called it.

I waited for Van Helsing to begin, but he stood as if thinking hard. Then he closed his bag with a snap and said, "I have changed my mind. I wish I could do now, at this moment, what is to be done. But there are other things to follow, and they may be far more difficult. This is simple. This Undead has not yet taken a life, although she will, and for us to act now would be to take this danger from her forever. But later we may need to involve Arthur, and how shall we tell him of this? Even you, who have seen all these things, even you have had trouble believing. Then how can I expect Arthur, who knows none of those things, to believe?

"If we tell him what we see, he will believe that his love was buried alive, and that our mistakes have killed her. He may try to believe, but he never can be sure, and he will suffer much. No! The poor fellow must live through one hour that will make the very face of heaven grow black to him. Then we can act for the good of all and send him peace. My mind is made up. Let us go. You return home for tonight. I shall spend the night here in this churchyard in my own way. Tomorrow night, meet me at the Berkeley Hotel at ten o'clock. I shall send for Arthur to come too, and also that good young American that gave his blood. Later we shall all have work to do. I come with you to get some dinner, for I must be back here before the sun sets."

So we locked the tomb, climbed over the wall of the churchyard, and departed.

Note left by Van Helsing in his briefcase,
Berkeley Hotel,
addressed to John Seward, M.D.
(not delivered)

September 27

Dear John,

I write this in case anything should happen. I go alone to watch in the churchyard. It pleases me that the Undead, Miss Lucy, shall not leave tonight, so that tomorrow night she may be more eager to get out. Therefore I shall put some things she will not like, garlic and a crucifix, to seal up the door of the tomb. She is just a young Undead, and will fear them. I shall be at the tomb from sunset till after sunrise, and if there is anything to learn there, I will learn it. I am not afraid of Miss Lucy, but

the one who made her so is another story. He
is skillful, as we know from the way he fooled
us when he gambled with us for Miss Lucy's
life. He already had the strength of twenty
men, and now he has the strength of we four
who gave our all to Miss Lucy. Besides, he can
call his wolf and who knows what else. So if he
comes looking tonight, he will find me.
Perhaps he will not. But if he does . . . take the
papers that are with this, the diaries of
Jonathan Harker and the rest, and read them,
and then find this great Undead and cut off his
head and burn his heart or drive a stake
through it, so that the world may rest from
him.

Farewell,
Van Helsing

Dr. Seward's Diary

September 28. A night's sleep has done me a
world of good. Yesterday, I had almost accepted Van Helsing's monstrous ideas, but now
they seem insane. Clearly he believes it all. I
wonder if his mind has become unhinged.
There has to be some rational explanation for
all these mysterious things. Is it possible that
the Professor could have done it himself? I

hate to think it, and it would be unbelievable to find that Van Helsing was mad, but anyhow, I shall watch him carefully.

September 29. Last night, at a little before ten o'clock, Arthur and Quincy came to Van Helsing's room where the doctor and I were waiting. Van Helsing began at once.

"I want your permission to do what I think is best. Even more, I ask you to give me that permission without knowing what those actions will be. This is so that afterwards, even though you may be angry with me for a time, you will not blame yourselves for anything."

"I don't quite see your drift," said Quincy, "but I know you're an honest man, and that's good enough for me."

"I thank you, sir," said Van Helsing proudly. He and Quincy shook hands.

But then Arthur spoke out, "Dr. Van Helsing, I don't like to work in the dark, as it were. Are you asking me to agree to anything which goes against my conscience as a gentleman and a Christian? If so, I cannot make such a promise. But if you can assure me that you are not, then I give you my consent, although for the life of me, I cannot understand what you are driving at."

"I accept your terms," said Van Helsing.

"All I ask of you is that later, if you think you must condemn any act of mine, you take the time to consider it well."

"Agreed!" said Arthur. "That is only fair. And now, may I ask what it is we are to do?"

"I want you to come with me, in secret, to the churchyard at Kingstead."

Arthur's face fell. "Where poor Lucy is buried?" he said in amazement.

The Professor nodded.

Arthur went on, "And when we get there?"

"We will enter the tomb."

Arthur stood up. "Professor, is this some monstrous joke? No, I see you are serious. And when we are in the tomb?"

"We will open the coffin."

"This is too much!" Arthur said angrily. "I am willing to be patient in all things that are reasonable, but in this . . . this . . ." His voice was choked with pain.

The Professor looked at him with pity. "If I could spare you this, my poor friend," he said, "God knows I would. But this night we must pass down thorny paths, or later and forever, the feet you love must walk in paths of flame!"

Arthur looked up, his face white with horror, and said, "Take care, Van Helsing. Do not go too far!"

"Shouldn't you at least hear what I have to say?" said Van Helsing.

"Yes, Art, that's fair enough," broke in Morris.

After a pause Van Helsing went on. "Miss Lucy is dead, is it not so? Yes! Then we can do her no harm. But if she be not dead . . ."

Arthur leaped again to his feet, "Good God!" he cried. "What do you mean? Has there been a mistake? Has she been buried alive?" He groaned in heartbreaking anguish.

"I did not say she was alive, my child. I say only that she might be Undead."

"Undead! Not alive! What do you mean? Is this all a nightmare?"

"There are mysteries which men can only guess at, and we are in the middle of one. But I am not finished. Lord Godalming, may I cut off the head of dead Miss Lucy?"

"Heavens and earth, no!" cried Arthur, enraged. "Not for the wide world may you mutilate her dead body! Dr. Van Helsing, you push me too far. What have I done to you that you should torture me so? What did that poor, sweet girl do that you should want to dishonor her? I have a duty to protect her grave from destruction, and by God, I shall do it!"

Van Helsing stood up and said, gravely and

sternly, "Lord Godalming, I too, have a duty. It is a duty to others, a duty to you, a duty to the dead, and by God, I shall do it! All I ask you now is that you come with me, and that you look and listen. Later, when I make the same request to you, you may be even more eager for it to be done than I am. But if you still refuse, I will hold myself completely responsible." His voice broke a little, as if he were on the verge of tears himself.

"But I beg you," he went on, "do not be angry with me. In all my long life, I have never faced such a difficult task as I do now. Just think. Why should I bring this horror on myself? I have come here from my own land, first to please my friend John, and then to help a sweet young lady, whom I, too, came to love. For her—I did not tell you before, but I say it in kindness—I gave the blood of my body. I gave her my nights and days, before death and after death. And now, if my death can help her, she shall have it freely."

Arthur, sobbing now, took the old man's hand and said in a broken voice, "Oh, it is hard, and I cannot understand, but at least I shall go with you and wait."

Chapter 16

Dr. Seward's Diary
(continued)

It was just before midnight when we got into the churchyard. The night was dark with occasional gleams of moonlight between the heavy clouds. We all kept close together, with Van Helsing leading the way. When we came close to the tomb, I looked at Arthur, afraid that the sight might upset him, but he bore up well.

The Professor unlocked the door and entered, the rest of us following. He lit a lantern and pointed to a coffin. Arthur stepped forward hesitantly. Van Helsing then said to me, "You were with me here yesterday. Was the body of Miss Lucy in that coffin?"

"It was."

He took his screwdriver and again took off the lid of the coffin. Arthur looked on, very pale but silent, and watched Van Helsing force back the leaden flap.

The coffin was empty!

For several minutes no one spoke a word. The silence was broken by Quincy Morris. "Professor, your word is all I want. I wouldn't ask such a thing ordinarily, but this is a mystery that goes beyond honor or dishonor. Did you remove the body?"

Van Helsing looked him in the eye. "I swear to you that I have not touched her. What happened was this. Two nights ago my friend John and I came here. I opened that coffin, which was then sealed up, and we found it as now, empty. We then waited and saw something white come through the trees. The next day we came here in daytime, and she lay there. Did she not, John?"

"Yes."

"That night we were just in time. Another small child was missing, and we found it, thank God, unharmed among the graves. Yesterday, I came here before sundown, for at sundown the Undead can move. I waited here all night, but I saw nothing. That was likely because I had placed garlic over the door, which the

Undead cannot bear, and I did other things which they fear. Last night nothing left the tomb, so tonight before sundown I took away my garlic and other things. And now we find this coffin empty. But bear with me. So far there is much that is strange. Wait with me outside, very quietly, and even stranger things will happen. Come." He put out the flame of his lantern, opened the door, and we filed out, with him locking the door behind us.

How fresh and pure the night air seemed after the horror of that tomb. Arthur was silent, and was, I could see, struggling to understand. Quincy Morris seemed to be calmly accepting all this in the spirit of cool bravery. Not being able to smoke, he cut himself a good-sized plug of tobacco and began to chew. As for Van Helsing, he was busy. First he took from his bag what looked like a thin biscuit, which was carefully rolled up in a white napkin. Next he took out a double handful of some whitish stuff, like dough or putty. He crumbled the biscuit and worked it into the doughy stuff between his hands. Then rolling the dough into thin strips, he began to lay them into the cracks between the door of the tomb and its frame. I was puzzled at this and asked him what he was doing. Arthur and Quincy drew near also.

He answered, "I am closing the tomb so that the Undead may not enter."

"What is that which you are using?" Arthur asked.

"The Communion Host. I brought it from Amsterdam. I have permission to so use it."

Van Helsing's answer was so earnest, it was impossible not to respect his sincerity, and we watched him work in silence. Then we went to the places he assigned, close by the tomb, but hidden from view.

There was a long spell of silence, big and aching, and then from the Professor a sharp hiss. He pointed, and far down the tree-lined avenue we saw a dim white figure which held something dark at its breast. A ray of moon-light pierced the clouds and revealed the figure to be a dark-haired woman in a white burial gown. We could not see her face, for it was bent down over the fair-haired child she was carrying. After a pause we heard a little cry. And then as we looked, the white figure moved forwards again. It was now near enough for us to see clearly in the moonlight. My own heart grew cold as ice, and I could hear Arthur's gasp, as we recognized Lucy Westenra. It was Lucy, and yet how changed! All the sweetness in her face had turned to hardest cruelty and her purity to something very different.

Van Helsing stepped out, and obeying his gesture, we all did the same. The four of us stood in a line before the door of the tomb. Van Helsing lit and raised his lantern. By the brighter light that fell on Lucy's face, we could see that her lips were crimson with fresh blood. The stream had trickled over her chin and stained her white death robe.

We shuddered with horror. I could see by the way the light was shaking that even Van Helsing's iron nerve had failed. Arthur was next to me, and if I had not grabbed his arm, he would have fallen.

When Lucy—I call the thing that was

before us Lucy because it bore her shape— saw us, she drew back with an angry snarl such as a cat gives when it is threatened. Her eyes ranged over us. They were Lucy's eyes in shape and color, but unclean and full of hell fire. At that moment, what remained of my love turned into hate and loathing. If I could have killed her then, I would have done it with savage delight. As she looked at us, her eyes blazed with unholy light, and the face broke into a sensual smile. Oh, God, how it made me shudder to see it! With a careless motion, she flung the child in her arms to the ground. It gave a sharp cry and lay there moaning. Her cruelty drew a groan from Arthur. She turned her eyes on him and advanced with outstretched arms and that same wanton smile. He backed away, hiding his face in his hands.

She drew nearer to him, with a lazy, sensual grace, saying, "Arthur, come to me. Leave these others and come to me. My arms are hungry for you. Come, and we can rest together. Come, my husband, come!"

There was something diabolically sweet in her tones, something like the tinkling of glass when it is struck by a piece of silver.

Arthur seemed under a spell. He took his hands from his face and opened his arms to her. She was moving swiftly towards him when

Van Helsing sprang forward, holding his little golden crucifix between them. She drew back with a hiss of rage, then dashed past him as if to enter the tomb.

When she was within a foot of the door, however, she stopped, as if she had struck an invisible wall. Then she turned, and her face showed quite clearly. I have never seen such hatred, and I hope I never shall again. If ever looks could kill, that was the moment.

And so for half a minute—which seemed an eternity—she remained caught between the lifted crucifix and the sacred closing of her tomb.

Van Helsing broke the silence by asking Arthur, "Answer me, my friend! Shall I do my work?"

"Go ahead. Do as you will. There can be no horror like this ever again." And Arthur groaned like a dying man.

Quincy and I moved forward together and held Arthur's arms. Van Helsing approached the tomb, stripping away the sacred materials which he had placed there to seal the door. When he stood back, we all watched with horrified amazement as the woman, whose body seemed as real as our own, passed through that gap, so slender a knife blade could barely have fit. We all felt a sense of relief when we saw the

Professor calmly restoring the strings of putty to the edges of the door.

When this was done, he lifted the child and said, "Come now, my friends. We can do no more until tomorrow. There is a funeral at noon, so here we shall all come after that. The mourners will be gone by two, and we shall remain after the caretaker locks the gate. As for this child, he is not badly hurt. We shall leave him on the policeman's path, as we did before, and he will be all right."

Coming close to Arthur, he said, "My friend, you have had a terrible shock, but when you look back, you will see it was necessary. You are now in bitter waters. By this time tomorrow, please God, this horror will be over."

Arthur and Quincy came home with me, and we tried to cheer each other up on the way. We had left the child behind in safety and were tired.

September 29, night. A little before noon, Arthur, Quincy, and myself, went to fetch the Professor. I noticed that all of us, without talking about it beforehand, had chosen to wear black. We got to the graveyard by half-past one and strolled about, keeping out of sight. Once the gravediggers had completed their work, the caretaker locked the gate.

Instead of his usual little black bag, Van Helsing had with him a long, heavy leather one. He unlocked the door of the tomb, and we entered, closing it behind us. Then he took from his bag the lantern and two candles, which he lit.

When he again lifted the lid off Lucy's coffin, we all looked and saw that the corpse lay there in all its death beauty. But there was no love in my own heart. There was nothing but loathing for the foul Thing which had taken Lucy's shape, without her soul. I could see even Arthur's face grow hard as he looked. Finally he said to Van Helsing, "Is this really Lucy's body, or only a demon in her shape?"

"It is her body, and yet it is not. But wait a while, and you shall see her as she was and will be again."

Van Helsing, in his usual calm manner, began taking items from his bag. There were a prayer book, his operating knives, and a round wooden stake, about three inches thick and three feet long. One end of it had been hardened by fire and was sharpened to a fine point. With this stake came a heavy hammer, such as is used for breaking lumps of coal.

When all was ready, Van Helsing said, "Before we do anything, let me tell you something. I know it from those who have studied the powers of the Undead. When a person becomes Undead, she is cursed with immortality. She cannot die, but must go on age after age, multiplying the evil of the world. For she who dies from the bite of an Undead becomes Undead herself, and hunts more victims, and the circle goes on widening like the ripples from a stone thrown in the water. My dear friend Arthur, if you had taken that last kiss from poor Lucy, or last night if you had embraced her, you would in time have become Nosferatu, as they call the Undead in Eastern Europe.

"The career of this unhappy lady has just begun. Those children whose blood she sucked are not yet badly hurt. But if she lives on, sucking more and more blood from them, they will become like her. But if she dies— truly dies, finds the peace of death—then all is ended. The tiny wounds of the throats disappear and the children go back to their play, innocent and unknowing. But the most blessed thing of all is this. When this now Undead become truly dead, then the soul of the poor lady whom we love shall be free. Instead of working wickedness, she shall take her place with the other angels. So, my friend, she will bless the hand that sets her free. I am very willing to do this, but is there someone who has the better right? Whose hand would she choose to send her free among the stars?"

We all looked at Arthur. He saw, as we all did, Van Helsing's kindness in suggesting that he should be the one to save Lucy. He stepped forward and said bravely, though his face was as pale as snow, "My true friend, from the bottom of my broken heart I thank you. Tell me what I am to do, and I will not fail!"

Van Helsing laid a hand on his shoulder and said, "Brave man! A moment's courage, and it is done. This stake must be driven through her. It will be dreadful, but it will be over soon, and you will rejoice even more than you have suffered. But you must not hesitate once you have begun. Keep in your mind always that we, your true friends, are around you, and that we pray for you all the time."

"Go on," said Arthur hoarsely. "Tell me what to do."

"Take this stake in your left hand, ready to place over the heart, and the hammer in your right. Then I shall read the prayer for the dead, and as we pray, you will strike in God's name." Arthur took the stake and the hammer with hands that never quivered. Van Helsing opened his book and began to read, and Quincy and I followed as well as we could.

Arthur placed the point over the heart and

then struck with all his might. The thing in the coffin twisted, and a hideous, bloodcurdling screech came from the opened red lips. The body shook and quivered and twisted wildly. The sharp white teeth snapped together until the lips were cut, and the mouth was smeared with crimson foam. But Arthur never paused. His steady arm rose and fell, driving the stake deeper and deeper, while the blood from the pierced heart spurted up around it. His face was strong and shining. The sight of it gave us courage, so that our voices seemed to ring through the little tomb.

And then the twisting and quivering of the body lessened, and the teeth stopped chattering. Finally it lay still. The terrible task was over.

The hammer fell from Arthur's hand. He staggered and would have fallen had we not caught him. Great drops of sweat sprang from his forehead, and his breath came in broken gasps. For a few minutes we were so busy with him that we did not look towards the coffin. When we did, however, a murmur of startled surprise ran among us. We gazed so eagerly that Arthur rose from his seat on the ground and came and looked too. A joyous light broke over his face, driving away the horror that had been there.

In the coffin lay no longer the disgusting Thing that we had grown to hate. Instead, there was Lucy as we had seen her in life, her face sweet and pure. True, we saw the marks of her illness, the pain that she had suffered. But we welcomed those marks, for they told us we were looking at a normal, mortal body. Holy calm lay like sunshine over the wasted face.

Van Helsing came and laid his hand on Arthur's shoulder, and said to him, "And now, Arthur my friend, am I not forgiven?"

Arthur took the old man's hand and kissed it, saying, "Forgiven! God bless you that you have given my dear one her soul again, and me peace." He put his head on the Professor's shoulder and wept like a child while we stood unmoving.

When Arthur raised his head, Van Helsing said to him, "And now, my child, you may kiss her. Kiss her dead lips if you wish. For she is not a grinning devil now. She is God's true dead, whose soul is with Him!"

Arthur bent and kissed her, and then we sent him and Quincy out of the tomb. The Professor and I sawed the top off the stake, leaving the point of it in the body. Then we cut off the head and filled the mouth with garlic. We sealed up the leaden coffin, screwed on the coffin lid, gathered up our belongings, and walked away. When the Professor locked the door, he gave the key to Arthur.

Outside the air was sweet, the sun shone, and the birds sang. There was gladness and peace everywhere, and we ourselves were glad, though it was with a bittersweet joy.

Before we left, Van Helsing said, "Now, my friends, one step of our work is done, the step most painful to ourselves. But there remains a greater job. We must find the author of all this sorrow and stamp him out. I have clues which we can follow. But it is a long task, and a difficult one, and there is danger in it, and pain. Will you help me? We have learned to believe, all of us, is it not so? Shall we go on to the bitter end?"

We all shook hands, making our promises. The Professor said, as we moved off, "The night after next, let us meet for dinner at seven. I shall ask two others, people that you do not yet know, and we will talk about our plans. John, please come home with me, for I need your help. Tonight I leave for Amsterdam but shall return tomorrow night. And then begins our great quest."

Chapter 17

DR. SEWARD'S DIARY
(continued)

When we arrived at the Berkeley Hotel, Van Helsing found a telegram waiting for him. It read: "Am coming up by train. Jonathan is in Whitby. Important news. Mina Harker."

The Professor was delighted. "Ah, that wonderful Madame Mina!" he said. "She arrives, but I cannot stay. She must go to your house, John. You must meet her at the station." As we had a cup of tea together, he told me about Jonathan Harker's diary. He gave me a typewritten copy of it as well as a copy of Mrs. Harker's journal kept at Whitby. "Take these," he said, "and study them well. When I have returned, you will know all the facts, and we will be well-prepared for our work. What is here"—and he laid his hand heavily on the packet of papers as he spoke—"may mean the death of you and me and many others. Or it may mean the end of the Undead who walk the earth." He then said goodbye, and I drove to Paddington Station to meet Mrs. Harker.

The crowd of passengers melted away, and I was beginning to be afraid that I might not find her, when a sweet-faced girl stepped up to me and said, "Dr. Seward?"

"And you are Mrs. Harker!"

"I knew you from Lucy's description . . ." She stopped suddenly and blushed. I blushed as well, for we both knew what Lucy must have written about me. I collected her luggage, which included a typewriter, and we set out for my house.

She is settling into her room now, but she said she would come soon to my study, for she has much to tell me. So now I am waiting for her. I have not had the chance of looking at the papers which Van Helsing left with me. I must get Mrs. Harker busy with something so that I may read them. She does not know what a hurry we are in. I must be careful not to frighten her. Here she is!

Mina Harker's Journal

September 29. After I had tidied myself, I went down to Dr. Seward's study. After a little general conversation, I came to the point.

"You were with my dear friend Lucy at the end. Please tell me how she died. I know nothing, and I would be very grateful."

To my surprise, he answered, looking horror-struck, "Tell you of her death? Not for the wide world!"

"Why not?" I asked, with a terrible feeling coming over me.

He paused, and I could see that he was trying to invent an excuse. Finally he stammered out, "Surely it would only make you sad. Wouldn't you rather remember her as she was, lively and healthy?"

By this time, I was convinced that his story had to do with the monster that Jonathan had written of. I said, as calmly as I could, "I can bear it. I want to know everything."

His face turned so white I thought he would faint. He said, "No! No! For all the world, I wouldn't let you know that terrible story!"

Then I knew I was right. For a moment, I looked about the room, thinking what to say next. I noticed a great pile of typewritten sheets on the table. His eyes followed mine.

"You do not know me yet," I said. "When you have read those papers, my own diary and my husband's also, you will know me better. Then, perhaps, you will trust me."

After a moment, he stood up and selected one notebook from a pile. He handed it to me. "You are right," he said. "Lucy trusted you, and so should I. I know that Lucy told you about me. She told me about you too. I apologize for hesitating to share this. Here is a portion of my diary. It describes Lucy's illness and . . . other things. Read it, and when you are done, dinner will be ready. In the meantime I will read over some of these papers, and then we will both understand each other better."

DR. SEWARD'S DIARY

September 29. I was so fascinated by the diaries of Jonathan Harker and his wife that I lost track of the time. Mrs. Harker was not down when the maid announced dinner, so I said, "She is probably tired. Let dinner wait an hour," and I went on reading. I had just finished Mrs. Harker's diary when she came in. She looked sweetly pretty, but her eyes were red with crying. This moved me very much. I have often wanted to cry lately, but I cannot, and the sight of those sweet, tearful eyes went straight to my heart. So I said as gently as I could, "I am so sorry. I am afraid I have upset you."

"Oh, no, do not apologize," she replied. "But I have been more touched than I can say by your grief and how you cared for my poor, dear friend. It makes me all the more determined to help rid the earth of this terrible monster. Won't you tell me the whole story? Your diary only took me to September 7, and told me about how ill Lucy was. Believe me, Jonathan and I have been working day and night to puzzle out this mystery since Professor Van Helsing saw us. Jonathan is in Whitby now, gathering more information, and he will be here tomorrow to help us. We can have no secrets from one another. Working together and with absolute trust, we will surely be stronger than we would be alone."

She looked at me with such courage that I gave in. "I will do what you ask. God forgive me if I am wrong! You will learn terrible, unspeakable things. But you have traveled this far on the road to understanding Lucy's death, and you will not be satisfied to stop here. Her end—her very end—may give you peace. Come, let us have dinner. We must keep one another strong for what is ahead of us. After you have eaten, I shall tell you everything."

MINA HARKER'S JOURNAL

September 29. After dinner I went with Dr. Seward to his study, and he gave me the rest of his notebooks.

As I finished the terrible story of Lucy's death, and all that happened later, I think I nearly fainted in my chair. When Dr. Seward saw me, he jumped up and brought me a glass of brandy. My brain was all in a whirl. If I hadn't known that my dear Lucy was finally at peace, I don't think I could have stood it. It is all so wild and mysterious and strange that if I had not known about Jonathan's experience in Transylvania, I could not have believed it. As it was, I didn't know what to believe, so I distracted my mind with work. I took the cover off my typewriter and said to Dr. Seward, "I have an idea. The dates on which everything occurred may be very important. I will look through all these documents and make a list of events, in chronological order. Then we will be ready for Dr. Van Helsing when he comes."

I went to work while Dr. Seward made his rounds to check on his patients. When he had finished, he came back and sat near me, reading, so that I did not feel lonely while I worked. How good and thoughtful he is. The world seems full of good men, even if there are monsters in it.

DR. SEWARD'S DIARY

September 30. Mr. Harker has arrived. He seems like a very clever man, full of energy. If his journal is true, and I believe it is, he is also a man of great courage.

After lunch he and his wife went back to their own room, and, as I passed it a while ago, I heard the click of the typewriter. They are hard at work. Mrs. Harker is knitting together every scrap of evidence we have into chronological order. Harker is now reading my diary. I wonder what he makes of it.

How stupid of me not to guess that Carfax, the house next to this one, might be the Count's hiding place! Goodness knows that we had enough clues from Renfield. Harker has the letters concerning the purchase of the house. Oh, if we had only had them earlier, we might have saved poor Lucy! Harker has gone back to Whitby for more material. He says that by dinnertime they will be able to show the entire list of dates, and that it will be very helpful. In the meantime, he wants me to see Renfield. He believes Renfield's behavior has signaled the comings and goings of the Count.

I found Renfield sitting peacefully in his room with his hands folded, smiling. He seemed as sane as anyone I ever saw. I sat down and talked with him about a lot of subjects. He then, all on his own, brought up the subject of his going home. I don't believe he has ever mentioned the possibility before. If I hadn't talked with Harker, I believe I would be ready to discharge him. But I left him without asking any questions. He is a little too sane right now. My questions might make him start to think, and then who knows? I don't trust these quiet moods of of his. I have put the attendant on alert, telling him to have a straitjacket ready, just in case.

JONATHAN HARKER'S JOURNAL

September 29. My trip to Whitby gave me the information I hoped for. I was able to trace the horrible cargo the Count sent, all the way from Transylvania to its place in London. I saw the original invoice, which listed "Fifty cases of earth, to be used for experimental purposes."

Step by step, invoice by invoice, I traced it from one shipping point to another, until I located the very workmen who had moved the fifty cases into Carfax. In the words of one of them, "That there house, guv'nor, was the strangest I ever was in. Blymie! Bet it ain't been touched in a hundred years. There was dust so thick in the place that you could sleep on the floor without hurtin' your bones. But the old chapel, where we left the boxes—that took the cake. Me and my buddy, we couldn't get out of there quick enough. You'd have to pay me a pound a minute to stay there after dark."

If he knew what I know, I think he would raise his price.

I am now satisfied that all those boxes which were shipped from Transylvania to Whitby in the doomed ship *Demeter* were safely placed in the old chapel at Carfax. There should be fifty of them there unless any have since been moved. Dr. Seward's diary makes me afraid this may have happened.

MINA HARKER'S JOURNAL

September 30. I was afraid to let Jonathan go to Whitby. I feared that thinking about the Count might reopen his terrible wounds and weaken his spirit. But the exact opposite has happened. He has come back calm, strong, and ready for battle. I could almost feel sorry for the Count now that Jonathan is so determined to hunt him down. I say "almost." Reading Dr. Seward's story of Lucy's death, and what happened afterwards, has dried up any pity I might have felt.

Lord Godalming and Mr. Morris have arrived. Meeting them was painful for me, as it made me remember all Lucy's hopes of just a few months ago. I gave them each a copy of the papers I have typed out. When Lord Godalming got his, he began to thank me for my help. But when he got to the words, "I know you loved my Lucy . . ." he turned away and covered his face with his hands. I could hear the tears in his voice. Mr. Morris kindly laid his hand on his shoulder for a moment and then walked out of the room. I suppose it was something about being with a woman, Lucy's friend, which allowed Lord Godalming to show his emotions as he did. He sank down on the couch, and I sat beside him and took his hand, for I could see his heart was breaking.

I said, "I did love Lucy, and I know how you two loved each other. She and I were like sisters. Now that she is gone, will you let me be like a sister to you?"

In an instant the poor man was over-whelmed with grief, and tears rained down his cheeks. I felt so sorry for him that without even thinking about it, I took him in my arms. With a sob he laid his head on my shoulder and cried like a child, shaking with emotion. I stroked his hair as though he were my own son, never thinking how strange it all was.

As he calmed down, he apologized, "It's been so many days and nights, and there hasn't been anyone I could talk to openly about it all. I can't thank you enough for your sweet sympathy today. You will let me be like a brother, won't you, all our lives, for Lucy's sake?" I promised, and I truly feel as though I have gained a brother today.

Leaving him, I met Mr. Morris in the hallway. He turned as he heard my footsteps. "How is Art?" he said. Then, noticing my red eyes, he went on, "Ah, I see you have been comforting him. Poor fellow, he needs it. Only a woman can help a man when he is in trouble of the heart, and he has had no one."

He spoke so bravely that my heart bled for him. I saw the manuscript in his hand, and I knew that when he read it, he would realize I know that he, too, had loved Lucy. So I said to him, "I wish I could comfort all who suffer.

Will you let me be your friend, and will you come to me for comfort if you need it? You will understand later why I am saying this."

He raised my hand to his lips and kissed it. Tears rose in his eyes as he said, "Little girl, I'll never forget your kindness as long as I live." Then he went back into the study to find Art.

Chapter 18

DR. SEWARD'S DIARY

September 30. I got home at five o'clock, and found Godalming and Morris studying the documents that the Harkers had prepared. Jonathan Harker was out on an errand. Mrs. Harker kindly prepared tea for us all, and when we had finished, she said, "Dr. Seward, may I ask a favor? I want to see your patient, Mr. Renfield. What you have said of him in your diary interests me a great deal."

I had learned not to second-guess Mrs. Harker's wishes, and I agreed. We went off together, and I went into Renfield's room, telling him that a lady would like to see him.

"Why?" he asked.

"She is touring the asylum and wants to see everyone in it," I answered.

"Oh, very well," he said, "let her come in, but just wait a minute until I tidy up the place."

His method of tidying up was peculiar. He simply swallowed all the flies and spiders in the boxes before I could stop him. When he had finished his disgusting task, he said cheerfully, "Let the lady come in," and sat down on the edge of his bed. His head was lowered, but he was looking upward so that he could see her as she entered. For a moment I thought that he might be planning to attack her. I remembered how quiet he had been just before he stabbed me in my own study, so I was careful to stand where I could grab him if he tried anything.

She came into the room, looking as relaxed and graceful as if she were entering a friend's parlor. Walking over to him, she smiled pleasantly and held out her hand.

"Good evening, Mr. Renfield," she said. "You see, I know you, for Dr. Seward has told me about you."

He didn't answer immediately, but looked at her, frowning. His frown then turned to a look of wonder as he said, to my astonishment, "You're not the girl the doctor wanted to marry, are you? You can't be, you know, for she's dead."

Mrs. Harker smiled sweetly as she replied, "Oh, no! I have a husband of my own, to whom I was married before Dr. Seward and I ever met. I am Mrs. Harker."

"Then what are you doing here?"

"My husband and I are visiting Dr. Seward."

"Don't stay," Renfield said.

"But why not?"

I thought this conversation would be unpleasant for Mrs. Harker, so I interrupted. "How did you know I wanted to marry anyone?" I asked.

He glanced at me for only a moment. "What an idiotic question!" he exclaimed. Then his eyes returned to his visitor.

Mrs. Harker came instantly to my defense. "I don't see that at all, Mr. Renfield," she said.

His reply to her was as polite as his remark to me had been rude. "You must understand, Mrs. Harker, that when a man is so respected and honored as Dr. Seward, everything about him interests the members of our little community. Dr. Seward is loved, not only by his friends, but even by his patients, even though some of us cannot express our affection in the ordinary ways."

My eyes opened wide at this. Here was my own patient, as mad a man as I had ever met, chatting courteously with the manners of a polished gentleman.

We continued to talk for some time. Seeing that he seemed quite reasonable, she began (glancing at me for permission) to lead him to his favorite topic. I was again astonished, for he talked about his own condition as matter-of-factly as a doctor. He even used himself as an example when he mentioned certain things.

"Why, I myself am an illustration of a man who had a strange belief. It's no wonder that my friends were alarmed and insisted that I be put in the asylum. I used to believe that by eating a great number of live things, no matter how low in the scale of creation, a person could live forever. At times I believed it so strongly that I actually tried to take human life. The doctor here will tell you that I even tried to kill him in order to take in his blood and strengthen my own powers. Isn't that true, doctor?"

I nodded in agreement, so amazed that I hardly knew what to think or say. It was hard to imagine that just minutes before, I had seen this man gobble up spiders and flies. Looking at my watch, I saw that I needed to go to the station to meet Van Helsing, so I told Mrs. Harker that it was time to leave. She rose and shook hands again with Renfield, saying, "Goodbye, and I hope I may see you again, under conditions that will be more pleasant for you."

To my astonishment, he replied, "Goodbye, my dear. I pray to God that I never see your sweet face again. May He bless and keep you!"

I went to the station to meet Van Helsing alone. The Professor jumped down from the train with the energy of a boy. He rushed up to me, saying, "Ah, friend John, how goes all? Well? So! I have been busy, for I come here to stay if need be. I've finished my business in Amsterdam, and I have much to tell. Madame Mina is with you? Yes. And her so fine husband? And Arthur and my friend Quincy, they are with you, too? Good!"

As I drove to the house, I brought him up to date, and told him of Mrs. Harker's work with the documents. The Professor interrupted me, "Ah, that good Madame Mina! She has a wonderful brain to go along with her kind heart. She has been a great help. But after tonight, in my opinion, she must not be involved with this terrible affair. The risk is too great. We men are determined to destroy this monster, but I do not want to involve her. She is a young woman and not so long married, and there may be a child to think of some time, if not now. Tonight she must consult with us, but tomorrow she should say goodbye to this work, no?"

I agreed with him, and then I told him what we had learned: that the house which Dracula had bought was the one beside my own. He was amazed, and more than a little sad.

"Oh, if only we had known it before!" he said, "for then we might have reached him in time to save poor Lucy. However, as you say, 'it is not to cry after the milk that is spilled.'" When we reached the house, the Professor took a copy of Mrs. Harker's document to study after dinner. We will all meet at nine o'clock to arrange our plan of battle with this terrible and mysterious enemy.

MINA HARKER'S JOURNAL

September 30. We met in Dr. Seward's study two hours after dinner, as though we were a sort of board or committee. Professor Van Helsing took the head of the table with me on his right. Jonathan sat next to me, and opposite us were Lord Godalming, Dr. Seward, and Mr. Morris.

The Professor said, "I take it that we are all acquainted with the facts that are in these papers. Then, I think, I should tell you more about the enemy with which we have to deal.

"There are such things as vampires. Even if we had not gone through our own tragic experience, the records of the past should convince any sane person. I once did not believe. If I had known at first what I know now, our precious friend might have been saved. She is gone, but we must work so that other poor souls do not perish.

"Now let us consider what we know about vampires in general, and this one in particular. We must turn for our help to traditions and superstitions. For, let me tell you, the vampire is known everywhere that men have ever lived. In old Greece, in old Rome, in Germany, France, India, China, there he is, and has always been. The vampire lives on, and cannot die by mere passing of the time. He will flourish when he can fatten on the blood of the living. Even worse, we have seen that he can even grow younger when his diet is plenty.

"But he cannot live without this diet, for he does not eat as others do. Even friend Jonathan, who lived with him for weeks, never saw him eat, never! He throws no shadow; he makes no reflection in the mirror. He has the strength of many, as Jonathan witnessed. He can change himself to wolf, as we know from when the *Demeter* arrived in Whitby and when he tore open the dog. He can become a bat, as we have all seen.

"He can come in fog which he creates, as that brave ship's captain wrote. He can come on moonbeams as particles of dust, as again, Jonathan saw those sisters in the castle of Dracula. He can become so small! We ourselves saw how Miss Lucy, before she was at peace, slipped through the space of a hair at the tomb door. He can see in the dark, and this is no small power.

"He can do all these things, yet he is not free. No, he is a prisoner like a galley slave, like a madman in his cell. He, who is not of nature, still has to obey some of nature's laws. He may not enter anywhere at first, unless someone of the household invites him to come. But afterwards he can come when he pleases. His power ends at the coming of the day.

"At certain times he has only limited freedom. He can do as he likes in his earth-home and at unholy places, as we saw when he went to the suicide's grave at Whitby. But at other places he can only change at noon or at exact sunrise or sunset. Then there are things which take away his power: the garlic, for one thing,

and sacred symbols, as this crucifix. There are other things, too, which I shall tell you of, in case we need them. Placing a branch of wild roses on his coffin will keep him from leaving it. A sacred bullet fired into the coffin will kill him so that he is truly dead. Then there is the stake through him—we know already of its peace—or the cut-off head that gives true rest. We have seen these with our own eyes.

"And so, when we find where this man-that-was lies, we can confine him to his coffin and destroy him. But he is clever. I have asked my friend Arminius, of Budapest University, to tell me who he was. He must have been the man named Voivode Dracula in ancient times. If that be true, then he was no ordinary man.

In his time, and for centuries after, he was spoken of as the cleverest, the most cunning, and the bravest of his people. The Draculas, says Arminius, were a great and noble family, although even in ancient times it was rumored they had dealings with the Evil One."

While Dr. Van Helsing was talking, Mr. Morris was looking steadily at the window. Now he got up quietly and went out of the room. The professor continued: "And now we must decide what we are to do. We know from Jonathan's investigation that fifty boxes of earth arrived at Whitby and were delivered to Carfax. We also know that at least some of these boxes have been removed. It seems to me that our first step should be to determine how many remain and how many have been removed. Then we must trace . . ."

Here we were interrupted in a very startling way. Outside the house came the sound of a pistol shot. The glass of the window was shattered with a bullet which struck the far wall of the room. I shrieked, and we all jumped to our feet. Lord Godalming ran over to the window and threw back the curtain. As he did, we heard Mr. Morris's voice outside, saying, "I'm sorry I frightened you. I shall come in and tell you about it."

A minute later he came in and said, "That

was an idiotic thing for me to do. But the fact is that while the Professor was talking a big bat came and landed on the windowsill. I've learned to hate the things recently, and I've gotten in the habit of taking a shot at them whenever I see them."

"Did you hit it?" asked Dr. Van Helsing.

"I guess not, for it flew away into the woods." Without saying any more, he took his seat, and the Professor began to resume his statement.

"We must trace each of these boxes. We must, so to speak, sterilize the earth so that he cannot return to it. Finally, we must find him in his human form between the hours of sunrise and sunset and so deal with him when he is at his weakest.

"And now for you, Madame Mina, this night is the end until we have succeeded. You are too precious to us to risk."

All the men, even Jonathan, seemed relieved to hear this. It did not seem right to me that they should leave me behind, but their minds were made up. It was a bitter pill for me to swallow, but I couldn't do anything but accept their care for me.

Mr. Morris was the next to speak, "There is no time to lose. I vote we have a look at his house right now." And off they went to Carfax.

Like typical men, they have told me to go to sleep. As if a woman can sleep when those she loves are in danger! I shall lie down and pretend to sleep, so that Jonathan won't worry.

DR. SEWARD'S DIARY

October 1, 4 a.m. Just as we were about to leave the house, an urgent message was brought to me. Renfield wanted to see me at once, claiming that he had something of great importance to say. I told the messenger that I would see him in the morning but that I was busy at the moment.

The messenger replied, "He is very insistent, sir. I have never seen him so excited. If you don't come, I believe he may have one of his violent fits." The attendant is a sensible fellow, so I agreed to come, asking the others to wait a few minutes. Instead, they all asked to come with me. I agreed, and we headed for the patients' quarters.

I found Renfield highly excited, but completely reasonable in his speech and behavior. He asked me to release him from the asylum and send him home. He argued that he was completely recovered and entirely sane.

"Please, ask your friends what they think,"

he said. "Perhaps they will not mind serving as a jury in this case. By the way, you have not introduced me."

He sounded so dignified, so normal, that I did as he asked. "Mr. Renfield," I said, "may I present Lord Godalming, Professor Van Helsing, Mr. Quincy Morris, of Texas, and Mr. Jonathan Harker."

He shook hands with each of them, speaking to them in turn. "Mr. Harker, a pleasure, sir. Lord Godalming, I have had the honor of meeting your father. He was loved by all that knew him, and I was sorry to hear of his passing. Mr. Morris, you should be proud of your great state. And what can I say of my pleasure in meeting the great Van Helsing? Your work in the sciences is revolutionary, sir. Gentlemen, you are all great and gifted men. I ask you to witness that I am as sane as most men who walk the streets. And you, Dr. Seward, are a humanitarian as well as a scientist. Don't you think it is your moral duty to release me?"

It was amazing. In spite of everything I knew about Renfield, I was tempted to tell him that I would see about his release in the morning. I knew, however, how quickly this patient could change, so I simply said that he appeared to be getting better very quickly and that I would talk with him more tomorrow.

But this did not satisfy him at all. He said quickly, "Dr. Seward, you do not understand. I want to leave now, this very hour, this very moment. Time is short. I must go at once."

"I cannot permit that," I answered.

There was a considerable pause, and then he said slowly, "I am begging to go, not for my own sake, but for the sake of others. I cannot tell you my reasons, but I promise you that they are good, unselfish ones. If you could look into my heart, Doctor, you would approve of my request. In fact, you would see that I am trying to be your true friend."

Again he looked at us appealingly. My thought was that this sudden change was, in fact, just another phase of his madness. I noticed that Van Helsing was gazing at him with a look of utmost intensity, his bushy eyebrows almost meeting over his nose. He asked Renfield, "Can't you tell me, honestly, your real reason for wishing to be free tonight? If you will do so, I will do my best to convince Dr. Seward to grant your wish."

Renfield shook his head sadly. The Professor went on, "Come, Mr. Renfield, think about this. You claim to be completely sane. Obviously we have reason to doubt that this is true. If you will not help us by speaking frankly, how can we help you?"

Renfield's expression did not change. "Dr. Van Helsing, I have nothing to say," he replied. "Your argument makes perfect sense. If I were free to speak, I would do so, but I do not have that freedom. I can only ask you to trust me. If I am refused, I cannot be responsible for what happens."

I thought it was now time to end the scene, which was becoming ridiculous. I went towards the door, saying, "Come, my friends, we have work to do. Goodnight."

But as I got near the door, a new change came over Renfield. He moved towards me so quickly that for a moment I thought he was going to attack me. I was wrong, however. Instead, he held up his hands in a motion of prayer and began to beg me to let him go. His attitude reminded me of when he had asked me for a cat. Remembering that time, I expected him to become quiet and sulky when I refused.

I was, again, quite wrong. When he saw that I was really going to leave without granting his request, he became absolutely frantic. He threw himself on his knees, holding up his hands, and poured forth a torrent of words while tears rolled down his cheeks.

"I am begging you, Dr. Seward, to let me out of this house at once. Send me anywhere you like. Send attendants with me. Let them keep me in a straitjacket with leg irons on. Even send me to jail, but let me leave this place. You don't know what you are doing by keeping me here. You don't know who you are hurting, or how, and I may not tell you. By all you hold sacred, by your love that is lost, take me away from here and save my soul from guilt! Can't you hear me, man? Can't you understand? Will you never learn? Can't you see that I am no lunatic, but a sane man fighting for his soul? Oh, hear me! Hear me! Let me go, let me go, let me go!"

It seemed the longer this went on, the wilder it would get, so I took him by the hand and raised him to his feet.

"Come along," I said sternly, "no more of this. Go to your bed and behave yourself."

He stopped and looked at me hard for several moments. Then, without a word, he walked to his bed and sat down.

When I was leaving the room, he said to me in a quiet, polite voice, "I hope that later on, Dr. Seward, you will remember that I tried to convince you."

Chapter 19

Jonathan Harker's Journal

October 1, 5 a.m. I went off with the other men to search Dracula's house at Carfax, feeling very glad that Mina had agreed to stay behind. She has done so much already, helping to put this story together. I am relieved to know she won't be involved in this dangerous work.

I think we were all a little upset by the scene with Mr. Renfield. When we came away from his room, we were silent until we got back to my study. Then Mr. Morris said to Dr. Seward, "Say, Jack, that man seems like the sanest lunatic I ever saw. Wasn't it pretty rough on him not to give him a chance?"

Dr. Van Helsing added, "John, you know more lunatics than I do, and I'm glad of it. I'm afraid that before that last hysterical outburst, I would have freed him. But we live and learn, and I'm sure you were right to take no chances."

Dr. Seward answered them both in a dreamy kind of way. "I just don't know. If Renfield had been an ordinary lunatic, I would have taken the chance. But he seems so mixed up with the Count that I am afraid to help him carry out his plans. I can't forget how he asked for a cat almost as persuasively, and then tried to tear my throat out with his teeth. Besides, he called the Count 'lord and master,' and he may want to get out to help the Count in some diabolical way. That monster already has wolves and rats to help him, so I suppose he isn't above trying to use a poor lunatic. I only hope we have done what is best."

The professor put his hand on his shoulder and said in a kindly way, "Don't be afraid, John. We are trying to do our duty in a very sad and terrible case, with God's help."

Lord Godalming had disappeared for a few minutes, but now he returned. He held up a little silver whistle, as he remarked, "That old place may be full of rats. If so, I've got the remedy here."

We passed the wall that Renfield had climbed and walked to the house, being careful to keep in the shadows so that no one might notice us. When we got to the porch, the Professor opened his bag and took out a collection of things, which he separated into four groups.

"My friends, we are going into terrible danger, and we need weapons of many kinds," he said. "Our enemy is not only spiritual, but physical as well. He has the strength of twenty men and he can hurt us easily. We must, therefore, protect ourselves from his touch. Keep this near your heart." As he spoke he gave a little silver crucifix to each of us. "Put these flowers around your neck," and here he handed out wreaths of withered garlic blossoms. "For other, more ordinary enemies, here are a pistol and a knife, and a small flashlight. Most important of all, here is a portion of a Communion wafer.

"Now, John," he said, "where are the skeleton keys? Let us see if one will work, so that we do not need to break a window." We were in luck, for Dr. Seward tried one or two of the keys and succeeded in opening the door.

The light from our tiny lamps dimly lit all

sorts of odd shapes. I could not shake the feeling that there was someone else here among us. I think everyone felt the same, for I noticed that the others kept looking over their shoulders at every sound, just as I was doing.

The whole place was thick with dust, inches deep on the floor. In the corners were masses of spiders' webs, so weighed down with dust that they looked like old tattered rags. On a table in the hall was a great bunch of keys, with a label on each. It was evident they had been used several times, for on the table were several marks in the blanket of dust.

The Professor said to me, "You have copied maps of this place, Jonathan. Which way is the chapel?"

I led the way, and after a few wrong turns I found myself opposite a low, arched oaken door, ribbed with iron bands. We found the proper key on the bunch and opened the door.

We were prepared for the air to be stale, but none of us expected the odor we encountered. When I had seen the Count, he was either in the non-eating stage of his existence or bloated with fresh blood in a ruined building open to the air. Here the place was small and close, and the air was stagnant and foul. But as to the odor itself—how can I describe it? It was not only the penetrating, burning smell of blood. It seemed as though evil itself had become a scent. It sickens me to think of it.

Doing our best to ignore the nauseating smell, we set to work examining the place. Our first task was to try to determine how many of the fifty boxes of earth were still there. We began to count—there were only twenty-nine!

Just then I saw Morris jump suddenly back from a corner. We all followed his movements with our eyes and we saw a mass of glowing dust, twinkling like stars. Then, somehow, the whole place was alive with rats.

For a moment or two we stood paralyzed— all except Lord Godalming. Rushing over to the great oaken door leading to the outside, he turned the key in the lock, drew the huge bolts, and swung the door open. Taking his little silver whistle from his pocket, he blew a low, shrill call. It was answered from behind Dr. Seward's house by the yelping of dogs. After about a minute, three terriers came dashing around the corner of the house. With every minute that passed, the number of rats increased greatly. The floor seemed alive with their moving dark bodies and glittering, hateful eyes. At the doorway the dogs suddenly stopped and snarled, and then, lifting their noses, they began to howl in a most mournful way.

Lord Godalming lifted one of the dogs

and, carrying him in, placed him on the floor. The instant his feet touched the ground, he seemed to recover his courage and rushed at his natural enemies. The other dogs followed his lead. In a few instants the little dogs had shaken the life out of several dozen of the creatures, and the rest were fleeing for their lives.

As the dogs went about their business, it seemed as if some evil presence had departed. The terriers frisked around as happily as if they were hunting rabbits in the woods. Their cheery activity helped raise our spirits. We closed the outer door and locked it, and bringing the dogs with us, began our search of the house. We found nothing throughout except pounds of dust untouched by any footprints, and the dogs showed no nervousness at all.

The sun was beginning to rise as we left the house. Dr. Van Helsing had taken the key of the hall door from the bunch and locked the door behind us.

"So far, so good," he said. "We are all yet safe, and we have discovered how many boxes are missing. We have learned, too, that the beasts which the Count can call to help him have no special powers, for these rats ran like any ordinary rodents from the brave little dogs."

The house was silent when we got back,

except for a low, moaning sound from Renfield's room. I tiptoed into our own room and found Mina asleep. She looks paler than usual. I hope the meeting tonight has not upset her. I am thankful that she is to be left out of our future work and even of our conferences. There may be things which would frighten her to hear. From now on, I will tell her nothing of our work until I can tell her that it is finished and the earth is free from a monster.

October 1, later. I suppose it was natural that we all overslept, for the day was a busy one and the night had no rest at all. Even Mina must have felt its exhaustion. Although I slept until the sun was high, I was awake before her and had to call two or three times before she woke up. Even then, she was so sound asleep that for a few seconds she did not recognize me, but looked at me with a sort of blank terror. She complained of being tired and rested much of the day. We now know that twenty-one boxes have been removed from Carfax, and I will attempt to discover where they have gone. Later today I shall look up Thomas Snelling, one of the movers whom Renfield attacked.

DR. SEWARD'S DIARY

October 1.   It was about noon when I was awakened by the Professor walking into my room. He was more jolly than usual and it is clear that last night's work has taken some of the worry off his mind.

After we talked of the night's adventure, he suddenly said, "Your patient, Renfield, interests me much. May I visit him with you this morning? Or if you are too busy, I can go alone. It is a new experience for me to find a lunatic to converse with so intelligently."

I had some work to do, so I told him go alone. I called an attendant and gave him the necessary instructions. Before the Professor left the room, I warned him against believing everything my patient said.

"Do not worry," he answered. "I want him to talk of himself and of his desire to consume live things. He told Madame Mina that he had once had such a belief. Why are you laughing, John?"

"Because," I said, "when our sane and well-behaved lunatic made that statement, he still had the taste in his mouth of the flies and spiders he had eaten just before Mrs. Harker entered the room."

Van Helsing smiled too. "But isn't it just

this type of behavior which makes mental disease such a fascinating study? Perhaps I learn more from the nonsense of this madman than I shall from the teaching of the most wise. Who knows?"

I went on with my work. In a very short time, there was Van Helsing back in the study.

"Do I interrupt?" he asked politely as he stood at the door.

"Not at all, "I answered. "Come in. I can go with you now, if you like."

"No need; I have seen him!" he answered.

"Well?"

"Our interview was short. When I entered his room, he was sitting on a stool with his elbows on his knees, looking most sullen. I spoke to him as cheerfully as I could. He did not answer. I asked, 'Don't you remember me?' He answered, 'I know you well enough. You are the old fool Van Helsing. I wish you would take yourself and your idiotic ideas somewhere else. Damn all thick-headed Dutchmen!' He wouldn't say another word. Needless to say, I didn't learn much, so I shall go now and cheer myself up with a few words with sweet Madame Mina."

So Van Helsing has gone to chat with Mrs. Harker, and Harker, Quincy and Art are all out following up the clues about the boxes of earth. I shall finish my work and we shall meet tonight.

MINA HARKER'S JOURNAL

October 1. It is strange for me to be kept in the dark like this. For years, Jonathan and I have had no secrets from one another.

This morning I slept late. Although Jonathan was very sweet, he never mentioned a word of what had happened in the Count's house. They have all agreed I should not be drawn further into this awful work. I understand they mean well. But to think that he keeps anything from me! And now I am crying like a silly fool. Some day, I know, Jonathan will tell me everything. But still I feel strangely sad and low-spirited today.

Last night I went to bed when the men had gone off to Carfax. I was too anxious to feel sleepy. Everything that I've done, no matter how right it seemed, seems awful to me now. If I hadn't gone to Whitby, perhaps Lucy would be alive now. She didn't start visiting the churchyard until I came, and if she hadn't come there in the daytime with me, she wouldn't have walked there in her sleep. And if she hadn't gone there at night, that monster couldn't have destroyed her as he did. There now, I'm crying again! I wonder what has come over me today.

I can't quite remember how I fell asleep last night. I do recall hearing the barking of the dogs and a lot of queer sounds, like very loud praying, from Mr. Renfield's room, which is somewhere under mine. And then there was silence over everything, silence so profound that it startled me. I got up and looked out of the window. Not a thing seemed to be stirring. I noticed a thin streak of white mist creeping across the grass towards the house. I went back to bed but still could not quite sleep, so I got up and looked out the window again. The mist was spreading and was now close to the house, lying thick against the wall. Poor Mr. Renfield was crying out more loudly than ever. Then there was the sound of a struggle, and I knew that the attendants were dealing with him. I felt so frightened that I got into bed and pulled the bedclothes over my head. I must have fallen asleep then.

My dreams were very peculiar. I seemed to know that I was asleep and that I was waiting for Jonathan to come back. The air was heavy and cold. I pulled my head out from under the blankets and found everything around me cloudy and dim. The light that I had left on for Jonathan seemed only a tiny red spark through the fog, which appeared to have come in through the window. I wanted to get up, to make sure I had closed the window, but my body felt as if it was made of lead, and I could not move. The mist grew thicker and thicker. I could see now that it was not coming in through the window but rather through the crack along the side of the door. It became sort of a pillar of cloud in the room, through the top of which I could see the light shining like a red eye. As I looked, the fire divided and seemed to shine on me through the fog like two red eyes.

Today I am so tired. I would like to ask Dr. Van Helsing or Dr. Seward to prescribe something for me to make me sleep, but I don't want to worry them. Tonight I shall try hard to sleep naturally.

October 2, 10 p.m. Last night I slept without dreaming. Yet my sleep has not rested me, for I feel weak and depressed. I spent all yesterday trying to read, or lying down, dozing. In the afternoon Mr. Renfield asked if he could see me. The poor man was very gentle, and when I left him, he kissed my hand and said, "God bless you." Somehow this touched me very much, and I am crying again. This is a new weakness which I do not understand.

Jonathan and the others were out until dinner time, and they all came in tired. After dinner they went off to smoke together, or so they said. I could tell they wanted to talk about what had happened during the day. Before they went, I asked Dr. Seward to give me something to make me sleep. He very kindly gave me something which he said was very mild and could not do me any harm. I have taken it and am waiting for sleep. As I grow sleepy, I begin to worry that I have been foolish. Perhaps I will not have the power to wake up if I need to. But that thought is too late. Here comes sleep. Goodnight.

Chapter 20

JONATHAN HARKER'S JOURNAL

October 1, evening. I found Thomas Snelling, the mover, at home, but unfortunately he was too drunk to be of any help. His wife told me, however, that he was only the assistant to Joseph Smollet, the other of the two workmen.

So off I drove to Walworth and found Mr. Smollet having his tea. He is a decent, intelligent fellow. He remembered all about the boxes, and from a wonderful dog-eared notebook, he gave me the details. There were, he said, six in the cartload which he took from

Carfax and left at 197 Chicksand Street, Mile End, New Town. He then delivered another six to Jamaica Lane in Bermondsey. My guess is that the Count intends to scatter these horrible "homes" of his all over London. I asked Smollet if any other boxes had been taken from Carfax.

He replied, "Well guv'nor, you've treated me very handsome" (I had by then given him twenty pounds), "and I'll tell you all I know. Four nights ago at the pub I heard a man by the name of Bloxam say that he and his mate had done a right dusty job in an old house at Purfleet. There ain't many such jobs dusty as this, an' I'm thinkin' that maybe Sam Bloxam could tell you something."

I asked if he could tell me where to find Bloxam and that I'd give him another ten pounds for his address. So he gulped down the rest of his tea and stood up, saying that he was going to begin the search then and there. At the door he stopped and said, "Look here, guv'nor, there ain't no sense in me keeping you waiting. I may find Sam soon, or I may not, but anyhow he ain't like to tell you much tonight. Sam is a rare one when he starts on the booze. If you can give me a stamped envelope with your address on it, I'll find out where Sam is and send you his address later tonight. Then you can be after him in the morning." This all made sense, so I made up an envelope as Smollet suggested.

I am tired tonight, and I want to sleep. Mina is fast asleep and looks a little too pale. Her eyes look as though she has been crying. Poor dear, it must worry her to be kept in the dark like this. But it is for the best.

October 2, evening. A long, difficult, exciting day. Early in the morning my envelope arrived. Inside was a dirty scrap of paper, on which was written, "Sam Bloxam, Korkrans, 4 Poters Cort, Bartel Street, Walworth." I left the house without waking Mina. She didn't look at all well. When I get back today, I'll suggest she should return to Exeter.

I drove to Walworth and found, with some difficulty, Potter's (not Poters) Court. Mr. Smollet's spelling misled me. However, when I had found the court, I recognized the boarding house, which is actually named Corcoran's.

The landlord who answered the door was helpful. Yes, Mr. Bloxam had stayed there last night, but he had left for work at five o'clock that morning. After asking a series of questions and getting bits of information from a series of people (helped along by a pound here and there), I finally located Bloxam, a rough-looking workman. After I promised to pay for his information, he told me that he had made two journeys between Carfax and a house in Piccadilly, and had moved nine great boxes, "heavier than you would believe," from the first house to the second.

I asked him the address of the house in Piccadilly. He couldn't remember. "It was a dusty old place," he added, "though nothing like the dirt of the house we took the boxes from."

"How did you get in if both houses were empty?" I asked.

"The old man that hired me was waiting in the house at Purfleet," he said. "He helped me lift the boxes and put 'em in the cart. God bless me if he wasn't the strongest man I ever saw, even though he was an old fellow with a white moustache, and so thin you wouldn't think he could throw a shadow."

Bloxam's words made me shudder.

"And how did you get into the house in Piccadilly?" I asked.

"He was there too. He must have started off and got there before me, for when I rung the bell he come and opened the door and helped me carry the nine boxes into the hall."

I made one last attempt. "But you can't

remember the number of the house?"

"No, sir. But you'll recognize it. It's a tall, high house with long steps up to the front door, just a few doors down from a white church." I thought that with this description I could find the house, so having paid Bloxam for his information, I started off for Piccadilly. I had learned something disturbing. The Count could, apparently, move the earth-filled boxes himself if need be. If so, time was precious, for he could finish scattering them across London with no witnesses.

I walked up and down Piccadilly until I located what I felt sure was the latest of Dracula's homes. The house looked as though it had been empty a long time. The windows were crusty with dust, and the paint was peeling. I was disappointed that there was no realtor's sign still up, for it would have been helpful to know who had sold or rented the house. I went around to the back to see if I could gather any more information. From talking to several of the grooms and servants walking about, I got the names of Mitchell, Sons, & Candy, Realtors. I was soon at their office in Sackville Street.

The gentleman who saw me was both polite and completely unhelpful. Once he told me that the Piccadilly house (which he insisted on calling a "mansion") had been sold, he clearly thought our interview should end. When I asked who had purchased it, he blinked rapidly, paused a few seconds, and repeated, "It is sold, sir."

"Pardon me," I said, with equal politeness, "but I have a special reason for wishing to know who purchased it."

Again he paused longer, and raised his eyebrows still more. "It is sold, sir," was again his reply.

"But surely," I said, "you won't mind telling me who bought it?"

"But I do mind," he answered. "Mitchell, Sons, & Candy do not discuss the affairs of their clients."

There was no use arguing with him. I decided to play his snobbish game. "Your clients are fortunate that you take such good care of them," I said, handing him my business card. "In this case, I am not merely curious," I said. "I am acting on behalf of Lord Godalming, who is interested in purchasing this or a similar property."

These words had a great effect on the man, who fell over himself to become cooperative. "Oh, my goodness, by all means, I would be pleased to help you, Mr. Harker, and even more so his lordship. If you will let me have his lordship's address, I will consult with my partners and will write later today to his lordship. It will be a pleasure if we can assist his lordship."

I wanted to secure a friend, and not to make an enemy, so I thanked him, gave him Dr. Seward's address, and left. It was now dark, and I was tired and hungry. I got a cup of tea and returned back to the asylum at Purfleet by the next train.

I found all the others at home. Mina was looking tired and pale, but she made an effort to be bright and cheerful. It makes me feel awful to know that I am causing her pain. Before I met with the others, I took her to our room so we could chat before she went to bed. The dear girl was more affectionate with me than ever, and clung to me as though she wanted me to stay, but there was so much to be talked about with the others that I left her there.

When I had finished giving the information I had gathered, Van Helsing said, "This has been a great day's work, Jonathan. We are on the track of the missing boxes. If we find them all in that house in Piccadilly, then our work is near the end. But if there are some missing, we must search until we find them, then hunt the wretch to his real death."

Mr. Morris broke in, "Say! How are we going to get into that house?"

"We got into the other house," answered Lord Godalming.

"But, Art, this is different. We broke into Carfax, but we had night and a walled park to protect us. It will be a mighty different thing to commit burglary in the middle of Piccadilly, either by day or night. I don't see how we are going to get in unless that realtor gives us a key."

Lord Godalming frowned. "Quincy is right. This burglary business is getting serious. We got off once all right, but we could get into real trouble here, unless we can find the Count's keys."

Nothing more could be done before morning, at least until Lord Godalming heard from the realtor. I am very sleepy and shall go to bed . . .

Dr. Seward's Diary

October 1. I am even more puzzled about Renfield. His moods change so rapidly that I can't keep track of them. This morning, when I went to see him after he had sent Van Helsing away, his manner was that of an all-controlling god. He had no use for a poor mortal like me. I tried to converse with him, but I found him full of riddles and dead-ends. At one point, trying to get him to talk about his new attitude, I said, "You are a god, I suppose?"

He smiled in a very superior way. "Oh no! Far be it from me to call myself a deity. If I am like anyone, it is Enoch."

This puzzled me. Enoch, I knew, was a character in the Bible, but I could not remember his story. Finally I asked, "And why Enoch?"

"Because he walked with God."

This meant nothing to me. Trying a new tactic, I asked him, "Would you like some sugar to catch some more flies?"

With a laugh he replied, "No! Flies are poor things, after all!" After a pause he added, "But I don't want their souls buzzing round me, all the same."

"Or spiders?" I went on.

"Hang spiders! What's the use of spiders? There isn't anything in them to eat or . . ." He stopped suddenly, as though reminded of a forbidden topic.

It occurred to me that this was the second time recently he had refused to say the word "drink."

Renfield seemed to realize he had made an

error, for he hurried on as though trying to distract me. "I'm past all that sort of nonsense," he said. "You might as well ask a man to eat molecules with a pair of chopsticks as to try to interest me in lesser creatures when I know what is ahead of me."

"I see," I said. "You want to get your teeth into big things, then? Perhaps you'd like to eat an elephant?"

"What ridiculous nonsense you are talking!"

"I wonder," I said reflectively, "what an elephant's soul is like!"

He at once lost his superior manner and became a child again.

"I don't want an elephant's soul or any soul at all!" he said. He jumped to his feet. "To hell with you and your souls!" he shouted. "Why do you bother me about souls? Haven't I got enough worry and pain to distract me already, without thinking of souls?"

He looked so hostile that I thought he was in for another violent fit, so I called for the attendant.

The instant I did so, he became calm and said apologetically, "Forgive me, Doctor. You are safe with me. I am so worried in my mind that I am irritable. If you only knew the problem I have to face, you would pity, and tolerate, and pardon me. Please do not put me in a straitjacket. I want to think, and I cannot think freely when my body is imprisoned."

He seemed in control of himself, so I told the attendant he could go. Once he had left, Renfield said to me, with great dignity and sweetness, "Dr. Seward, you have been very considerate. Believe me that I am very grateful to you!"

I thought it was best to leave him in that mood, so I left. I must think about what is happening with him. Here are the points that seemed clear today:

He will not mention "drinking."

He hates the thought of being burdened with the "soul" of anything.

He looks down on lower forms of life.

Merciful God. Has the Count gotten to him again? Is there some new horrible plan afoot?

Later. I went to chat with Van Helsing and told him about my visit with Renfield. He grew very serious and, after thinking the matter over for a while, asked me to take him to Renfield. I did so. As we came to the door, we heard the man singing gaily.

When we entered I saw with amazement that he had spread out his sugar again. The flies were beginning to buzz into the room. We tried to get him to pick up our previous conversation, but he would not. He went on with his singing, just as though we had not been present. We went away as ignorant as we went in.

He is a curious case indeed. We must watch him tonight.

Letter from Mitchell, Sons & Candy
to Lord Godalming

October 1

My Lord,

We are only too happy to meet your wishes and to supply the following information concerning the sale of No. 347, Piccadilly. The purchaser is a foreign nobleman, Count de Ville. He paid cash for the property, and beyond this we know nothing at all about him.

Yours most sincerely,
Mitchell, Sons & Candy

Dr. Seward's Diary

October 2. I assigned a man to spend last night in the hallway. I gave him instructions to pay special attention to Renfield's room and to call me if anything strange happened.

After dinner, when Mrs. Harker had gone to bed, we all gathered round the fire in the study to discuss the day. Before going to bed, I went by Renfield's room and looked in through the observation window. He was sleeping soundly.

This morning the man on duty reported to me that a little after midnight, Renfield was restless and began praying loudly. I asked him if anything else had happened, and he replied that that was all he heard. There was something suspicious about his manner, so I asked him point blank if he had been asleep. He denied sleeping but said he may have "dozed" for a while. It is too bad that men cannot be trusted unless they are watched.

Today, Harker is out following up on some clues, and Art and Quincy are making sure we have horses ready. We must sterilize all the Transylvanian earth between sunrise and sunset. Then we shall catch the Count at his weakest and without a refuge to go to. Van Helsing is off to the British Museum, where he will do some research on ancient medicine. He hopes to find some witch and demon cures which may be useful to us later.

I sometimes think we must be all mad and

that we shall awake someday in straitjackets.

Later. We have met again. We seem at last to be on our way, and our work tomorrow may be the beginning of the end. I wonder if Renfield's quiet mood means anything. If we could only get some hint as to what he was thinking about, it might be valuable. He has been silent for some hours. But just now I heard a wild yell—was that from his room?

The attendant came bursting in here and told me that Renfield had somehow had an accident. He had heard him yell, and when he went to Renfield, found him lying on his face on the floor all covered with blood. I must go at once . . .

Chapter 21

DR. SEWARD'S DIARY

October 3. Let me write down what has happened, as well as I can remember. I must not forget a detail. I must stay calm.

I found Renfield lying on the floor in a glittering pool of blood. When I went to move him, I saw that he was badly injured. His face was horribly bruised as though it had been beaten against the floor. The blood had come from the wounds in his face.

"I think his neck is broken," said the attendant, kneeling beside him. "See, both his right arm and leg and the whole side of his face are paralyzed. I can't understand how both things could have happened. I suppose he could mark his face like that by beating his own head on the floor. I saw a young woman do it once at the Eversfield Asylum. And it's possible he could have broken his neck by falling out of bed. But if his neck was broken, he couldn't beat his head, and if his face was like that before the fall out of bed, there would be blood in the bed."

I told him to run and get Dr. Van Helsing. Within a few minutes, the Professor appeared in his bathrobe and slippers. When he saw Renfield on the ground, he said calmly, "Ah, a sad accident! I will get dressed and join you in a few minutes."

The patient was now breathing in harsh gasps. It was easy to see that he was near death.

Van Helsing returned quickly, carrying his surgical case. He whispered to me, "Send the attendant away. We must be alone with him in case he becomes conscious and speaks."

I said, "That will do now, Simmons. Go about your rounds, and Dr. Van Helsing will operate."

The man left and we examined the patient. The wounds of the face were bloody but not severe. The real injury was a dreadful fracture of the skull.

There was a soft tapping at the door. Arthur and Quincy stood there in their pajamas and slippers. "I heard your man call Dr. Van Helsing and tell him of an accident. So I woke Quincy and we came. Things are moving too quickly for any of us to sleep well. May we come in?"

I nodded. When Quincy saw the patient and the horrible pool on the floor, he said softly, "My God! What has happened to the poor devil?" I told him briefly and added that we expected he might regain consciousness after the operation. He and Godalming sat down on the edge of the bed.

"We shall wait," said Van Helsing, "until I can guess the best spot for drilling into the skull, so as to relieve the pressure of the blood that is building up there."

The minutes passed with awful slowness. I felt a horrible sinking in my heart, and from Van Helsing's face I could tell that he too feared what was going to happen. I dreaded hearing the words Renfield might speak.

It became obvious that the patient was slipping away quickly. The professor said, "There is no time to lose. His words may save many lives. We shall operate here, just above the ear."

Without another word he began to cut

through the bone. For a few moments Renfield's condition seemed unchanged. Then there came a long intake of breath, so deep it seemed it would tear open his chest. Suddenly his eyes opened, and he glared about with a wild, helpless stare. This look then softened to happy surprise, and from his lips came a sigh of relief. He moved awkwardly, saying, "I'll be quiet, Doctor. Tell them to take off the strait-jacket. I have had a terrible dream, and it has left me so weak that I cannot move. What's wrong with my face? It feels all swollen and it hurts dreadfully."

He tried to turn his head, but the effort made his eyes grow glassy again. Then Van Helsing said in a quiet tone, "Tell us your dream, Mr. Renfield."

As he heard the voice, his face brightened through its bruises, and he said, "That is Dr. Van Helsing. How good it is of you to be here. Give me some water—my lips are dry—and I shall try to tell you. I dreamed . . ." His voice faded away.

We moistened his parched lips, and Renfield became more awake. It seemed, however, that his poor injured brain had been working all the time, for he looked at me with an agonized confusion and said, "I must not fool myself. It was no dream. It was reality."

For an instant his eyes closed, as though he were trying hard to concentrate. When he opened them, he said hurriedly, "Quick, Doctor, quick, I am dying! I only have a few minutes. Give me more water. I have something that I must say before I die. Thank you!

"It was that night after you left me, when I begged you to let me go away. I couldn't speak then, for I felt my tongue was tied. But I was as sane then as I am now. I was in despair for a long time after you left me. Then I felt a sudden peace. I heard the dogs bark behind our house, but that was not where the Count was!"

As he spoke, Van Helsing's eyes never blinked, but he put his hand out and gripped mine, hard. He nodded slightly and said, "Go on," in a low voice.

Renfield proceeded. "He came up to the window in the mist, as I had seen him often before. He was laughing with his red mouth. I saw the sharp white teeth glinting in the moonlight. I wouldn't ask him to come in at first, although I knew he wanted to, just as he had wanted all along. Then he began promising me things—not just in words, but by doing them."

He was interrupted by the Professor, "How?"

"By making them happen," Renfield said. "Just as he used to send in the flies for me, great big fat ones. And big moths, in the night, with skulls and crossbones on their backs. He began to whisper, 'Rats, Renfield! Hundreds, thousands, millions of them, and every one a life. And dogs to eat them, and cats too. All those lives for you! All that red blood, with years of life in it—much better than buzzing flies!'

"I laughed at him, for I wanted to see what he could do. He motioned me to come to the window. I looked out, and he raised his hands, and seemed to call out without using any words. A dark mass spread over the grass. And then he moved the mass to the right and left, and I could see that there were thousands of rats with their eyes blazing red, like his, only smaller. He held up his hand, and they all stopped, and he seemed to be saying, 'All these lives will I give you, yes, and many more, through countless ages, if you will fall down and worship me!' And then a red cloud, like the color of blood, seemed to close over my eyes. Before I knew it, I found myself throwing open the window and saying to Him, 'Come in, Lord and Master!' The rats were all gone, and he slid into the room."

His voice was weaker, so I moistened his

lips again, and he continued. "All day I waited to hear from him, but he did not send me anything, not even a fly, and when the moon rose, I was pretty angry with him. When he did slide in through the window, I got mad. He just sneered at me. He acted as though he owned the whole place, and I was nobody. He didn't even smell the same as he had before. It smelled, somehow, as though Mrs. Harker had come into the room."

When the Professor heard this, his hand began to tremble. Renfield went on without noticing, "When Mrs. Harker came in to see me this afternoon, she was different. She was like tea that had been watered down. I don't like pale people. I like them with lots of blood in them, and hers all seemed to have run out. After she left I began to think, and it made me angry to realize that he had been taking the life out of her. So when he came tonight, I was ready for him. I saw the mist stealing in, and I grabbed it tight. I have heard that madmen have unnatural strength, and since I am a madman, sometimes at least, I decided to use my power. I thought I was going to win, for I didn't want him to take any more of her life. But then his eyes began to burn into me, and my strength became like water. He picked me up and threw me onto the floor. Then there was a red cloud before me, and a noise like thunder, and the mist seemed to creep away under the door."

His voice was becoming fainter and his breath more gasping. Van Helsing stood up. "We know the worst now," he said. "He is here and we know what he is after. Let us be armed, the same as we were the other night, and go quickly."

We all hurried to our rooms and gathered the garlic, crucifixes, and other things that we had taken into the Count's house. The Professor had his ready, and as we met in the hallway he pointed to them as he said, "They never leave me, and they will not until this unhappy business is over. Be wise also, my friends. It is no ordinary enemy that we deal with. Oh, it is too hard that dear Madame Mina should suffer!"

Outside the Harkers' door, we paused and looked at one another. Van Helsing touched the handle. "If the door is locked, we must break it in. All of you, if the door does not open, put your shoulders down and shove. Now!"

He turned the handle as he spoke, but the door did not yield. We threw ourselves against it. With a crash, it burst open, and we almost fell into the room. The Professor actually did fall, and I looked across him as he gathered himself up from his hands and knees. What I saw filled me with horror. I felt my hair rise like bristles on the back of my neck, and my heart seemed to stand still.

The moonlight through the window was so bright that we could see clearly. On the bed lay Jonathan Harker, his face flushed, breathing heavily as though he were in unconscious. Kneeling on the edge of the bed nearest us was Mrs. Harker, wearing a white nightgown. By her side stood a tall, thin man, dressed in black. We all recognized the Count, right down to the scar which Jonathan's shovel had left on his forehead. With his left hand he tightly held both Mrs. Harker's hands. His right hand gripped her by the back of the neck and he was forcing her face down onto his bare chest, which showed through his ripped shirt. The position of the two reminded me, horribly, of a child forcing a kitten's nose into a saucer of milk to make it drink.

As we burst into the room, the Count turned to us, and a hellish look leaped into his face. His eyes flamed red, the nostrils of the great arched nose flared wide, and the white sharp teeth snapped together like those of a wild beast. He violently threw Mrs. Harker back upon the bed, then turned and sprang at us. But by this time the Professor had gotten on his feet again, and he held up the envelope which contained the Communion wafer. The Count stopped, just as poor Lucy had done outside the tomb, and cowered back. Further and further back he shrank as we advanced, lifting our crucifixes. The moonlight dimmed as a great black cloud sailed across the sky. By the time Quincy had hurriedly lit the lamp, we could see nothing but a faint vapor seeping under the door.

Mrs. Harker drew in a great breath and gave a scream so wild and ear-piercing that I believe it will ring in my ears until my dying day. Her face was horribly white, a whiteness that was accented by the blood which smeared her lips and cheeks and chin. From her throat trickled a thin stream of red, and her eyes were mad with terror. She put her poor crushed hands before her face, and from behind them came a low, agonized wail. Van Helsing stepped forward and gently covered her body with a blanket, while Art ran out of the room.

Van Helsing whispered to me, "The Vampire has put Jonathan in a stupor. We can do nothing with poor Madame Mina for a few moments. I must wake him!"

He dipped the end of a towel in cold water and began to flick it in Jonathan's face. Mrs.

Harker continued to hold her face between her hands and sob in a way that was heart-breaking to hear. I looked out of the window. In the moonlight I could see Quincy run across the lawn and hide himself in the shadow of a great tree. Before I could wonder what he was doing, I heard Harker's exclamation as he began to awaken. On his face was a look of wild amazement. He seemed dazed for a few seconds, and then he leaped up.

His wife felt his movement. She turned to him with her arms stretched out, as though to embrace him. Instantly, however, she pulled them back. Once again she held her hands before her face, shuddering until the bed beneath her shook.

"In God's name, what does this mean?" Harker cried out. "Dr. Seward, Dr. Van Helsing, what is it? What has happened? Mina, dear, what is it? What does that blood mean? My God, my God!" And raising himself to his knees, he shouted wildly, "Good God help us! Help her! Oh, help her!"

He jumped from the bed and began to pull on his clothes. "What has happened? Tell me!" he insisted. "Dr. Van Helsing, you love Mina, I know. Oh, do something to save her. Guard her while I look for him!"

Mrs. Harker seized hold of him and cried

out, "No! Jonathan, you must not leave me! I have suffered enough tonight without him harming you, too. You must stay with me!" She was frantic with fear. Giving in, he sank down by her side.

Van Helsing and I tried to calm them both. The professor held up his golden crucifix and said, "Do not fear, my dear. We are here, and while this is close to you, no evil thing can come near. You are safe for tonight, and we must be calm and think."

She shuddered and was silent, laying her head on her husband's shoulder. When she raised it, his white shirt was stained with blood where her lips had touched and where the open wound in her neck left drops. The instant she saw it, she drew back with a low wail and whispered, "Unclean, unclean! I must not touch or kiss him again. I am now his enemy!"

"Nonsense, Mina," Jonathan objected. "I won't listen to such words. Nothing will ever come between us!" He pulled her close and she rested against him, still weeping. He held her gently until she was quieter and then said, "And now, Dr. Seward, tell me everything. Exactly what did you see?"

I told him and he listened calmly, but I could see the emotion in the twitching muscles of his face. It touched me deeply to see him, even in that awful moment, continue to gently stroke his wife's hair. As I finished, Quincy and Godalming returned to the room.

"I could not see him anywhere in the hallway, or in any of our rooms. But he had been in the study . . ." He stopped, looking at the poor drooping figure on the bed.

Van Helsing said gravely, "Go on, Arthur. No more secrets. Our hope now is in knowing all. Tell freely!"

So Art went on, "He had been there. All the manuscript had been burned; I could still see bits of the pages in the fire."

Here I interrupted. "Thank God there is another copy in the safe!"

His face brightened at that, but fell again as he went on. "I ran downstairs then, but could see no sign of him. I looked into Renfield's room, but there was no trace there except . . ." Again he paused.

"Go on," Harker said hoarsely.

So he bowed his head, adding, "except that the poor fellow is dead."

Van Helsing turned to Quincy and asked, "And you, friend Quincy, have you anything to tell?"

"A little," he answered. "I wanted to see where the Count would go when he left the house. A bat rose from Renfield's window and flew to the west. I expected to see him, in some shape, go back to Carfax, but apparently he went to another of his dens. He will not be back tonight, for it is nearly sunrise."

Van Helsing placed his hand tenderly on Mrs. Harker's head and said, "And now, Madame Mina, poor dear, tell us exactly what happened. God knows that I do not want to cause you further pain, but we must know all."

The poor lady shivered but then raised her head and held out one hand to Van Helsing, who held it tightly. The other hand was locked in that of her husband, who held his arm around her protectively. Then she began:

"I took the sleeping medicine which you had given me, but it took a long time to work. Finally I must have slept, and I didn't wake when Jonathan came in. The next thing I remember, I was aware of a thin white mist in the room. I felt afraid, and I tried to wake Jonathan, but I could not. Then, beside the bed, I saw a man. It was as if he had stepped out of the mist—or as if the mist had turned into the man. I knew him at once from the descriptions I had heard. My heart stood still, and I would have screamed out, only I found I could not move or make a sound. Then he spoke in a fierce whisper, pointing to Jonathan.

"He said, 'Silence! If you make a sound, I shall take him and dash his brains out before your eyes.' Then he smiled and placed one hand upon my shoulder. He pulled the neck of my gown open and said, 'First, I will have a little snack. Don't look so surprised, my dear. It is not the first time, or the second, that you have fed me!' I was bewildered, but strangely enough, I did not want to stop him. I suppose it is a part of his horrible spell. And then, oh, my God, pity me! He put his mouth on my throat!" Her husband groaned. She looked at him with pity, as if he were the injured one, and went on.

"I felt my strength fading away, and I was nearly fainting. It seemed that a long time passed before he took his foul, awful mouth away. I saw it drip with fresh blood. Then he spoke to me mockingly. He said, 'And so you try to defeat me. You help these men to hunt me! Now you know the price for crossing my path. The stupid men should have been watching their own home, not looking for me out there! While they were out playing detective, I was taking their best beloved one and making her flesh of my flesh, blood of my blood. Later you will become my companion and my helper. But first, you will be punished for what you have done. You will come whenever I want you. When I say "Come!" you will cross land or sea to do whatever I say. Start with this!'

"He pulled open his shirt, and with his long, sharp nails, he cut open a vein in his chest. When the blood began to spurt out, he pressed my mouth to the wound, so that I must either suffocate or swallow . . . Oh, my God! What have I done? God pity me! And pity those who love me!" She began to rub her lips as though she could clean the Count's blood from them.

We have arranged that one of us is to stay all day with the Harkers until we can meet together and plan our next step.

Of this I am sure. The sun will not rise today on a more miserable house than ours.

Chapter 22

JONATHAN HARKER'S JOURNAL

October 3. I must do something or go mad, so I am writing in this diary. It is now six a.m., and we are to meet in the study in half an hour. Just now Mina told me that it is when we are in the worst trouble that we must have the most faith. We must keep trusting that God will aid us up to the end. The end! Oh my God! What end? . . . I must not allow myself to think!

Over breakfast, we agreed first of all that Mina must be told everything from now on. "There must be no more secrets," she said.

"We have had too many already. I wish to know everything."

Van Helsing asked her, "But dear Madame Mina, aren't you afraid after what has happened?"

Her face was very serious, but her eyes shone as she answered, "I am not afraid. I know what I must do."

"And what is that?" he asked gently. We were all very still, for we had some idea what she meant.

She answered directly. "If I see any sign that I might hurt someone I love, I will die."

"You would not kill yourself?" Van Helsing asked hoarsely.

"I would, unless a friend who loved me would save me from doing it myself." She gave him a look whose meaning we all understood.

He was sitting down, but he rose and came close to her and put his hand on her head. "My dear, if I could help you by making that promise, I would. But my child . . ."

His voice broke, and a great sob rose in his throat. He gulped it down and went on, "My dear Madame Mina, you must not die. You must not die at all, least of all by your own hand. Until the Count, who has fouled your sweet life, is dead—truly dead—you must not die. Don't you see—if he is still Undead, and you die, you will become what he is. No, you must live! You must fight death with all your strength. You may not even think of death until this great evil is past."

The poor girl grew paper-white and shook like a beech tree in the wind. We were all helplessly silent. Finally she grew more calm and sadly said, "I promise you, my dear friend, that if God will let me live, I shall struggle to do so."

We then turned to our plans for the day. Our task was to sterilize all the boxes of earth that we could find, so that the Count would have no safe haven to return to.

"What are we waiting for? Let us go to the house in Piccadilly and destroy the boxes of earth there!" I exclaimed. I was wild to begin, but Van Helsing held up his hand.

"No, my friend," he said, "think a minute. How are we to get into that house in Piccadilly?"

"Any way!" I cried. "We shall break in."

"And the police? Where will they be and what will they say?"

"Then what shall we do?" I demanded.

"Well," the Professor said, "suppose that you were, in truth, the owner of that house, and you could still not get in. What would you do?"

"I would hire a locksmith to pick the lock for me," I said.

"And the police, wouldn't they stop you?" he asked.

"No, not if they believed that I was really the owner and the locksmith was working for me," I answered.

"Ah, then, the only problem is convincing the policemen that we are, indeed, the owners of the house," Van Helsing said. "Do you know, I have read of a gentleman who owned a fine house in London. He happened to go to Switzerland for the summer. While he was gone, some burglar came and broke in through a back window and got in. He threw open the shutters and began walking in and out through the front door, before the very eyes of the police. Then he had an auction and sold every stick of furniture in the house. And finally he sold off the house itself, with the agreement that it would be knocked down to make way for another building. And the police helped him all they could. So when our poor owner returned from Switzerland, all he found was a hole in the ground. All because this burglar did not behave like a burglar! We should, I think, act like that clever burglar. We shall not go so early that the policemen will think it is strange. Let us go late in the morning, when there are many people around, just as we would if we were truly owners of the house."

He was right. I saw Mina's face grow more relaxed to hear his good advice.

Van Helsing went on, "Once we are in that house, we may find more clues. And some of us can remain there while the others go to the houses in Bermondsey and Mile End, where your Mr. Smollet delivered the other boxes."

Mina became interested in our plans and made some good suggestions. I was glad to see that she could, for a moment, forget the terrible experience of last night. She was very, very pale, and so thin that her lips were drawn back, showing her teeth more than usual. I did not mention this, but it made my blood run cold to remember what had happened with poor Lucy. At least her teeth did not seem to be growing sharper. But there was no time to lose and plenty of time for fear.

We decided to go to Carfax first and then on to the house in Piccadilly. The two doctors and I would stay there while Lord Godalming and Quincy found the earth boxes at Bermondsey and Mile End and destroyed them. The Professor thought it was possible that the Count might appear in Piccadilly during the day. If so, we might be able to deal with him then and there. I didn't want to go along at all, preferring to stay behind to protect Mina. But Mina would not listen. She said my experience in Transylvania might be useful during the day.

"I'm not afraid to be alone here," she said. "Things cannot be worse for me. Go, Jonathan! If God wishes it, he will guard me."

"We are prepared then," said Van Helsing. "Now, Madame Mina, you are quite safe here until sunset. And before then we shall be back if . . . We shall return! But before we go, let me arm you. I have prepared your room with the garlic and other things he cannot bear. Now let me guard you. On your forehead I touch this piece of Communion wafer in the name of the Father, the Son, and . . ."

There was a fearful scream which almost froze our hearts. As he had placed the wafer on Mina's forehead, it burned into the flesh as though it had been a piece of white-hot metal. She sank to her knees on the floor in an agony of shame. Pulling her beautiful hair over her face, she wailed out, "Unclean! God Himself cannot bear my polluted flesh!"

Van Helsing rushed to comfort her. "Madame Mina, my dear, I hope that we who love you will be there to see that scar pass away and leave your forehead as pure as your heart is. Surely the mark will disappear when God lifts this burden from us."

There was hope in his words, and comfort. We prayed for help in the terrible task which lay before us. So I said farewell to Mina, a parting which neither of us shall forget to our dying day, and we set out.

One thing I have decided. If we fail—if we find out that Mina must be a vampire in the end—then she shall not go alone into that unknown and terrible land.

We entered the estate at Carfax without any trouble. Everything was just as it had been when we were there before. It was hard to believe that among all that ordinary dust and dirt there was something so terrible. We found no papers or any sign that the house had been used. In the old chapel the great boxes looked just as we had seen them last.

Dr. Van Helsing said to us solemnly as we stood before him, "And now, my friends, we have a duty here to do, as we sterilize this earth."

He took a screwdriver and a wrench from his bag, and quickly opened the top of one of the cases. Taking from his box a piece of the Communion wafer, he laid it respectfully on the earth. Then he shut the lid and screwed it down again.

One by one we treated each of the boxes in the same way. As we passed across the lawn on our way to the train station we could see the front of the asylum. Mina was standing in the window of our room. I waved my hand to her and nodded to tell her that our work there was finished. She nodded to show that she understood. The last I saw, she was waving her hand in farewell. I felt sad and worried as we caught the train.

Piccadilly, 12:30 p.m. Just before we arrived, Lord Godalming said to me, "Quincy and I will find a locksmith. It will attract less attention if there are not too many of us. My title will impress the locksmith and any policeman that may come along. You had better go with Jack and the Professor and sit in the park across from the house. When you see the door is open and the locksmith has gone away, come across."

Godalming and Morris hurried off in a cab, while the rest of us strolled into Green Park. My heart beat hard as I saw the house, looking so grim and silent between its more lively, tidy-looking neighbors. We sat on a bench facing the house and began to smoke cigars so as to look as ordinary as possible. The minutes passed like hours as we waited for the others.

At length we saw a cab drive up. Out of it got Lord Godalming, Morris, and a heavy-set working man with a box of tools. The work-man took off his coat leisurely and hung it on one of the spikes of the rail, saying something to a policeman who just then wandered by. The policeman nodded agreeably and the man knelt down and went to work. In a very short time he had opened the door. Lord Godalming took out his wallet and gave him something. The man touched his hat, took his tools, put on his coat and left. Not a soul had paid any attention to the "burglary."

Once the locksmith was gone, we three crossed the street and knocked at the door. It was opened by Quincy Morris. Lord Godalming stood beside him, lighting a cigar. "The place smells so awful," he said, and indeed it did smell as bad as the old chapel at Carfax. Clearly the Count had been using the house.

In the dining room we found eight boxes of earth. Only eight out of the nine! Our work was not over and would not be until we found the missing box. Hurriedly we opened each of them and treated them as we had treated those at Carfax.

A search of the house revealed that only the dining room contained any of the Count's possessions. There were ownership papers to the Piccadilly house and deeds to the houses at

Mile End and Bermondsey as well. There were writing paper, envelopes, and pens and ink. In addition, we found a clothes brush, a hairbrush and comb, and a jug and basin. The basin contained water which was reddened, as if with blood. Last of all was a heap of keys of all sorts and sizes, probably those belonging to the other houses.

Quincy and Morris wrote down the addresses of the other houses, took the keys, and set out to destroy the boxes. The rest of us are, as patiently as possible, waiting for either them or the Count to return.

Chapter 23

DR. SEWARD'S DIARY

October 3. It seemed as if we waited endlessly for Arthur and Quincy. The Professor kept talking, obviously trying to keep our minds busy. I could see what he had in mind from the way he kept glancing at Harker. That poor fellow is overwhelmed with misery. Just last night he was a youthful, happy-looking man, full of energy. Today he looks exhausted and old, with hollow, desperate eyes. His energy, however, is still present; he burns with it. Perhaps this energy can take him through this period of despair. Poor fellow, I thought my own trouble was bad enough, but his . . . !

The Professor sees his agony and is doing his best to keep his mind active. As well as I can remember, this is what he was saying:

"I have been studying all the papers relating to this monster. The more I study, the greater seems the necessity of stamping him out. As I learned from my friend Arminius of Budapest, Dracula was a most wonderful man in his lifetime. He was a soldier, statesman, and scientist. He had a mighty brain, learning beyond compare, and a heart that knew no fear and no remorse . . ."

While he was speaking, we were startled by a knock at the door. We all moved out to the hall and Van Helsing answered the knock. It was only a boy delivering a telegram. The Professor opened it and read aloud.

"It is from Madame Mina. She writes, 'Look out for D. It is 12:45, and he has just left Carfax in a great hurry, traveling south.'"

There was a pause, broken by Jonathan Harker's voice, "Now, God be thanked, we shall meet him soon!"

Van Helsing answered, "God will act in His own way and time. Do not fear, and do not rejoice as yet. And be careful what you wish for."

"I don't care about anything now!"

Harker answered hotly, "except to wipe out this monster from the face of creation. I would sell my soul to do it!"

"Oh, hush, my child!" said Van Helsing. "God does not buy souls in this way. The Devil may buy them, but he does not keep his bargains. God is merciful, and he knows how you are suffering and how devoted you are to Madame Mina. Think how it would hurt her to hear your wild words. Believe me, the time for action is coming. See, it is twenty minutes past one. We must hope that Arthur and Quincy get here before the Count."

About half an hour after we had received the telegram, there came a quiet knock at the door. It was just an ordinary knock, but it made my heart stand still. Together we all moved out into the hall, each with our weapons ready. Van Helsing pulled back the latch, and holding the door half open, stood back. Our happiness must have shown upon our faces when we saw Arthur and Quincy. They came in quickly and closed the door behind them.

"It is all right," Arthur said, "We found both places. Six boxes in each, and we destroyed them all."

"Destroyed?" asked the professor.

"Destroyed for his use!"

Quincy said, "There's nothing to do but to wait here. But if he doesn't turn up by five o'clock, we must start for home. We can't leave Mrs. Harker alone after sunset."

"He will be here," said Van Helsing. "Madame's telegram said he went south from Carfax. I judge that he has gone to Mile End and Bermondsey and discovered you had been there before him. We shall not have long to wait now, so we should prepare our plan of attack . . . Hush, here he is! Prepare your weapons!" I heard a key turning in the lock of the door.

I noticed how, even in such a moment, a leader appeared. On our hunting trips and adventures in different parts of the world, Quincy had always been the one to arrange the plan of action, and Arthur and I automatically obeyed him. The same happened here. With a swift glance around the room, Quincy moved us each into position: Van Helsing, Harker, and I behind the door, with Arthur and Quincy standing just out of sight. We waited in suspense, hearing the slow, careful steps coming along the hall. The Count was evidently prepared for some surprise.

Suddenly he leaped into the room. There was something so inhuman, so cat-like in his movement, that it shocked us all. Harker was the first to react. With a quick movement, he threw himself between the Count and the exit door. As the Count saw us, he grinned in a horrible way, showing his long, pointed teeth. But the evil smile quickly passed into a cold stare, like that of a lion gazing at a rabbit. It was a pity that we did not have a better organized plan of attack. I did not know whether our guns or knives would have any effect on him.

Harker apparently decided to find out, for he lunged forward with his great knife and made a sudden, powerful stab. With diabolical quickness, the Count leaped back, and the blade sliced harmlessly through his coat. A bundle of paper money and a stream of gold coins fell out. The expression on the Count's face was so hellish that I was afraid for Harker. I moved forward protectively, holding the crucifix and wafer in my left hand. I felt a mighty power fly along my arm, and I was not surprised to see the monster cower away from me.

I cannot begin to describe the expression of hate, anger, and hellish rage which came over the Count's face. His skin actually seemed to change color and become greenish-yellow, and his burning eyes and the red scar on his forehead pulsed like fresh wounds. He dove under Harker's arm, avoiding the next blow. Grabbing a handful of the money from the floor, he dashed across the room and threw himself through the window. Amid the falling glass, he tumbled into the paved area below. I could hear the "ting" of the gold as some of the coins fell around him.

We ran over and saw him leap up unhurt from the ground. He raced across the yard and pushed open the stable door. There he turned and shouted back at us.

"You think you can defeat me? You, with your pale faces all in a row, like sheep in a butcher shop? You shall be sorry yet! You think you have left me without a place to rest, but I have more. My revenge has just begun, and time is on my side. The girls that you love are mine already. Through them you will be mine as well. You will do as I say, all of you, and you will be my banquet when I want to feed! Bah!"

He passed quickly through the door, and we heard the rusty bolt creak as he fastened it behind him. A door further in also opened and shut. Realizing the difficulty of following him through the stable, we moved toward the hall.

"We have learned something important," the Professor said. "For all his brave words, he is afraid of us, and he is afraid of being in need. For if not, why does he hurry so? Why does he take the money? Go and follow him. John and

I will stay here and take away anything that may be of use to him if he returns."

As he spoke he put the remaining money in his pocket. He took the ownership papers for the houses and swept everything else into the fireplace, which he lit with a match.

Arthur and Quincy had rushed out into

the yard, and Harker lowered himself from the window to follow the Count. But by the time they entered the stable, there was no sign of him. Van Helsing and I asked the passersby at the back of the house, but no one had seen him depart.

It was now late in the afternoon, and sunset was not far off. With heavy hearts we agreed to return home to Mina. "We can do nothing more here, and there we can at least protect her," said Van Helsing. "But do not despair. There is only one more box of earth, and we must find it. When that is done, everything may still be all right."

I could see that he spoke as bravely as he could to comfort Harker. The poor fellow was quite broken down and groaned whenever he thought of his wife. With sad hearts we returned to my house, where we found Mrs. Harker waiting for us. She saw from our faces that we had been unsuccessful. She forced herself to smile and praise our efforts.

Over supper, we told her everything which had happened. She listened and said nothing until the story was done. Then, without letting go of her husband's hand, she spoke.

"Jonathan," she said, and the word sounded like music on her lips. "Jonathan dear, and all you beloved friends, I want you to remem-

ber something. I know that you must fight.
You must destroy the Count, even as you
destroyed the false Lucy so that the true Lucy
might live forever. But my dear friends, do not
work in hate. That poor soul who has caused
all this misery is the saddest case of all. Just
think how great his joy will be when his worst
part is destroyed, so that his better part may
have true immortality. You must pity him,
even as you destroy him."

As she stopped speaking, Jonathan leaped
to his feet, almost tearing his hand from hers
as he spoke.

"Pity him, never! I would take joy in sending his soul to hell forever!"

Mrs. Harker seized his hand and spoke pas-
sionately. "Oh, hush! Hush in the name of God.
Don't say such things, my husband, or you will
crush me with fear and horror. Just think, my
dear—I have been thinking all day about this—
that perhaps, some day—oh, Jonathan, someday, I too may need such pity! And someone as
angry as you might deny it to me!"

We men were now all in tears. Mrs. Harker
wept, too. Her husband knelt beside her and,
putting his arms around her, hid his face in her
lap. Van Helsing beckoned to us, and we stole
out of the room, leaving the two of them alone.

The Professor protected their room

against the coming of the Vampire and promised Mrs. Harker that she might rest in peace. Van Helsing left a bell beside their bed, which either of them could ring in case of emergency. When they had gone to bed, Quincy, Arthur, and I arranged that we should sit up, protecting their room in shifts. The first watch is Quincy's, so the rest of us shall be off to bed as soon as we can.

Jonathan Harker's Journal

October 3 or 4, for it is near midnight. I thought yesterday would never end. I kept wishing I could sleep, hoping that when I awoke things would be changed for the better. We simply do not know what to do next. All we know is that one earth box remains and that the Count, alone, knows where it is. He may baffle us for years.

Later. I must have fallen asleep, for I was awakened by Mina, who was sitting up in bed. She placed a warning hand over my mouth and whispered in my ear, "Hush! There is someone in the hallway!" I got up softly and gently opened the door.

Just outside, stretched on a mattress, lay

Quincy, wide awake. He whispered to me, "Go back to bed. It is all right. One of us will be here all night. We aren't going to take any chances!"

I came back and told Mina. She sighed as she put her arms around me. "Thank God for good men!" she said, and sank back into sleep.

October 4, morning. Once again during the night I was wakened by Mina. This time the sky was just beginning to lighten. She said to me hurriedly, "Go, call the Professor. I want to see him at once."

"Why?" I asked.

"I have an idea. Go quickly, dearest."

I went to the door. Dr. Seward was resting on the mattress and seeing me, he jumped to his feet.

"Is anything wrong?" he asked, in alarm.

"No," I replied. "But Mina wants to see Dr. Van Helsing at once."

Two or three minutes later, Van Helsing was in the room in his bathrobe, and Quincy, Arthur, and Dr. Seward were at the door. Turning to Mina, the Professor said cheerfully, "And what can I do for you? For at this hour you do not want me for nothing."

"I want you to hypnotize me!" she said. "I have the Count's blood in my veins, don't I?

Perhaps I can share some of his thoughts. Do it before the dawn, for I feel that I can speak freely until that time. Hurry!"

Without a word, Van Helsing motioned her to sit up in bed. Looking deeply into her eyes, he began moving his hands in front of her, from the top of her head downward. Mina gazed at him for a few minutes, during which my own heart beat like a trip hammer. Gradually her eyes closed and she sat very still. The Professor made a few more movements with his hands, then stopped. His forehead was covered with great beads of perspiration.

Mina opened her eyes, which had a far-away look in them. She barely seemed to be breathing. The stillness was broken by Van Helsing's voice speaking very quietly.

"Where are you?" he asked.

"I do not know. It is all strange to me!"

"What do you see?"

"I can see nothing. It is all dark."

"What do you hear?" I could hear the tension in the Professor's patient voice.

"I hear . . . water. It is lapping against the outside, and little waves leap."

"Outside . . . then you are on a ship?'"

We all looked at each other, startled.

The answer came quickly. "Yes. A ship."

"What else do you hear?"

"The sound of men stamping overhead. There is the creaking of chains and men shouting as they carry heavy objects aboard."

"What are you doing now?"

"I am still, oh so still. It is like death!" Mina's voice faded away into a deep breath, and her open eyes closed again.

By this time the sun had risen. Dr. Van Helsing gently lowered Mina to her pillow. She lay like a sleeping child for a few moments and then, with a long sigh, awoke and stared in wonder at us all around her.

"Have I been talking in my sleep?" Then she remembered what had happened and eagerly asked what she had said. The Professor repeated the conversation, and she said, "There is not a moment to lose. It may not be too late!"

Mr. Morris and Lord Godalming started for the door, but the Professor's calm voice called them back.

"Wait, my friends. That ship, whichever it was, must have been weighing anchor in the Port of London. But which ship? God be thanked, we have once again a clue, though where it may lead only He knows. But now, at least, we know what was in the Count's mind when he seized that money. He meant escape! He saw that with only one earth box left, and a pack of men following him like dogs after a fox, London was no place for him. He has taken his last box on board a ship, and he is leaving this country. He thinks he will escape, but no! We will follow him, as hunting dogs drive a fox to its death. Our old fox is very clever, but we are clever too. So we must rest today and try to think as he is thinking. Then the hunt continues."

Mina looked at him in confusion. "But Professor," she asked, "we have won, haven't we? Why must we keep chasing him, now that he is going away?"

He took her hand as he replied, "Because my dear, now more than ever must we find him, even if we have to follow him to the gates of Hell!"

She grew paler as she asked, "But why?"

"Because," he answered sadly, "he can live for centuries, and you are a mortal woman. Time has become your enemy since he put that mark upon your throat. We must find and destroy him before your own life ends."

I was just in time to catch her as she fainted.

Chapter 24

Note from Van Helsing to Jonathan Harker

Today, I ask you to stay here with your dear Madame Mina. We shall go to make our search. Search is perhaps the wrong word. We go to confirm what I believe I already know.

Our enemy has gone back to his castle in Transylvania. I know this as surely as if the words were written on the wall in letters of fire. Somehow he has prepared for this, and that last box of earth was ready to ship somewhere. This is why he took the money. This is why he hurried so, in case we should catch him before the sun goes down. He knew that his game here was finished, and so he decided to go back home. He found a ship going by the route he wanted, and he left in it.

So now we go off to discover that ship. When we have our answer, we will come back and tell you all. Then we will comfort you and Madame Mina with new hope. For think of what we have done already. It took hundreds of years for this creature to get so far as London. He learned a new language, new customs, new skills to prepare to do so. He purchased many properties and made such great preparations. And yet in one day we drove him out. He is very powerful, but he has his limits.

JONATHAN HARKER'S JOURNAL

October 4. When I read Van Helsing's note to Mina, the poor girl brightened up considerably. The knowledge that the Count is out of the country has given her comfort. And comfort is strength to her. She tries to share that comfort with me by saying that perhaps we may yet become instruments of great good in all this. I am trying to think as she does.

MINA HARKER'S JOURNAL

October 5, 5 p.m. Here is the report of our meeting:

Dr. Van Helsing described what he and the others have done to discover the boat on which Count Dracula made his escape. Here is what he said:

"As I knew that he wanted to get back to Transylvania, I assumed that he would return by the route he took to arrive here. And so we looked to find what ships left for the Black Sea last night. We went to the shipping office, which has records of every ship that sails, and found only one such ship. She is the *Czarina Catherine*, and she is to sail from Doolittle's Wharf to Varna, Bulgaria, and then on to other ports. 'So!' said I, 'this is the Count's ship.' And off we went to Doolittle's Wharf. There we found a man in the office. From him we inquire about the departure of the *Czarina Catherine*. He swears a lot, and is very red-faced and loud-voiced, but he is a good fellow all the same. And after Quincy gives him a few pounds, he is an even better fellow! He comes with us, and asks many men working on the wharf, and they tell us what we want to know.

"They say that yesterday afternoon at

about five o'clock, a man came in a great hurry. He was a tall man, thin and pale, with a great strong nose and sharp white teeth. He asked what ships are sailing for the Black Sea. So they took him to the office and then to the ship, but he would not go aboard. He insisted that the captain leave the ship and come to him. The captain did so, and the man made arrangements to pay him well. Then the thin man left to find a horse and cart to hire. He returned, driving the cart himself, hauling a great box. This box he himself lifted down, although it took several strong men to carry it onto the ship. He was very particular, they said, about just how and where the box is to be placed. The captain became impatient and told him to come on board himself if he was so concerned. But the man said no, that he could not come yet, as he had business to attend to. The captain told him that he had better hurry, for the ship would leave very soon, before the tide could turn. But the thin man smiled and said that he would be surprised if it sailed quite so soon. Then the man went away.

"No one knew where he went 'or bloomin' well cared' as they said, for they had something else to think about. For it soon became apparent that the *Czarina Catherine* would not sail as was expected. A dense fog enveloped the ship. The captain swore in seven languages, but he could do nothing. He was in no friendly mood when, just at full tide, the thin man came up the gangplank again and asked to see where his box had been stowed. He went down with the mate and saw where the box was placed and came back up and stood on the dock in the fog. He must have left soon after that, they said, for no one saw him again. Indeed they forgot all about him, for soon the fog began to melt away and all was clear again. The men laughed as they told us how the captain raged and cursed when he learned from the crews of other ships that none of them had had any trouble with fog at all. At any rate, the ship soon sailed and is now well out at sea.

"And so, my dear Madame Mina, we have some time to rest. Our enemy is on the sea with the fog at his command, and on his way to Varna."

Tonight, we shall all sleep on the facts. Tomorrow, at breakfast, we shall decide on some definite cause of action.

I feel a wonderful sense of peace tonight. It is as if some haunting presence were removed from me. Perhaps . . . but no. I just looked in the mirror and caught sight of the red mark upon my forehead. I am still unclean.

Dr. Seward's Diary

October 5. We all got up early, and I think that the good night's sleep did much for each of us. When we met at breakfast, we were more cheerful than any of us had ever expected to feel again. Even Mrs. Harker seemed to forget her troubles for a few minutes.

We are to meet here in my study in half an hour and decide what to do next. One problem is troubling me very much. It is more a feeling than anything else. I sense, somehow, that poor Mrs. Harker is no longer able to speak completely freely. I suspect that some of that horrid poison which has gotten into her veins has begun to work. The Count had his reasons when he gave her what Van Helsing called "the vampire's baptism of blood."

Later. When the Professor came in, we talked over the state of things. I could see that he had something on his mind but he seemed hesitant. He finally said, "Friend John, there is something that you and I must talk of alone, at least for now. Later, we may have to speak with the others."

Then he stopped, so I waited. He went on, "Madame Mina, our poor, dear Madame Mina is changing."

A shiver ran through me to find that Van Helsing shared my fears. He continued:

"We learned much from our sad experience with Miss Lucy, and we must not let things go too far. I can see some changes, the signs of the vampire, coming to her face. It is now but very, very slight. Her teeth are sharper, and at times her eyes are more hard. But that is not all. More worrisome to me is that she is often silent, as Miss Lucy was. My fear is this: Madame Mina can, in a hypnotic trance, tell us what the Count sees and hears. Is it not possible, then, that he who hypnotized her first, and who has drunk her blood and made her drink his, can read her thoughts as well?"

I nodded. He went on, "What we must do is keep her ignorant of our plans. She cannot tell him what she does not know. This breaks my heart, but it must be. When we meet today, I must tell her that for reasons which I cannot say, she must not be part of our talks, but that she will be guarded by us."

The poor man's forehead was damp with sweat, which had broken out at the thought of the pain he would have to give the poor, tortured woman. To comfort him, I told him that I had come to the same conclusion. I wanted to take away the pain of any doubts he might feel.

It is now nearly time for our meeting. Van Helsing has gone away to prepare. I believe his real purpose is to be able to pray alone.

Later. At the very beginning of our meeting, something happened which relieved both Van Helsing and me very much. Mrs. Harker sent a message to say that she would not join us. She thought it would be better for us to meet without her.

Van Helsing put the facts before us. "The ship *Czarina Catherine* left London yesterday morning," he explained. "Ordinarily it takes her at least three weeks to reach Varna. But we can travel by land to the same place in three days. Now, let us allow two days less for the ship's voyage, due to the fact that we know the Count can influence the weather. Let us add a day and a night for any delays which may slow our trip. We still have a margin of nearly two weeks.

"Thus, in order to be quite safe, we must leave here on the 17th at the latest. Then we are sure to be in Varna a day before the ship arrives."

Here Quincy Morris added, "I understand that the Count's country is full of wolves. I suggest that we add Winchester rifles to our supplies. I have great faith in a Winchester when there is trouble of that sort around."

"Good!" said Van Helsing, "Winchesters it shall be. And here is another thought. None of us are familiar with Varna, am I right? So why should we not go sooner? We might just as well wait there as here. Tonight and tomorrow we can get ready. Then we four can set out on our journey."

"We four?" asked Harker.

"Of course!" answered the Professor. "You must remain here to take care of your sweet wife!"

Harker was silent for a while, then said, "Let's talk about that in the morning. I want to consult with Mina."

I thought it was time for Van Helsing to warn him not to tell her our plans, but he said nothing. I gave him a hard look and coughed. He put his finger to his lips and turned away.

JONATHAN HARKER'S JOURNAL

October 5, afternoon. Mina's decision not to take any part in our discussion puzzles me. The way the others happily accepted that decision puzzles me as well. The last time we talked of the subject, we agreed that we would tell her everything. Right now, Mina is sleeping, calmly and sweetly. Thank God she can still have such happy moments.

Later. As I sat watching Mina sleep, she opened her eyes and gave me a loving look. She said, "Jonathan, I want you to promise me something. It is a promise that you must not break, even if I go down on my knees and beg you with bitter tears. Quick, you must promise me at once."

"Mina," I said, "I can't make such a promise without knowing what it is. It might not be right for me to make."

"It is right," she said calmly. "You may ask Dr. Van Helsing if it is not. If he disagrees, you may do as you wish and forget your promise."

"Very well, what is it?" I said.

She said, "Promise me that you will not tell me anything about your plans to find and destroy the Count. Not a word, or even a hint, as long as this remains visible." And she solemnly pointed to the scar.

"I promise!" I said sadly. As I said the words, I felt as though a door had slammed shut between us.

October 6, morning. Another surprise. Mina woke me early, about the same time as yesterday, and asked me to call Dr. Van Helsing. I thought she wanted to be hypnotized again, so I was not too surprised. He thought so too, and said so as he hurried into our room.

"No," she said quite simply, "that is not it. I needed to tell you that I must go with you to Transylvania."

Dr. Van Helsing was as startled as I was. After a moment's pause he asked, "But why?"

"You must take me with you. I am safer with you, and you shall be safer, too."

"But why, dear Madame Mina? You know that your safety is our greatest concern. We are going into great danger, more dangerous to you than to any of us."

In answer, she pointed to her forehead. "I know. That is why I must go. I can tell you now, before the sun is coming up. I may not be able to say this again. I know that when the Count calls me, I must go. To go to him, I will lie, I will deceive—even Jonathan." She turned to me with a look in which love, shame, and pride were equally mixed. I could only squeeze her hand.

She went on. "Together, you men will be stronger than one man alone. Besides, I may be able to help, since you can hypnotize me and so learn things that I don't even realize I know."

Dr. Van Helsing said gravely, "Madame

Mina, you are, as always, most wise. You shall come with us. And together we shall succeed."

After he left the room, Mina fell back on her pillow asleep. She did not even wake when I had pulled up the blind and let in the sunlight. Van Helsing and I went to his room, where we met with Lord Godalming, Dr. Seward, and Mr. Morris.

He told them the new development. "She suffers much, but her soul is still pure. She has warned us in time. In Varna we must be ready to act the instant the ship arrives."

"What, exactly, shall we do?" asked Mr. Morris.

"We shall board that ship," Van Helsing replied. "When we have found the box, we shall place a branch of wild roses on it. This will fasten the box, keeping the Count safely inside. Then, when none are near to see, we shall open the box, and . . . and all will be well."

"I will not wait," said Morris hotly. "The moment I see the box, I shall open it and destroy the monster. I don't care if there are a thousand men watching and I am hanged for it!"

"You are a brave man," said Dr. Van Helsing. "God bless you for it. We all shall do what we must do. But, indeed, many things may happen that we cannot foresee. Now, let us put our affairs in order. I have made my own will and other legal arrangements, so I shall go make arrangements for the travel."

Later. It is done. My will is made. It is nearly time for sunset. Mina seems very uneasy, and I am sure that there is something on her mind. I must go—she is calling to me.

Dr. Seward's Diary

October 11, evening. Jonathan Harker has asked me to write this; he says he does not have the heart and he wants it added to the record.

None of us were surprised when Mrs. Harker asked to see us all a little before sunset. We have seen that sunrise and sunset are the times she can speak most freely. This condition lasts only about half an hour. Afterwards, she falls back into an unnatural silence.

Motioning her husband to sit beside her on the sofa, she asked the rest of us to bring chairs up close. She took Harker's hand in hers and began.

"We are all here together in freedom, perhaps for the last time," she began. "In the morning we go out on this terrible task, and God knows what may happen. You are taking the risk of bringing me along—I, whose soul perhaps is lost. No! Not lost yet, but at risk," she said as Harker tried to interrupt. "No matter how much you love me, you must remember that I am not like you. There is a poison in my blood which will destroy me unless we find the cure. Oh, my friends, you know as well as I do that my soul is at stake. There is only one way out, and that is a way that I may not take!

"It is bitter," she said, "because we all know that if I ended my life, you could set my immortal spirit free, as you did poor Lucy's. If the fear of death were the only thing standing in my way, I would not hesitate. But I can't believe that it is God's will that I die while we still have hope. There is one thing I will ask of you today."

She looked at our faces, one at a time, and we listened with all our hearts for her request.

"What will each of you give me? I know you would give your lives," she added quickly, "for that is easy for brave men. Your lives are God's and you can give them back to Him, but what will you give to me?" Seeing the puzzlement in our faces, she continued. "I shall tell you plainly what I want, for there must be no doubt in your minds. You must promise me—even you, my beloved husband—that if the right time comes, you will kill me."

"What is that time?" The voice was Quincy's, but it was low and strained.

"When you are convinced that I am so changed that I am better off dead. After my body dies, then you will, without a moment's delay, drive a stake through me and cut off my head and give me rest!"

One by one, we knelt beside her, kissed her hand, and gave her this strangest of all promises. All but Harker. He turned to her, his eyes hollow and his skin the color of ashes, and asked, "And must I, too, make such a promise, my wife?"

"You too, my dearest," she said, with infinite pity in her voice and eyes. "You most of all. You are nearest and dearest to me. If I must meet death at any hand, let it be at the hand of him that loves me best."

Unable to speak, Harker promised with a nod.

JONATHAN HARKER'S JOURNAL

October 15, Varna. We left London by train on the morning of the 12th, got to Paris the same night, and continued by train on the Orient Express. We traveled all night and through the next day, arriving here in Varna at about five o'clock. Mina is well and looks stronger. Her color is coming back. She slept through almost the entire journey. Before sunrise and sunset, however, she was very alert. It has become a habit for Van Helsing to hypnotize her at such times. He always asks her what she can see and hear.

Her answer to the first question is, "Nothing; all is dark."

And to the second, "I can hear the waves lapping against the ship and the water rushing by. The wind is high . . . I can hear it in the sails."

It is evident that the ship *Czarina Catherine* is still at sea, hurrying on her way to Varna. Lord Godalming has just returned from the telegraph office. His agent back in London is sending him a telegram every day, reporting whether the *Czarina Catherine* has been seen anywhere. Four telegrams were waiting for Godalming, each saying the same: "Not yet reported."

We had dinner and went to bed early. Tomorrow we will meet with city officials to see about getting on board the ship as soon as she arrives. Our plan is for Godalming to say that a box on board contains goods stolen from a friend of his. This is a country in which anything can be accomplished with a bribe, and we do not expect any trouble with the officials or the seamen. We are well supplied with money.

October 16.   Mina's report is still the same. Lapping waves and rushing water, darkness and high winds. When we hear news of the *Czarina Catherine*, we shall be ready. Soon she must pass through the Dardanelles, a narrow stretch of water between Europe and Turkey. She will be noticed there, and we are sure to have some report.

October 17.   Everything is pretty well fixed now, I think, to welcome the Count home from his vacation. Godalming's money had its desired effect, and he has papers allowing him to board the ship and open the box. We have arranged what to do at that point. If the Count is there, Van Helsing and Seward will cut off his head at once and drive a stake through his heart. Morris and Godalming and I shall prevent anyone else from interfering. The Professor says that once we do as we have planned, the Count's body will turn into dust. If that is true, there will be no evidence against us if anyone tried to accuse us of murder.

October 24. A whole week of waiting. Daily telegrams to Godalming, but only the same story: "Not yet reported." Mina's morning and evening hypnotic report is always the same. Lapping waves, rushing water, and creaking sails.

October 24. Godalming has received a telegram. The *Czarina Catherine* was reported this morning passing through the Dardanelles.

DR. SEWARD'S DIARY

October 25. We were all wild with excitement yesterday when Godalming got his telegram. Now I know what soldiers must feel when they hear the call to battle. Only Mrs. Harker did not show any signs of emotion. She could not, because we were careful not to let her know anything about it. Van Helsing and I are very worried about her, and we talk about her often. We have not, however, said a word to the others. It would break poor Harker's heart if he knew that we were so suspicious. Van Helsing examines her teeth carefully while she is in her hypnotic trance. Thank God, there is no further change there. If the teeth begin to sharpen, it will be necessary to act. We both know what that action would have to be, but we do not say the words, even to each other.

It should take only about 24 hours for the *Czarina Catherine* to sail from the Dardanelles to here. She should therefore arrive tomorrow some time around noon. We shall go to bed early and be ready to move at a moment's notice.

October 25, noon. No news yet of the ship's arrival. Mrs. Harker's hypnotic report this morning was the same as usual, so we may get news at any moment. We men are all in a fever of excitement, except Harker, who is calm. His hands are cold as ice, and an hour ago I found him sharpening the knife which he always carries with him.

Van Helsing and I were alarmed about Mrs. Harker today. About noon she became very drowsy. She had been restless all morning, so we were glad at first to know that she was sleeping. When her husband mentioned that she was sleeping so soundly that he could not wake her, we went to her room to see for ourselves. She was breathing naturally and looked so well and peaceful that we agreed that sleep was better for her than anything else. Poor girl, she has so much to forget that it is no wonder that she sleeps when she can.

October 26. Another day and no news of the *Czarina Catherine*. She ought to be here by now. We know she is still sailing somewhere, for Mrs. Harker's hypnotic report at sunrise was still the same. We must continue watching, as the ship may now be sighted at any moment.

October 27, noon. Very strange. No news yet of the ship. Mrs. Harker reported last night and this morning as usual. "Lapping waves and rushing water," though she added that "the waves sound very faint." The telegrams from London have been the same: "No further report." Van Helsing is terribly anxious.

October 28. Telegram from Godalming's man in London. "*Czarina Catherine* reported entering port of Galatz, Romania, at one o'clock today."

Dr. Seward's Diary

October 28. When the telegram came announcing the arrival in Galatz, it was less of a shock than might have been expected. I think we all expected that something strange would happen. When we heard the news, Van Helsing raised his hand over his head for a moment, as though to argue with the Almighty. But all he said was, "When does the next train start for Galatz?"

"At 6:30 tomorrow morning." We all were surprised, for the answer came from Mrs. Harker.

"How on earth do you know?" said Art.

"You don't know, although Jonathan and Dr. Van Helsing do, that I am a train fiend. At home in Exeter, I always memorized the train schedules so as to be helpful to my husband. I found it so useful that I got into the habit of looking them up wherever we go."

"You wonderful woman!" murmured the Professor. "Now, let us organize. You, friend Arthur, go to the train and get the tickets. You, friend Jonathan, go to the shipping agent and get letters from him to the agent in Galatz, giving us permission to search the ship, as we had here in Varna. John will stay with Madame Mina and me, and we shall consult."

"And I," said Mrs. Harker brightly, "shall try to be useful, writing for you as I used to do. Something is shifting in me in some strange way, and I feel freer than I have lately!"

The younger men looked happy to hear

this. but Van Helsing and I exchanged a worried look.

When the three men had gone out, Van Helsing asked Mrs. Harker to look up the copy of the diaries and find him the part of Harker's journal that describes the Castle. She went away to get it.

When the door was shut upon her he said to me, "Now, quickly. Speak out!"

"There is some change," I said.

"There is. Do you know why I asked her to get the manuscript?"

"No!" I said, "unless it was to get an opportunity of seeing me alone."

"You are right, friend John. I want to tell you something. As Madame Mina said those words about feeling a change inside, an idea came to me. This is what I believe: In her trance three days ago, the Count sent his spirit to read her mind. He learned then that we are here. Now he is making his greatest effort to escape us. At present, he does not want her. He has cut her off, so that she will not come to him. Here comes Madame Mina!"

In his excitement, Van Helsing told her his theory. Mrs. Harker clapped her hands together in excitement. "You are right, I feel that you are!" she exclaimed. "He has gone from me in some way!"

"And yet—and this is most important—he has made an error," Van Helsing continued. "He thinks that since he cut himself off from knowing your mind, then you can know nothing of him. There is where he is wrong! That terrible baptism of blood which he gave you makes you able to go to him in spirit, as you have been doing in your times of freedom, when the sun rises and sets. To protect himself from this power, he has cut himself off from even knowing where we are. Friend John, this has been a great hour, and it has done much to advance us on our way. You must be the secretary and write this all down so that when the others return from their work, you can give it to them."

Chapter 26

DR. SEWARD'S DIARY

October 29. This is written in the train from Varna to Galatz. Last night we all met a little before sunset. Each of us had done his work as well as he could, so we are prepared. When the usual time came around, Mrs. Harker prepared herself to be hypnotized. The process was more difficult than usual. Usually she speaks freely, but this time the Professor had to ask her questions repeatedly before we could learn anything. At last her answer came.

"I can see nothing. We are still. There are no waves lapping, but only a steady swirl of water. I can hear men's voices calling and the roll and creak of oars. A gun is fired somewhere. There is tramping of feet overhead, and ropes and chains are dragged along. What is this? There is a gleam of light. I can feel the air blowing upon me."

Here she stopped. She had risen from where she lay on the sofa and raised both her hands, palms upwards, as if lifting a weight. Van Helsing and I looked at each other with understanding. Quincy raised his eyebrows, while Harker's hand closed round the hilt of his knife.

Suddenly she sat up and, as she opened her eyes, said sweetly, "Would anyone like a cup of tea? You must all be so tired!"

We wanted only to make her happy, and so agreed. She went off to get tea. When she had gone Van Helsing said, "You see, my friends. He is close to land. He has left his chest of earth. But he is not yet on shore. You see, the Vampire cannot cross running water himself. If he is not carried onto the shore, or if the ship does not touch it, he cannot reach the land. As a result, he will lose at least a whole day. We may then arrive in time. For if he does not escape at night, we shall come on him in daytime, boxed up and at our mercy."

There was no more to be said, so we waited

in patience until the dawn, at which time we might learn more from Mrs. Harker.

Early this morning we listened, with breathless anxiety, for the words she might say in her trance. It was even more difficult than before to make her speak. Finally, though, a few words came: "All is dark. I hear lapping water, and some creaking as of wood on wood."

And so we are traveling towards Galatz in an agony of suspense. We were due to arrive between two and three in the morning, but already we are running three hours late, so we cannot possibly get in until after sunup. By then we may have two more hypnotic messages from Mrs. Harker. Either or both may throw more light on what is happening.

Later. Sunset has come and gone. Mrs. Harker was harder to hypnotize than ever before. I am afraid that her power of reading the Count's mind may die away just when we need it most.

When she did speak, her words were puzzling. "Something is going on. I can feel it pass me like a cold wind. I can hear, far off, confused sounds. There are men talking in strange tongues, falling water, and the howling of wolves." She stopped, and a shudder ran through her. She said no more, even when the Professor questioned her insistently.

October 30, 7 a.m. We are near Galatz now, and I may not have time to write later. Knowing that Mina's trances were becoming more difficult, Van Helsing began trying earlier than usual. Nothing happened, however, until only a minute before the sun rose. The Professor lost no time in his questioning.

Her answer came equally quickly. "All is dark. I hear water swirling, at the same level as my head, and the creaking of wood on wood. Cattle are calling far off."

The whistles are sounding. We are nearing Galatz. We are on fire with anxiety and eagerness.

JONATHAN HARKER'S JOURNAL

October 30. At nine o'clock this morning Dr. Van Helsing, Dr. Seward, and I went to see the shipping agents. Having heard from their colleagues in Varna, they were eager to help us. They took us on board the ship *Czarina Catherine*, which lay at anchor out in the river harbor. There we saw the Captain, a man named Donelson, who told us of his voyage. He said that in all his life he had never had so fast a run.

"Man!" he said, "it almost scared us, for

we kept expecting to have a piece of bad luck to make up for it. It's unheard of, the way we ran from London to the Black Sea with a wind behind us every step of the way, as though the Devil himself were blowing on our sails. And much of the time we couldn't see a thing. Every time we got near another ship, or a port, or land, a fog fell over us and traveled with us. At first I was tempted to lower our sails and wait a bit until the fog lifted. But then I thought, no, if the Devil wants to get us into the Black Sea quick, he'll do it whether we agree or not."

The skipper went on. "When we got past the Bosporus Sea, the men began to grumble. Some of them, the Romanians, asked me to heave a big box overboard which had been put on board by a queer lookin' old man just before we left London. I had seen them staring at the fellow, and putting out their two fingers to guard against the evil eye. Man! but the superstition of foreigners is ridiculous! I sent them about their business pretty quick, but, just after that, the fog closed in again. I began to feel a bit the same way they did, although I wouldn't say it was because of the big box.

"Well, on we went, and as the fog didn't let up for five days, I just let the wind carry us, for if the Devil wanted to get somewheres, he would fetch us up there all right. Sure enough, we had a fair wind all the time. Then, two days ago, when the morning sun came through the fog, we found ourselves in the river opposite Galatz. The Romanians were frantic, I tell you. They wanted me to take out the box and fling it in the river. I had to argue with them with a club in my hands. And when the last of them picked himself up off the deck, I had convinced them that, evil eye or no evil eye, the property of my clients was better in my hands than in the river. By then they had brought the box up on the deck, ready to throw it overboard. I thought I'd let it lie there until we unloaded in the port. We didn't do much unloading that day, but in the morning, an hour before sunup, a man came aboard with an order to receive a box marked for one Count Dracula. Sure enough, it was that box he was after. He had his papers ready, and I was glad to be rid of the damn thing. I'm beginning to think we were carrying the Devil's own luggage!"

"What was the name of the man who took it?" asked Dr. Van Helsing eagerly.

"Let me get the receipt," he answered, and stepped down to his cabin. A moment later he produced the paper, signed "Immanuel

Hildesheim," with an address in the city.

We found Hildesheim in his office. He told us he had received a letter from Mr. de Ville of London, telling him to receive a box which would arrive at Galatz on the *Czarina Catherine.* He was to pick it up before sunrise so that he would not have to go through customs. He was to then hand the box over to a man named Petrof Skinsky, a trader who did business with the gypsies. He had done so, and that was all he knew.

We then looked for Skinsky but were unable to find him. One of his neighbors, who seemed to dislike him, said that he had disappeared two days before. We were at a standstill again.

But while we were talking, another neighbor came running. He breathlessly gasped out that the body of Skinsky had just been found inside the wall of a churchyard. His throat had been torn open. The people we had been speaking with ran off to see the horror. We hurried away, in case anyone should think we were somehow involved.

MINA HARKER'S JOURNAL

October 30. They were so tired and worn out when they returned that I sent them all to lie down while I write down everything up to the moment. I have asked Dr. Van Helsing for new information, and he gave me all the papers that I have not yet seen. While they are resting, I shall go over them carefully.

Later. I do believe that with God's help I have made a discovery. I shall get the maps and look over them.

I am more sure than ever that I am right. I will gather the men together and read it to them.

MINA HARKER'S NOTES

Problem: Count Dracula's needs to return to his own castle.

Issues to consider:

(a) He must be brought back by someone. This is clear. If he had the power to move alone, in the form of a man, a bat, a wolf or another creature, he would do so. He is helpless between dawn and sunset, trapped in his wooden box.

(b) How is he to be taken? There are several possibilities to consider.

1. *By road.* This would be extremely difficult. For one thing, there are people. And people are curious and investigate. If they had a hint as to what was in the box, they would

destroy him. There might be customs officers to pass. Worst of all, his pursuers might follow him. He is so afraid of this that he has tried to cut ties with me, his victim.

2. *By rail.* No one would be traveling with the box and watching over it. He would have to take the chance of having the box delayed. This would be fatal to him, with enemies on his track. True, he might escape at night. But then he would be in a strange place with no safe refuge to fly to. He does not want to risk this.

3. *By water.* This is the safest way, in one sense, but most dangerous in another. On the water he is powerless except at night. Even then he can only summon fog and storm and snow and his wolves. If there was a shipwreck, he would be trapped helplessly in the living water. However, we know from his history that traveling by water is his first choice. From that, and from what I have picked up during my hypnotic trances, I think we should assume that he has continued to travel by water.

My belief is that the Count decided back in London to return to his castle by water, as the most safe and secret way. When he left Transylvania, he was transported from the castle by gypsies. Therefore the Count knows people who could arrange this service for him.

I have examined the map, and I find that there are two rivers running from Galatz up to the area of the Count's castle. One is the Pruth and the other is the Sereth. In my trance, I heard cows moo, water swirling at the same level with my head, and the creaking of oars. I believe this means that the Count was on a river in an open boat near the riverbank and being rowed upstream. So far, those conditions could apply to either the Pruth or the Sereth. But by looking at the map further, I see two things. One is that the Pruth is more easily traveled. But the other is that at the town of Fundu, the Sereth is joined by the Bistritza River. The Bistritza runs around the Borgo Pass. The loop it makes runs very close to Dracula's castle, as close as one can get by water.

MINA HARKER'S JOURNAL
(continued)

When I had finished reading, Jonathan hugged and kissed me. The others kept shaking my hand, and Dr. Van Helsing said, "Our dear Madame Mina is once more our teacher. Her eyes are clear where ours were blind. Now we are on the track once again, and this time we may succeed. Our enemy is at his most helpless. If we can find him by day on the water, our task will be over. He has a head start, but he is traveling slowly. And he may not leave his box, for if the men who are carrying him would throw him in the water, he would perish. Now, quickly! We must plan what each of us shall do."

"I shall get a boat with a steam engine and follow him," said Lord Godalming.

"And I will take horses and follow along on the riverbank in case he lands," said Mr. Morris.

"Both good!" said the Professor, "But neither of you must go alone. The gypsies are rough, and they carry weapons."

Dr. Seward said, "I think I had better go with Quincy. We have hunted together often, and the two of us will be a match for whatever may come along. But you must not be alone, Art. It may be necessary to fight the Count's men. We must not take any chances this time. We shall not rest until the Count's head and body have been separated."

He looked at Jonathan as he spoke, and Jonathan looked at me. I could see that the poor man was struggling. Of course he wanted to stay with me, to protect me. But the men in the boat would most likely destroy the . . .

Vampire (Why is it even hard for me to write that word?)

He was silent, and during his silence Dr. Van Helsing spoke. "Jonathan, I want you to go on the boat. You are young and brave and can fight. And more importantly, it is your right to destroy Dracula, after all he has done to you and Madame Mina. Do not be afraid; I will watch over her. I am old and I cannot run as quickly as I once could. But I can help in other ways. And I can die, if I need to, as well as younger men. You and Arthur go in your swift little steamboat up the river, John and Quincy guard the bank, and I will take Madame Mina right into the heart of the enemy's country. While the old fox is tied in his box, we shall follow the same path Jonathan took, from Bistritz over the Borgo, to the Castle Dracula. Here, Madame Mina's hypnotic power will surely help, and we shall find our way to that fateful place. There, we will wipe out that nest of snakes."

"Do as you will," said Jonathan with a sob that shook him; "we are in the hands of God!"

Later. I am thankful for the wonderful power of money. It is fortunate that Lord Godalming and Mr. Morris are both rich, and both willing to spend it so freely. For if they were not, we would not be nearly so well prepared. It has been only three hours since we decided what each of us would do. And already Lord Godalming and Jonathan have their steamboat, and Dr. Seward and Mr. Morris have half a dozen good horses. We have all the maps and supplies that we need. Professor Van Helsing and I are to leave by train tonight for Veresti, where we will buy a carriage and horses for our trip to the Borgo Pass. We will drive ourselves, for we have no one whom we can trust to go with us. We've got all the weapons, including a pistol for me. The weather is getting colder every hour, and there are snow flurries.

Jonathan Harker's Journal

October 30, night. I am writing this in the light from our little boat's furnace door. Arthur is firing it up with fuel. He is an experienced sailor, as he has had a boat of his own for years in London. We should be able to travel at good speed up the river, even at night. The river is plenty wide with deep water. Quincy and Dr. Seward left on their long ride before we started. They will ride along the right bank, far enough off to get on higher lands where they can see a good stretch of river. It is a wild adventure we are on. We are drifting into unknown places and unknown ways. Godalming is shutting the furnace door . . .

October 31. Still hurrying along. The day has come and Arthur is sleeping. I am on watch. The morning is bitterly cold, so I am thankful for the furnace heat and our heavy fur coats. We have passed a few open boats, but none of them had on board any box of the size we seek.

November 1, evening. No news all day. We have found nothing. We have now left the Sereth and passed into the Bistritza, so if our guess of the Count's route was wrong, we have lost our chance. Some of the sailors we have passed tell us that a big boat passed them going at more than usual speed. This was before they came to Fundu, so they could not tell us whether the boat turned into the Bistritza or continued on up the Sereth. At Fundu there was no news of any such boat, so she must have passed there in the night. I am feeling very sleepy. Godalming insists that I rest while he keeps the first watch. God bless him for all his goodness to Mina and me.

November 2, morning. It is broad daylight. Bless Arthur's heart, he would not wake me for my shift. He says it would have been a sin to, for I was sleeping peacefully and forgetting my troubles. It seems selfish to me to have slept so long, but I do feel like a new man this morning. I wonder where Mina and Van Helsing are now. They should have arrived at Veresti about noon on Wednesday. It would take them some time to buy the carriage and horses. So if they had started and traveled hard, they might be at the Borgo Pass now. God guide and help them! I am afraid to think what may happen. If we could only go faster! But we can't. The engines are doing their best.

DR. SEWARD'S DIARY

November 2. Three days on the road. No news, and no time to write it if there had been, for every moment is precious. We rest only when the horses must. But we are full of energy. We will not feel happy until we get Art and Jonathan's boat in sight again.

November 3. We heard at Fundu that the boat had turned up the Bistritza. I wish it wasn't so cold. There are signs of snow coming.

November 4. Today we heard Art's boat was

slowed by an accident when it tried to force its way up the rapids. The local boats get through the rapids all right, by aid of a rope and their captains' knowledge of the area. The locals tell us that the boat kept stopping even after she got back into smooth water, so the damage must be considerable. We must push on harder than ever. Our help may be needed soon.

MINA HARKER'S JOURNAL

October 31. Arrived at Veresti at noon. The Professor tells me that this morning he could hardly hypnotize me at all, and that all I could say was, "dark and quiet." He is off now buying a carriage and horses. We have more than 70 miles to travel. The country is lovely and most interesting. If Jonathan and I were driving through it for pleasure, what a joy it would be. To stop and see people, and learn something of their life, and to fill our minds and memories with the color of the whole wild, beautiful country—but no.

Later. Dr. Van Helsing has returned. He got the carriage and horses. We will have some dinner and start in an hour. The landlady is preparing us a huge picnic basket. It seems like enough food for an army. The Professor encourages her and whispers to me that it may be a week before we can get any food again. He has been shopping too, and has bought fur coats and all sorts of warm things. There will not be any chance of our being cold.

We shall soon be off. I am afraid to think what may happen to us. We are truly in the hands of God. I pray Him to watch over my beloved husband. Whatever may happen, I want Jonathan to know that I loved him and honored him more than I can say, and that my last thoughts were of him.

Chapter 27

MINA HARKER'S JOURNAL

November 1. All day long we have traveled quickly and it looks as though the journey may be easy. Dr. Van Helsing tells the farmers we pass that he is hurrying to Bistritz. They give us hot soup, or coffee, or tea, and off we go. It is a lovely country, full of beauty. The people seem brave and strong, and full of kindness. They are, however, very superstitious. In the first house where we stopped, the woman who served us saw the scar on my forehead. She crossed herself and put out two fingers to keep off the evil eye. I believe they put an extra amount of garlic into our food, and I can't stand garlic. Since then I have left my hat on to hide the scar.

The Professor never seems tired. All day he did not rest, though he made me sleep for a long time. At sunset he hypnotized me, and he says I answered as usual, "Darkness, lapping water and creaking wood." So our enemy is still on the river.

November 2, morning. We took turns driving all night, so the Professor could sleep. Now the day is on us, bright and cold. Only our warm furs keep us comfortable. At dawn Van Helsing hypnotized me. He says I answered "darkness, creaking wood and roaring water," so the river is changing as they go upstream.

November 2, night. The country gets wilder as we go and the great peaks of the mountains seem to gather around us and tower in front. Dr. Van Helsing says that by morning we shall reach the Borgo Pass.

Note from Van Helsing to Dr. Seward

November 4. This to my old and true friend John Seward, M.D., of Purfleet, London, in case I may not see him again. It is morning, and I am writing by the fire which Madame Mina and I have kept burning all night. It is terribly cold, and the gray sky is heavy with snow. The weather seems to have affected Madame Mina, who has done literally nothing all day. She sleeps, and sleeps, and sleeps. She has lost her appetite, and she has not even written in her little diary which she usually keeps so faithfully. Something whispers to me that all is not well. Tonight, though, she seems more lively. At sunset I tried to hypnotize her, but with no success.

We got to the Borgo Pass just after sunrise yesterday morning. When I saw the signs of the dawn, I stopped the carriage and got ready for the hypnotism. She answered as usual, "Darkness and the swirling of water." Then she woke, bright and energetic. Some new power is in her, for she pointed to a road and said, "This is the way."

"How do you know that?" I asked.

"Of course I know it," she answered dreamily. At my questioning look, she added, "Jonathan wrote about it in his journal."

We drove on for long, long hours. Madame Mina slept all the time. I finally became suspicious and tried to wake her, but I could not. It is not long until sunset. The sunlight is a yellow flood over the snow, and we throw great long shadows. We are going up, and up, and it is as wild and rocky as the end of the world.

I finally woke Madame Mina, and then I tried to hypnotize her. I continued to try without success until I found us in the dark—the sun had gone down. Madame Mina laughed out loud. She is now wide awake and looks as healthy as I have ever seen her. I am amazed and uneasy as well. But she is so kind and thoughtful that I try to forget my fear. I lit a fire, and she prepared food while I unharnessed the horses and fed them. When I returned to the fire, she had my supper ready. I urged her to join me, but she told me she had eaten already. I did not like that, or believe it. But I said nothing. I ate alone, and then we wrapped up in our furs and lay beside the fire. I told her to sleep while I kept watch. But every time I checked, she was awake, looking at me with bright eyes. At sunrise, again, I could not hypnotize her. Then once the sun was up, she slept so heavily I could not wake her. I actually had to lift her up and place her, sleeping, in the carriage. I am afraid, afraid, afraid!

November 5. Let me be accurate in everything, for though you and I have seen some strange things together, you may think that I am mad.

All yesterday we traveled, always getting closer to the mountains. Madame Mina still sleeps and sleeps. And though I ate, I could not waken her, even for food. I begin to fear that the fatal spell of the place is upon her, poisoned as she is with vampire blood. "Well," I said to myself, "if she sleeps all day, I do not sleep at night." So as the horses obediently jogged along the road, I slept.

I woke with a sense of much time passed and found Madame Mina still sleeping, and the sun low down. We were near the top of a steep hill, and there stood the castle, just as Jonathan had described in his diary. I rejoiced and feared at the same time. For good or bad, the end was near.

I woke Madame Mina and again tried unsuccessfully to hypnotize her. Before it became too dark, I unharnessed the horses, fed them, and built a fire. I made Madame Mina, now awake and more charming than ever, comfortable nearby. I prepared food, but she would not eat. Then, with the fear of what might happen, I drew a big ring around where she sat. All along the ring I crumbled bits of the Communion wafer. She sat still all the time, so still as one dead. And she grew whiter until she was the same color as the snow. But when I came near to her, she took my arm, and I could feel the poor soul tremble from head to foot.

I wanted to test her, so after a bit I said, "Won't you come sit by the fire?" She rose obediently, but as she tried to step forward over the ring, she stopped.

"Why don't you come?" I asked. She shook her head and returned to sit in her place.

"I cannot," she said simply. I rejoiced, although I wept for her inside. For if she cannot pass out of the ring, those whom we fear cannot pass into it either. I joined the poor lady within the circle.

As we sat there in the dark, the horses began to scream and tore at their ropes until I came to quiet them. When they felt my hands on them, they whinnied low as if in gratitude and licked at my hands. Many times through the night I came to them, and every time they grew quiet.

In the coldest hour of the night, the fire began to die. The snow was coming in flying sheets, and along with it came a mist. The snow reflected the little light available, and it seemed to me that the flurries and mist gathered into strange shapes—the shapes of women in long gowns. The horses whinnied and trembled in fright. These terrifying figures drew near, circling around the ring that held Madame Mina and me. I looked at her, but she sat calm, smiling. At one point I began to go to add wood to the fire, but she caught me and held me back, whispering, "No! No! Do not go. Here you are safe!"

I turned to her, saying, "But you? I am afraid for you!"

She laughed a strange, low laugh, saying, "Why fear for me? No one in the world is safer from them than I am." As she spoke, she pointed to the red scar on her forehead. If I didn't understand what she meant, I soon learned.

The figures of mist and snow came closer, closer, but never stepping within the holy circle. Then they took more solid form until— unless God has taken away my sanity—I saw them clearly. They were without a doubt the same three women that Jonathan saw in the castle, the ones who would have kissed his throat. I knew their seductive, swaying hips, their bright, hard eyes, their white teeth, their pouting lips. They smiled at Madame Mina. Beckoning to her, they said in those sweet, tinkling tones that Jonathan had written of, "Come, sister. Come to us. Come!"

In fear I turned to Madame Mina, and my

heart leaped with gladness. For her sweet eyes were full of revulsion and horror, not welcome. I took up a piece of the wafer and held it out towards them as I walked towards the fire. They laughed at me, but they drew back and left me alone. I fed the fire and my fear lessened. For I knew that we were safe within the ring, which Mina could not leave and they could not enter. The horses had stopped moaning and lay on the ground, where snow was swiftly covering them. I knew their terror was at an end.

And so we remained until the red of the dawn began to pierce through the snow. I had been feeling an immense sadness and despair. But as that beautiful sun climbed the horizon, life seemed to return to me. At the first rays of sunrise, the horrible figures melted from sight. The whirling mist moved towards the castle and was lost.

Automatically, with the dawn coming, I turned to Madame Mina, hoping to hypnotize her. But she lay in a deep and sudden sleep, from which I could not wake her. I am afraid to move. I have made my fire and checked on the horses. They are all dead. Today I have much to do, and I am only waiting until the sun is high in the sky. For the sunlight is my only safety.

I will have breakfast and then go on with my terrible work. Madame Mina still sleeps, and God be thanked! She is calm . . .

JONATHAN HARKER'S JOURNAL

November 4, evening. The accident to the boat has been a terrible setback for us. If not for that, we would have overtaken the Count's boat long ago, and my dear Mina would be free. I can't stand to think of her near that evil castle. We have left the boat and gotten horses, and we are following along the track. I note this while Godalming is getting ready. If only Quincy and Dr. Seward were with us. We must only hope! Goodbye, Mina! God bless and keep you.

DR. SEWARD'S DIARY

November 5. At dawn we saw the gang of gypsies ahead of us, dashing away from the river. Most of them are on horseback, but they have with them a wagon. The snow is falling lightly, and there is a strange excitement in the air. Far off I hear the howling of wolves. The snow brings them down from the mountains, and we are all in danger. The horses are nearly ready, and we will leave soon. We are riding to the death of someone.

Note from Van Helsing to Dr. Seward

November 5. I know now, at least, that I am sane. I am glad for that, although proving it has been a dreadful task.

I left Madame Mina sleeping within the holy circle and walked to the castle. The doors were open, but still I used the blacksmith's hammer I carried to break off all the rusty hinges. That way, no one can close the doors after me and trap me here.

Jonathan's diary was of much use to me. By remembering his description, I found my way to the old chapel where my work lay. The air was heavy, and breathing it made me dizzy. Far off I heard the howl of wolves. I thought of dear Madame Mina with a shudder of fear. Yes, I had left her safe from the Vampire in the holy circle. And yet she was in danger from wolves! But what could I do? In my judgment, it is better to perish in the jaws of a wolf than rest in the grave of a vampire. So I continued with my work.

I knew that there were at least three

graves—occupied graves—in that chapel. So I searched and searched, and eventually found one of them. The woman inside lay in her vampire sleep, so full of life and seductive beauty that I shuddered, as though I had come to murder her. Surely, many a man who tried to do this task has found his heart failing him. How easy it would be for a man to look, and look, until the beauty and the fascination of the lovely Undead had hypnotized him. And he would remain on and on until sunset came and the vampire sleep was over. Then the beautiful eyes would open and look lovingly at him and the passionate lips invite a kiss and the man would be weak . . . and there is one more victim—one more member in the unholy family of the Undead!

Yes, for I am such a man—I, Van Helsing, with all that I know of these creatures. Even in a tomb, heavy with the dust of centuries, I felt desire grow within me. Looking at that lovely face, I found myself slipping into something like open-eyed sleep. But then through the cold air came a long, low wail, so full of sadness that it woke me like the sound of a trumpet. For it was the voice of dear Madame Mina.

I shook off the spell that had crept over me and wrenched off the tops of more tombs until

I found the grave of one more sister, the other dark-haired one. I did not pause to look at her, for fear that I would weaken once again. But I went on searching until I found in a high great tomb that final, fair-haired woman. She was so radiantly beautiful, so exquisite, that my foolish man's head whirled with emotion. Thank God that Madame Mina's wail had not yet died out of my ears. Before I could weaken further, I went on searching. I found no other Undead in the remaining tombs. I did, however, find one great tomb, high and lordly, labeled with just one carved word: DRACULA.

This then was the Undead home of the King Vampire. Before I began to set these women free, I laid some of the Communion wafer in Dracula's tomb, thus to banish him from it forever.

Then I began my terrible task. If there had been just one body, it would have been comparatively easy. But three! To begin twice more after I had been through such horror . . .

Oh, my friend John, I felt like a butcher. I needed every ounce of my strength and knowledge to go on. If I hadn't seen the first woman's look of peace at her last moment, I could not have continued. I could not have stood the dreadful screaming as I hammered the stake in, the agonized twisting of the body, and the lips foaming with blood. I would have run away in terror, leaving my work undone. But it is over! And the poor souls, I can now weep with pity for them. For, friend John, the moment my knife beheaded each body, the poor corpse crumbled into the dust that should have claimed it centuries ago.

When I returned to Madame Mina, I found her sleeping in the circle. She awoke when I stepped into it and cried out in joy to see me. "Come!" she said, "let us leave this awful place! Let us go to meet Jonathan!" She looked thin and pale and weak. Understand me when I say I was glad to see her illness, for my mind was full of the horror of that pink-cheeked vampire sleep.

And so with trust, hope, and fear, we go eastward to meet our friends.

Mina Harker's Journal

November 6. It was late in the afternoon when the Professor and I began walking eastward. We did not go fast, even though we were traveling downhill, for we had to carry our heavy blankets and food. There would be no place to get more supplies here. When we had gone about a mile, I was tired and sat down to rest.

We could hear the distant howling of wolves. They were far off, but even so the sound was terrifying. Dr. Van Helsing began searching for a place where we would have some protection against attack.

In a little while he called to me, so I got up and joined him. He had found a wonderful spot, a sort of natural hollow in a rock, with an entrance like a doorway between two boulders. He took me by the hand and drew me in.

"See!" he said, "here you will be in shelter. And if the wolves do come, I can meet them one by one."

He brought in our furs and made a snug nest for me, and got out some food. But I could not eat, as much as I wanted to please him. He looked very sad but said nothing. Taking his binoculars from the case, he stood on the top of the rock, and began to search the horizon.

Suddenly he called out, "Look! Madame Mina, look!"

I stood beside him as he handed me the binoculars and pointed. The snow was now falling more heavily and swirled fiercely in the high wind. However, there were brief periods when the wind would die away and I could see a long way off. Far off, beyond the white fields of snow, I saw the river lying like a curling

black ribbon. Straight in front of us, not far away at all, came a group of men on horseback. In the middle of the group was a cart, a long wagon which swept from side to side, like a dog's tail wagging. I could see from the men's clothes that they were peasants or gypsies of some kind.

On the cart was a great square box. My heart leaped as I saw it, for I felt that the end was coming. The day was nearly done, and I knew that at sunset the Thing which was imprisoned there would be free to take many forms and escape. I turned to the Professor, but to my surprise he was not there. An instant later, I saw him below me. Around the rock he had drawn a circle, such as he had done the night before.

When he had completed it, he said, "At least you will be safe from him here!" He took the binoculars from me, and at the next pause in the snow, he took in the whole sight. "See," he said, "they move quickly. They are whipping the horses and galloping as hard as they can."

He paused and went on in a despairing voice, "They are racing for the sunset. We may be too late. God's will be done!" Down came another blinding rush of snow, and the whole landscape was blotted out. It soon passed, however, and once more he examined the plain below.

He cried out, "Look! Look! See, two horsemen are following fast, coming up from the south. It must be Quincy and John. Take the binoculars. Look before the snow blots it all out!" I took them and looked.

I saw the pair riding, and then I spotted two other men, racing after them at breakneck speed. One of them was Jonathan, and I was sure the other was Lord Godalming. When I told the Professor, he shouted in joy like a schoolboy. After watching until the snow made sight impossible, he laid his rifle against the boulder at the opening of our shelter.

"They are all coming together," he said. "When the time comes, we shall have gypsies on all sides." I got out my pistol, for the howling of wolves was drawing closer.

Every instant we waited seemed to last an hour. The wind came in fierce bursts, and the snow was driven around us with fury. At times we could not see an arm's length before us. We had become so accustomed to watching for sunrise and sunset that we knew almost exactly when each would occur. And the sun would set very soon.

Closer and closer the riders and wagon came. The Professor and I crouched behind our rock, holding our weapons ready. I could see that he was determined that the wagon should not pass. All at once two voices shouted, "Halt!" One was Jonathan's, the other Mr. Morris's. The gypsies may not have known the language, but there was no mistaking the meaning of the word. They halted automatically as Lord Godalming and Jonathan dashed up on one side and Dr. Seward and Mr. Morris on the other.

The leader of the gypsies, a splendid fellow who looked as though he'd been born on horseback, waved them back. In a fierce voice, he ordered his companions to continue, and they all dug in their spurs. But the four men raised their rifles and in that unmistakable way again commanded them to stop. At the same moment, Dr. Van Helsing and I rose behind the rock and pointed our weapons at them. Seeing that they were surrounded, the men again halted. Their leader spoke again, and every man pulled out either a knife or a pistol.

The leader threw his horse out in front and pointed first to the sun, now sinking down on the hilltops, and then to the castle. He said something which I did not understand. In answer, all four of our men leaped from their horses and dashed towards the cart. The gypsies circled around the cart to prevent them from reaching their target.

In the middle of all this, I could see Jonathan on one side of the ring of men and Quincy on the other, both shouldering and elbowing their way through the crowd. It was clear that they were determined to finish their task before the sun set. Nothing would stop them. They did not seem to notice the pistols, the flashing knives, and even the howling of the wolves. Jonathan's determination must have impressed the gypsies, who instinctively stepped out of his path. In an instant he had jumped upon the cart and with a strength which seemed inhuman, lifted the great box and flung it to the ground.

In the meantime, Mr. Morris was fighting his way through the ring of men. Out of the corner of my eye, I saw the knives of the gypsies flash as they cut at him. He defended himself with his great bowie knife, and at first I thought that he had come through in safety. But as he reached Jonathan's side, I could see that he was clutching at his ribs and that blood was spurting through his fingers. Even this did not slow him. Together, he and Jonathan attacked the lid of the box with their knives. The screeching sound of the nails being pulled from their places told me that their desperate efforts were successful. They threw the top of the box back.

By this time the gypsies had given up, seeing Lord Godalming and Dr. Seward's rifles aimed at them. The sun was almost down behind the mountain tops, and the shadows of the whole group fell upon the snow. I saw the Count lying within the box. When the box had fallen, some of the earth within it had scattered over his body. He was deathly pale, just like a wax figure, and the open red eyes glared with the horrible, hateful look which I knew so well.

As I looked, the eyes saw the sinking sun, and the look of hate in them turned to triumph.

But in that same instant came the sweep and flash of Jonathan's great knife. I screamed as I saw it rip through the throat, instantly severing the head. At the same moment, Mr.

Morris's bowie knife plunged into the heart.

It was like a miracle. Before our very eyes, in the time it takes to draw a breath, the whole body crumbled into dust and vanished from our sight.

As long as I live, I'll remember that in that final moment, the dreadful face took on a look of unimaginable peace.

The Castle of Dracula stood out against the red sky. The gypsies, who had witnessed the extraordinary disappearance of the dead man, turned without a word and galloped away as if for their lives. The wolves followed them, leaving us alone.

Mr. Morris had sunk to the ground, leaning on his elbow and pressing his hand to his side. The blood still seeped through his fingers. I ran to him, for now the holy circle did not keep me back. The two doctors reached him first. Jonathan knelt behind him, and the wounded man laid his head back on Jonathan's shoulder. With a sigh he took my hand in his unstained one.

He must have seen the anguish in my face, for he smiled at me and said, "I am so happy that I have been able to help. Oh, God!" he cried suddenly, struggling to a sitting position and pointing to me. "This is worth dying for! Look!"

All the men stared at me, and with one movement they sank on their knees. The dying man spoke, "God be thanked, this has not been in vain. See! Her forehead is as stainless as the snow. The curse has passed away!"

And with a smile he died, a gallant gentleman.

Note from Jonathan Harker

Seven years ago we all went through the flames. Our joy since then is as great as the pain that we endured. It makes Mina and me very happy that our little boy was born on the anniversary of Quincy Morris's death. I know his mother believes that some of our friend's brave spirit has passed into him. He has a whole string of names which link our little group of men together. But we call him Quincy.

Last summer, we took a trip to Transylvania and retraced our previous journey. It was almost impossible to believe that the things which we had seen with our own eyes and heard with our own ears were true. All we saw was a pleasant country, full of beauty and good people.

When we got home, we were talking of old

times with our friends. Our little group now includes two new members, for both Godalming and Seward are happily married. I took the papers from the safe, where they have been since our return. As we read them over, we realized what an unbelievable story they make. We could hardly expect anyone to accept our collection of journals and letters as proof of so wild a tale.

Van Helsing put it well. Holding our son on his knee, he said, "We want no proof. We don't ask anyone to believe us! This boy will some day know what a brave woman his mother is. Already he knows that she is sweet and loving. Later on he will understand that some men loved her greatly, and dared much for her sake."

by Beth Johnson

About the Author

How do you imagine the man who wrote *Dracula*? If you're like most people, you picture him as strange and mysterious, even a little frightening. You might think of him hidden away in a dark, cobweb-filled attic, working away on his masterpiece of terror, only coming out at night for a little . . . bite.

If so, you might be disappointed if you saw the bearded, cheerful-looking Irishman named Abraham "Bram" Stoker. He was a businessman as well as a writer, a husband and a father who (as far as anyone knows) didn't ever have the urge to sink his teeth into anyone's neck. But in its own way, Stoker's life was a strange one.

He was born on November 8, 1847, in Dublin, Ireland. His parents were neither rich or poor, but just average. Bram was the third of seven brothers and sisters. Now here's the first odd thing about his life: As a child, some sort of illness kept him in bed nearly full-time. No one has ever really explained what was the matter with little Bram, but he told friends that until he was seven, he couldn't walk without someone helping him. During what must have been long, boring years, while other children ran and played, Bram's mother entertained him with stories of Irish goblins, ghosts, and leprechauns. Perhaps that's when the idea of writing horror stories first came into Bram's mind.

Bram's mysterious illness seemed to go away permanently; in college he even became a star soccer player. He studied mathematics and graduated with honors. Although he had dreamed of being a writer, his father encouraged him to go to work for the Irish government, believing that it was a safer job. Bram went along with his father's wishes and became a kind of government clerk. He held that job for eight years. But in his free time, he wrote stories. He also became the unpaid the-